THE GREAT GULAXA

ALISTAIR ROUND

Design, typesetting and publishing by UK Book Publishing

www.ukbookpublishing.com

ISBN: 978-1-916572-49-2

THE GREAT GULAXA

ACKNOWLEDGEMENTS

Thank you to all my family and friends who continue to support me throughout my journey. Without your love and guidance I wouldn't be able to carry on conquering my fears and fulfilling my dreams.

To Vicki, my beautiful little rosebud, my soul mate. Thank you for showing me the meaning of true love. You give me another reason to be, you showed me light when I had given up hope, I love you with all that I have.

For Mum, the best mother a son could wish for.

So, I guess you're all wondering what happened with my little Grandfather Paradox experiment? Well, because I am continuing with my first person narrative then things must have gone pretty smoothly, right? Not exactly. Strange things happen when you travel through time, even stranger things happen when you try to eradicate the source of your own existence, but did I really expect anything different? I think in my own distorted way of thinking I imagined things would iron out like softened silk and the fabric of space and time would envelope my life as a mother smothers her new-born baby with pure, unadulterated love. My problem is I should really stop thinking, or maybe I just stop acting on instinct all the bloody time! If I was to count to ten before jumping into silly situations, maybe life would go a hell of a lot more smoothly. But if I did then you would have nothing to read to amuse yourself and that would be downright blasphemous. So, here we have it, the continuation of the silliest saga ever known. Buckle up my friends, things are about to get weird.

THE GRANDFATHER PARADOX

...I pulled the trigger.

Hmm, nothing happens, this was definitely not in the script, I feel like a right idiot. Quick, think, say something cool.

"Hold on grandad, just a little blockage in my shooting iron me old chap, what?"

My grandad, who stares at me with the personification of coolness, blinks, sighs heavily and shakes his head.

"Idiot."

Wait, guns have safety switches don't they, just flick the switch and we're good to go. Hmm, no switch anywhere, maybe the barrel is blocked? I'll just have a look down! No, all clear, well not clear, but certainly no blockage, maybe if I whack it against my head that'll release something.

"What in God's name are you doing you idiot?" my grandad screams as I whack myself on the side of the head with a loaded weapon, which hurts like a bastard, and sends a deafening roar right through my cerebral cortex with venomous fury. A bullet whistles behind me and ricochets off a lamp post before finally thudding into my grandads shin.

"Oops," I mutter coyly. "Sorry grandad."

Grabbing his shin as blood spurts everywhere, my battle hardened grandad begins crying like a little baby; what a way to shatter his once untarnished image! Unsure of what to do I crouch down and begin patting his back like trying to soothe a wailing toddler.

"There, there, big fella," I coo softly. "It's just a lickle scratch."

"A little scratch!" he booms, his baby like wailing eradicated in an instance. "You've put a bloody bullet through my shin you bumbling buffoon."

"Yeah but, like, you were being a dick, so you deserved it." I reply matter-of-factly. "Hey, at least you have some flowers for when you get to hospital," I say as I hand him the once discarded but now rejuvenated bunch of flowers – good old Mitch, always knows how to make the best of a bad situation, what a guy.

As I'm congratulating Mitch, or myself, I don't know any more, my for some reason angry grandad snatches the gun from my hand and points it at my head, which kinds of makes me snap back into the present moment.

"You shot the wrong guy soldier, see you on the other side."

Well this wasn't part of the bloody script, it seems as though the tables have turned on my mind bending experiment, it was kind of fun while it lasted. I ponder, if the hero dies at the beginning of the story, is there still a story?

My grandad pulls the trigger...

SLEEPING BEAUTY

W atching him sleep always brings me a sense of calm, as though the very core of my being is floating away on a sumptuous white cloud, heaven bound on some marvellous journey towards peace and serenity. That is until the dumb fool starts drooling and farting, what a disgusting animal. Good job my time here will be brief. I can't wait to torture this idiot's mind, this is going to be awesome. The power I have at my fingertips (well actually my mind, but fingertips sounds way cooler) is truly staggering. Passed down through generations of travellers I am one of the last and fully intend to use it as a tool for chaos rather than good. Who wants to be a foolhardy hero anyway? Boring if you ask me.

By the way, if you haven't guessed already, I'm Gulaxa, and I'm taking over this first person narrative. The other guy is, well, obsolete, so good riddance to the pondering fool. This is my story now, he's had his time. Get it – time – I'm way cooler than that waste of space, and my jokes are more awesome. Am I the bad guy? Guess that depends on where your line sits my friends, or how bloody soft you are. The thing is, I really don't give a shit if you like me or not, this is not a popularity contest, this is a time war, and one I intend on winning. You think I died when that bomb went off? Think again bitches, The Great Gulaxa never dies!

Anyway, back to watching sleeping beauty and sniffing his disgusting odour I ponder my next move, time is all in my hands and I intend to make every second count. But first things first I'd better make myself invisible, yep I can do that, cos I'm way better than that idiot. Funny thing about invisibility, you can still see yourself so you can't actually see if it worked. The first time I attempted it I just assumed I had mastered the skill and ran down the street with no clothes on and got arrested for flashing, not a great look, but we learn from our mistakes. So, best way to make sure it has worked is a trusty mirror. You see, there's no overwhelming sense of anything changing, no shimmering of light or head wobbles, just one second people can see you and the next they can't, it's quite magical really.

Checking in the mirror I see that I am invisible, well I don't actually see I'm invisible, I just see that I'm not visible, which is the same thing, I think. What I'm getting at is that it actually worked. I am no longer see-able by other people – I have vamoosed – wait, where have I heard that phrase before? Must be from some movie. Anyway, I digress, I have vanished out of existence, well not existence because I'm still alive. Look, I mean don't look, oh bloody hell! People can't see me, OK! I wonder if animals can though? I mean, they do have a sixth sense and are all super perceptive, so it would sort of make sense. Then, right on cue, that irritating cat with the same name as me appears from under the bed and begins hustling around me like a slithering snake.

"Piss off!" I hiss while giving it a little boot towards the open door.

The meowing moggy departs and I close the door softly behind it, stupid cat, how dare it have the same name as me! Come to think of it, I wonder who was named first? I mean, I am older so surely me. But, what if the cat is from the past and was actually born before me, making me the second Gulaxa? This thought does not please me, although it does make me younger so it's sort of a win-lose situation. Then again, it only looks about five years old, and dogs' years are seven to every human, so I guess felines are about the same. That makes the little bastard younger than me, making this a lose-lose situation. God I hate that stupid cat!

Another toot from the sleeping angel brings me back from my incessant inward rambling (when did I become such a constant over-thinker?), smelly little bugger, I feel like smothering him right there and then, but that would be too easy. I'm gonna make this little bitch pay. I decide to have a little fun before the ensuing chaos and pinch his nose tightly, watching him cough and splutter, then fart which sends an unwelcome waft catapulting out of a tiny gap in the bedsheets straight up my waiting nostrils. Dirty bugger, it'll be all those microwave meals the lazy git keeps eating, I dig him in the ribs for good measure, forcing out another trump in the process.

Stepping back out of smell range, I almost come into contact with the incoming him as he opens the door and saunters in like he owns the place, which he does, maybe, not actually sure on that one. He probably got the house given to him by his idiot parents. A silver spoon fed bastard who had a life of luxury, well not any more pal, I'm about to mess up your life. Tip-toeing over like some pretend ninja he gawps idiotically at himself sleeping, probably trying to grasp the whole concept of time travel in his pea-sized brain – good luck with that one pal!

As he bends over and places the envelope on the bedside table I expertly and quietly enter the walk-in wardrobe without making any sound whatsoever because, well, I am actually a trained ninja, in a fashion. I mean, I have watched lots of movies like Crouching Tiger Hidden Dragon, and also played many a stealth adventure game on my games console, so that counts as training to me. Anyone disagrees, well I say screw you and all your friends (if you have any!)

As he struggles to comprehend the handwriting on the envelope I giggle inwardly, this was (or will be) my first inference to him that we are the same person, it was so easy to get him to believe this, he is so bloody gullible. Feeling the change in the air that warns him of his incoming self he darts into the walk-in wardrobe, right beside his enemy who is waiting in the darkness like the evil bastard he is, or I am.

I study him closely for a while, seeing the utter panic and frustration on his face, it brings me immense satisfaction to see him so screwed up, and this is just the beginning, well it isn't because I saw him earlier, or later. Oh screw it, you'll find out in due course. As I see him open his mouth about to let all his emotions blow, I lean closer to him and whisper into his ear, timing it to perfection.

"It's OK," I coo softly. "It'll all be over soon."

And then, he is gone.

BACK TO THE DRAWING BOARD

W ell! That didn't go as expected, did it!? Guess I had better think of a better way to test my theory. Also, maybe this wasn't the thrilling introduction to the newest adventure you wanted. Oh well, I can't exactly change what happens in my own story, can I? I'm not a novelist, I'm a bloody time traveller (and a nurse, detective, counsellor amongst other things. No wait, Mitch is all those things. Come to think of it, is Mitch me? Am I Mitch? Are those questions the same?)

So, as the awesome chapter title suggests it's back to the drawing board, which means...I have no bloody idea what to do now! I am however extremely hungry, again, time travel certainly drains the old energy reserves. Maybe if I ate better food I could last longer, and I don't mean sexually, or do I? Wait, what? No time to be horny, or is there?

"Excuse me, sir," a gentlemen asks from my left, (or is it my right? No it's my left, God I'm such a weirdo these days!) startling myself out of my sexual pondering. "Are you ready to order?"

Looking around I see I am back at Chino's, the only question is when? Doesn't take me long to figure this out though as I see my dear mum waving at me from a few tables away. Bloody hell! I wave back with what I hope is my best 'everything is fine' expression, when the other me appears out of nowhere holding a bunch of flowers and wearing those God awful coveralls. My mum doesn't even bat an eyelid. Glancing around I see no-one else does either. I'm guessing everyone is bloody blind in this restaurant, or stupid. Not me though, I'm proper clever, got an IQ of probably like seventy-two at least. Wait, is that clever?

"I have an IQ of seventy two!" I blurt out at the waiter, who is still standing there patiently.

"I see," he replies slowly. "That explains a lot. Do you have enough IQ to order sir? Or shall I call for your carer?"

"Hmm, I think I have enough. Can I have the most expensive thing on the menu please my good man?" I order confidently.

"You would like the £300 bottle of French champagne sir? Do you require any food? You were muttering earlier about being famished?" This he asks with a hint of irritation.

"Hmm, I meant the most expensive food please Mr butlering man" I retort with all the grace of an obese penguin.

"Very well sir, the £72 lobster, and the price matches your IQ, how quaint. Anything to drink?"

"Yes please, I'll have a pint of lemonade mixed with a pint of coke, and a slice of lemon."

He looks at me for a little longer than is necessary.

"Sorry sir, you want a pint of lemonade and a pint of coke, so two pints of separate drinks?" he enquires slowly.

"Erm, no, but yes. Thank you Mr butlering dude. Oh, and I don't like lobster so just bring me a nice hot curry please."

"Very well sir. And I'm not a butler I'm a waiter, there's a difference," he huffs, as he rips up another page from his notepad and scribbles down my newest order. Guess this guy has some sort of bee up his bum or something, very strange the waiters in this here establishment, guess they're not used to time travelling legends like good old Mitch here.

After the waiter brings my two drinks over, I glance around the room, seeing myself and my mum deep in conversation. This is where I told her all about my time travelling shenanigans, and she already bloody knew it, cheeky devil that she is. Watching them intently, I'm suddenly overcome once more by how slightly abnormal this situation is. I am watching a previous version of myself approximately twenty years in the past tell my dead mother that I can travel through time, but she already knows anyway, and she just waved at me before the other me arrived. My head hurts! And then they both vanish and no-one in the restaurant bats a God damn eyelid, I mean come on! Does no-one in here use their eyes? There must be at least twenty customers in here and then all the waiters and not one of them notices. In fact, one of the waiters is now walking over and begins clearing away our dishes, we didn't even bloody pay!

"Bloody blind bastards," I mutter.

"Excuse me sir?" my friendly waiter enquires from beside me holding a tray of tasty fodder.

"I have a question me old mucker. There was, or were, two very nice people sat just over yonder way," I point for emphasis. "One was a decent looking chap, the other a very nice lady, where have they vamoosed to?" I hold my chin for effect.

"Ah, the stinky man and his mum. Yes, they have just left the building sir. Your food." He places the steaming curry in front of me, all remonstrations immediately forgotten.

"Thank you, o man of waiting, muchly appreciated." I stand up and bow for no reason whatsoever.

"Of course sir," he replies, walking backwards away from me.

I take a sip of my lemonade, and then my coke, and wonder why he didn't put them in the same glass, or why I would want that anyway. Maybe it's Mitch's favourite drink, maybe it's my favourite drink. Wait, what? Sod it, time to get munching. I scoff the food down with all grace of a starving rhinoceros and burp loudly while pushing my plate away.

"Ah, that's better!" I exclaim loudly, inviting numerous stares in my direction.

"Oh right!" I boom. "I exclaim loudly and everyone notices, but when two people disappear into thin air no-one bats an eyeball! Idiots!"

Then an explosion happens, which sends me flying out of my chair hurtling towards the wall at tremendous speed. Before I have a chance to inspect the incoming inanimate object, I pass a rather good looking gentlemen on the way, is that...me?

CLEANING OUT MY CLOSET

A h alone once more, well apart from sleeping beauty that is, who should be waking up any time now. I exit the wardrobe with all the grace of the invisible man and there we go, right on cue! The sleeping angel awakens from his slumber. Opening his eyes, he is the picture of happiness, content after a night of restful sleep. Well, his life is about to head into the shit storm of all shit storms, trundling right down into shit alley to fester amongst the feral faeces of ferocity (when the hell did I become so poetic?)

Picking up the envelope clumsily placed in front of the clock the idiot glances at it with a bemused expression on his face and retrieves the nothingness from within. I wonder inwardly, what the actual point of this was? I guess the envelope was placed there because it always had been, but what was its purpose? I'm guessing this was the first time this had happened, but then again, was it? Time travel kind of creates a loop that goes on ad infinitum where the beginning and the end merge into one. It really messes with the old grey matter. I guess pointlessly overthinking this shit is, well, pointless.

I'm dragged out of my reverie by a girlish squeal; I guess that bastard cat has just bitten my nemesis. Maybe he has his uses after all, and suddenly I don't quite hate him so much. I still hate him but just like maybe one percent less, or maybe half a percent which is like zero point five, or something. What the hell am I waffling on about? I have a moron to abuse. Not sexually by the way, in case you get any ideas, I know what you lot are like. Wait, who am I talking to? God I am going slightly insane with all this time travelling tomfoolery. Better give my head a shake, which I do, and knock my head off the side of the wardrobe, which kind of hurts. More importantly did anyone hear me? I guess not as I can hear the tap running in the bathroom. I then spot that freaky feline staring in my direction so I hiss as loudly as I can and give him a little pinch on his fat butt, sending him into a sort of demonic frenzy. That was kind of unexpected, but the results are fascinating as he heads his way out of the bedroom towards the bathroom in ultra stealth mode, almost as good as my expert ninja skills. Almost.

As I round the corner I see the back of idiot boy, and I mean all the back of him, he's only got no clothes on the dirty bugger. As if I need to see his stinky butt winking at me. I follow on tip toes like some sort of creeping Jesus just in case some of the floorboards are noisy, I really don't want to miss whatever happens next. I hope that fat little arsehole of a cat scratches the idiot's eyes out, that would be fun. Shit, I made the floorboards creak like an old man slowly expelling himself from his comfy chair! I hesitate and hunker down on my haunches for no reason whatsoever as the moron turns around, his tiny pecker now staring at me, dirty sod. Kind of a good job he did as fat cat was readying for the deadly pounce. I wonder if I actually prevented him from getting even more injured? Or if my actions may have an impact on future events? Who even cares!

Time seems to stand still for a moment as they are both caught in a trance, like two warriors ready to do battle, each one waiting for the other to make the first deadly move. Chubby checker makes the first move as it leaps with unbelievable power from a crouching position into a full length jump straight toward dickhead's face. Go on ravage his stupid features with those razor sharp claws, I want to see him bleed! I want the world to hear his screams as his blood runs rivers of crimson throughout the ravages of time! Alas, no. With expert precision he clocks chubs on the side of the head sending him smashing into the shower glass to land heavily on the floor with a dull thud. Shattering shards of sharpened splinters pour down on him like reflecting rain.

Well that was fun, I'm kind of enjoying this new voyeuristic life of mine, and no I am not getting any perverse sexual gratification out of this you dirty bastards! This is a clean narrative, cleanse your dirty minds you heathens! My newfound friend looks utterly dismayed and leans against the sink for support. That's it, suffer you moronic imbecile.

Just as he is gathering some sort of composure, fatso begins emitting a low rumbling sound. Here we go again, ding ding, round two, go get him tiger! And then the unexpected happens, he kneels down and snaps the fat cat's neck in one swift movement, I'm kind of liking this guy now, good move soldier, about time someone finally shut that stupid obese smoggy up. I stare into the idiot's eyes and can actually see some form of darkness encroaching over his vision. It's almost a physical entity, threatening to pull him down into the abyss of depression. I like that look, it makes me feel good. Again, not in a sexual way, before you get any ideas!

A ringing startles the darkness away as it recedes back to whence it came. The phone on the wall on the landing (why is called a landing? Not exactly an ideal place for planes to touch down is it!) His glumness trudges towards the receiver with the weight of the world on his shoulders and picks it up. He says hello a few times, asks a stupid question, and then puts down the phone with an even more bemused expression on his face.

As he walks back into the bathroom, I decide enough is enough, time to take this buffoon on a magical mystery tour, which could prove quite troublesome as I have to get near to his naked torso which is not going to be a pleasant experience. As he opens the blinds, I reluctantly touch his arm while avoiding everything else and prepare to transport him to another place, but not before the older (newer? Previous? Younger?) version of yours truly stands before me. He hands me some clothing sneakily, which I think is kind of odd, and then I realise why when I look at the naked idiot before me. We give each other a little devious smile coupled with a sinister wink, then off we go.

THE MEETING

"...and I'm an alcoholic," I hear someone mumble, where in holy hell am I now?

"Hi Bill," comes a cacophony of voices, before they all turn around and stare in my direction.

Seems I am in some sort of church hall as I spot a large wooden crucifix staring straight at me from the far wall. Maybe this is my shot at redemption, or maybe it is my one way ticket to see the bad man downstairs. Around fifteen people are seated in a circle of sorts, most with kindly, loving faces, but some with pure terror in their eyes.

"Is this your first meeting?" a smartly dressed man asks while coming over to greet me with his hand outstretched.

I shake it and his grip is firm and true like a soldier's, but the feeling I get from him is one of pure warmth. I hesitate with my reply: it is my first meeting, but I'm not an alcoholic (or am I? Maybe Mitch is a secret alki and is hiding it from me, wait, what!), what do I say?

"Erm, sort of," I reply quietly while giving my nails a cursory glance, good old Mitch, always knows how to look cool.

"My name is Bob, what's yours?" he asks politely.

"Mitch, Mitch Branning," I reply coolly, checking my nails once more, anticipating the ladies' hearts fluttering at a double nail checking encounter.

"No surnames here," Bob says. "Welcome Mitch, please, take a seat."

I do as commanded, although it wasn't really a command, and Mitch Branning takes orders from no man, so I do as he asked, or as he stated, which is kind of an order, I think. Wait, am I just overthinking as per usual?

"Are you OK Mitch?" Bob asks with an air of concern.

I realise I am halfway between sitting and standing while I contemplate whether I am taking orders or not, and that everyone is staring at me, but not with any form of malice, just with smiling interest in this obvious disturbed individual.

"Yeah, cool as ice," I reply with utmost suaveness.

As I sit down I realise I forgot to check my nails, but probably triple checking would send the females into a full on fainting session, and I really need to take a proverbial back seat here to find out my reason for arriving in this location. Is someone trying to tell me to lay off the hard stuff? I don't really have time for drink any more, too busy gallivanting all over the space time continuum. Also, probably not a good idea to be drinking excessively on the job, don't want to get pulled over by the Time Cops, wait, wasn't there a movie about that?

"Please continue Bill," Bob says politely.

"Thanks Bob, yes so my name is Bill and I'm an alcoholic."

I turn to look at the speaker and my heart nearly explodes. It's my dad. My father is sat directly opposite me wearing exactly what I remembered him wearing on the day we visited him at the morgue: light cream trousers, black shoes, and his favourite John Lennon t-shirt. He looks to be about forty years old, although the bags under his eyes and the yellowness of his skin makes him look a hell of a lot older. It takes all of my inner strength not to walk over to him and give him a massive hug, my heart throbs with pain and loss. I never knew he was an alcoholic, I knew he drank a bit when I was younger, he always had that smell about him, like a pub sort of odour, I just thought it was how all dads smelled.

He begins to share a story so dark and depressing that I hang onto his every word like a mountain climber clinging on for dear life after a near death fall. I hear things that probably no son should ever hear from their father. I hear of fear, pain and a crippling remorse that threatens to overwhelm his already frayed senses. What he said, I will not repeat, for this is the code in AA meetings all over the world, but what I will say is his words cut deep into every fibre of my being with all the subtlety of a roaring chainsaw. I felt as though I was being sliced open like a ripe tomato as my heart and soul pour out into the room to be soaked up by all the love from everyone in there. Is this what heaven feels like?

After about fifteen minutes, he finishes speaking and a nice blonde lady to my right asks if I am OK while passing me a tissue. It was only at this point I realised I had been crying all this time and my face was dripping with tears of total despair and some form of relief. I understood now, I finally knew why my dad took his life and although it didn't make it any easier, at least I had a reason now; he was broken, and no amount of meetings in the world could save him from his inner demons. But maybe I could. Maybe that's why I was here, to save my father from taking his own life and leaving his wife without a husband and his children orphaned.

I dabbed at my face and blew my nose with all the grace of a spitting cobra and gathered myself into some sort of composure. I tried not to stare at my dad as other people were speaking from the floor to share their experiences. It was difficult. I always looked up to my dad, and although he died when I was very young, I always remembered him as the strong silent type, but the guy sitting across from me was a broken shell of the man I aspired to be. He caught me staring at him once and I looked away sheepishly, feeling my cheeks burning bright crimson like they used to at school when I was asked to read.

As the meeting wrapped up we all held hands and everyone joined together in some sort of weird chant like we were in a cult. I kind of felt like a proper outsider, which I was, and kind of mumbled my way through whatever God or devil they were offering themselves to. A kind old guy approached me and shook my hands strongly once the sacrificial words had been uttered.

"Nice to meet you Mitch, I'm Roger," he said in a thick Yorkshire accent. "My grandfather told me a funny story once about a guy named Mitch Branning, says he vanished into thin air after he took him to the cop shop, must be where I got my drinking from, tally ho what!" He bursts out laughing. "Keep coming back Mitch, you're amongst friends here," he says as he walks away.

I'm guessing, with my awesome detective skills, that that was Reginald's grandson. Life doesn't get much more messed up than this folks. I guess I should have brought his jumper with me, come to think of it, where did I leave it? I was kind of hoping for a museum of my time travelling outfits to share with my adoring fans one day. Oh well, I guess I have bigger fish to fry at the moment. Time to go and speak to my dear old dad, who is actually about my age, so not really that old. This could get weird, but what else did I expect in the ever-changing chaos of the life I lead these days? A tap on the shoulder startles me from my ongoing inward commentary.

"Hi Mitch, I'm Bill," my father says as he shakes my hand firmly. "Great to see you at your first meeting."

I return his handshake,meekly as my hand shakes from the nervous tension.

"Thanks Dad, I mean Bill," I fumble. Come on Mitch get a grip. "Sorry, I call everyone Dad, you know like dad dad daddy-o. Well not everyone, like I don't call my cat dad, well because he's dead, I killed him." What the shit Mitch? Better to say nothing than blurt out you're a cat murdering psychopath.

"OK," he replies with a hint of worry. "Hey, it's OK to be nervous you know, I was petrified at my first meeting. And I'm sure you didn't mean to murder your cat. We used to have a right horrible bastard of a moggy years ago, wiped out pretty much all the local bird population. Hmm, what was his name again?"

"Zeus!" I blurt out, once more without bloody thinking.

He looks at me dumbfounded. "Yeah, Zeus, but how did you know? Have we met before, you look kind of familiar?"

Time to get my thinking cap on and say something clever to get us out of this insane scenario.

"I have an IQ of seventy two," I say while looking extremely pleased with myself.

Before he has a chance to reply Bob walks briskly over, just in the nick of time.

"Come on guys meeting's over, time to lock up."

As we are ushered out I turn round to thank Bob for the meeting and the warm welcome. I also attempt to say I am not an alcoholic and he just laughs and says "keep coming back" as he walks away down the street. I turn around to my father but he is nowhere be seen. He'd better not be a God damn time traveller as well, but he seems to have vamoosed. Very strange. Tell you one thing though, I could murder a drink after this crazy escapade! As I turn around, I feel a wet rag pressed against my nose and mouth. As I instinctively inhale I am sent into the sweet oblivion of unconsciousness.

BAITING THE IDIOT

fter arriving at our destination, which will henceforth be known as No-Time (in fact it is just a massive grassed area on a secluded island), the moron passes out, which is quite unfortunate as I have to dress the dirty bugger. I kind of like the out-of-fashion clothing my doppelganger has chosen, although I would have just left him naked to mess with his head more. Saying that, then he would just get arrested everywhere he went which, although it would be humorous, it wouldn't quite have the same effect as what I have planned for him. Come to think of it, what is my actual plan?

As I muse inwardly on varying degrees of psychological torture for my new best friend, I hastily dress him, which is an arduous task. As he's a total dead weight (literally as well as figuratively) I fling him over trying to pull his stupid shorts up and his elbow catches me in the nether regions. I punch him in the gut which makes him fart right into my open mouth. Dirty bloody bastard! Now my balls ache and my mouth literally tastes like shit! I hope all this hassle is going to be worth it. And before you ask (or think it, which I bet you are you dirty bastards!) I didn't touch his privates! I just scooped up his shorts and everything fell into place, so no, I'm not a disgusting pervert!

I think that little dig in his stomach has awoken the sleeping fart machine, time to get my invisibility on, which I do (I think, I have no mirrors to check!). Having done this numerous times now you'd think I would have thought to bring a little pocket mirror with me, wouldn't you? And then, as if by magic, a little mirror falls out of Farty Pant's pocket, that bloody Gulaxa thinks of everything. And he is me, so actually I think of everything, or I will, in the future, or the past. So, I make myself visible (I think), pick up the mirror, then make myself invisible again (which definitely happens because I now can't see my reflection in the dinky mirror).

Now you may be wondering why I had to make myself visible to pick up the mirror and then reverse the process. Well, my reading fools, this is because if I did not then he would see the mirror floating about and realised something was up. Only items you hold or are wearing follow you into the realm of invisibility. If you pick something up or put on some clothes while unvisible (is that the same as invisible? Sounds plausible so screw it I'm going with yes) then they just stay in the normal universe of see-able things. Makes sense, right?

Looking down I see my two-legged idiot breathing heavily while scrunching his eyes up. I wonder if my punch to the gut caused him some sort of winding. Awesome, I love causing him pain and misery. Sitting up he glances around with that perplexed look on his face like a little lost girl. I can almost see the internal struggle going on in his tiny mind. After a while he stands up and does some sort of weird rotational inspection of the area, looking like some sort of mechanical scanning device. If only he could see himself now. The glint way off in the distance catches his eye. If only he knew that was him sending himself an eternal time travelling message! Well, he will eventually.

I bet you're wondering why I don't just jump over there and stop the nuclear explosion. Well, it's just not that simple. You'll understand in due course my idiotic reading companions. Turning back towards dumbo, I see he has noticed that he is in fact dressed and has another confused look upon his moronic face. I wonder if he is questioning whether someone was messing about with his tackle? I know I would! I'll just let him contemplate that one for now, no harm in giving him something like this to mull over before more fun and games commence.

Metaphorically pulling up his socks he begins walking in the direction of the glinting. Good boy, get some exercise in those legs you lazy bugger, work off some of that microwave shit you keep stuffing in your fat belly. I saunter beside him doing the occasional moonwalk, looking cool as a cucumber. Wait! Do I actually look cool? I mean can you really look cool while you're invisible? Because to look you have to see, but if you're not visible then you can't be seen, so not sure on that one. I decide to retrieve my mirror to check myself and yeah, I look pretty damn good.

"Hello," I say suavely to myself. Shit! Better make myself visible before tosspot thinks there's an invisible man here, which there is, but he doesn't need to know that.

As he turns to face me, I adopt a dopey demeanour as he comically crouches down pretending to be some sort of special forces hard ass. Actually, he looks like a downright tosspot. I have to struggle to keep my composure as he maintains his idiotic stance whilst checking out how sexy I look. Can't blame him to be honest, I mean I am probably the sexiest man alive, so keep wishing you were me you dumb fool.

"Erm, who are you?" he asks suspiciously.

I ponder my reply, and then in the most stupid, dumbest voice I can conjure up, I lure him into my trap:

"I am your friend, do not be afraid, I only want to help you."

As I utter these words, I almost burst out laughing at his stupid face. This is just too much God damn fun.

"Okay then, why do you want to help me?" he asks seriously.

"You are in great danger. Your life is in great peril. I am your saviour. I am your guide. Come with me, and do not be afraid."

My reply is monotone and serious as I try to keep the same deadpan expression while trying not to burst out laughing. I deserve an Oscar for this shit. He continues to look at me with that same stupid expression and I can see the inward cogs inside his dopey brain slowly turning like a dismantling clock. He's trying to fathom out the meaning behind this cool individual stood before him. He demands answers from me in a shrill voice, obviously trying to act all tough but ending up sounding like a little girl. Time to bring out the big guns.

"If you can't trust me then you will die, the choice is yours. Why did you kill your cat?" I utter these words with more confidence, emphasising each word while still trying to maintain the charade of being a bit abnormal. I'd better get a call from the academy after this, damn I'm good!

Again the internal struggle is evident on his dumb face. I can almost see the inner workings of his thick brain as the worry lines on his face ebb and flow like rain cascading down a filthy window. Just when I think his equilibrium would snap a steely resolve comes over him. A look of sheer determination is etched across his brow. Interesting, maybe this won't be as easy as I thought.

"How do you know about my cat? Did you bring me here? Are you the reason I'm in this bizarre, but also beautiful, place? I want answers buddy, or there'll be trouble, trouble I tells ya!" he blurts out. Whoa there cowboy, take a God damn breath! Jesus this guy is so highly strung right now, which of course makes me chuckle (inwardly of course, I don't want to give the game away). I will have to admit it is very hard not to laugh my arse off at his words, he sounds like a 1920's gangster. What a buffoon. I reply monotonously in my best robotic voice, imagining I am reading from a script, which I'm not. I don't think. I suggest he best follow me, which he does, because what other choice does he have?

I walk away from the moron towards wherever the glinting was, which has now stopped for some reason. I guess us two best friends are now conversing and that idiot has stopped flashing himself in the past. That kind of sounds like some perverted time travel shenanigans, and I wouldn't put it past him the dirty git. I kind of feel a little bit of nervous tension as he doesn't follow me at first. I resist the urge to look back over my shoulder. After a few moments he trudges after me and just stares at me like some creepy uncle; proper freaks me out. But I keep my composure and adopt a dopier looking demeanour, trying not to overdo it by dragging my arms and lolling my tongue, which would of course be hilarious but might make him suspicious. Once he has checked me out in his perverted way, he cheerfully asks my name, as though we were two strangers and he is trying to be charming. Weirdo.

"My name is Gulaxa," I say slowly, which is true so no lie there. And then it hits me how messed up this must make him feel. He's just pretty much brutally decapitated his best (and only) friend in the whole wide world and this sexy, awesome chap appears and says he has the same name as his deceased companion, this is just perfect, or should I say purrfect. Again I employ all my strength not to giggle. I do however allow myself a slight smirk when he seems to slightly look down and ponder this newfound information, but soon regain my deadpan expression. He looks up and questions me once more, this time with a bit of anger in his voice. Way to go tiger, go get em!

"Let me get this straight, you're saying that your name is the same as my deceased cat?"

"Affirmative," comes my awesome robotic reply.

He seems to take this in his stride for now (quite literally as we are still walking). Maybe he thought I was taking the piss, which I was, sort of. We continue walking a little further before he states abruptly that everything looks the same, which is true. That's why I brought him here in the first place and why we end up here later on, or earlier. I can't be sure to be honest. I reply with an affirmation that he is indeed correct and he stops dead in his tracks. He folds his arms across his chest like a toddler and refuses to go any further until I give him some valuable information. This could work out perfectly, I need something prophetic to say, something momentous and inspiring that will mess with his head but also plant a seed of what is to come in the future, or is it the past? I've got it! Switching to my normal voice I muster all the bravado and fearful emotion I can possibly garner and utter these immortal words:

"We have no time to waste, for time is what is giving us chase." God I am so dashingly cool!

The expression on his face says it all; confusion, fear, and then a sort of realisation that these words have some sort of meaning in his life. Then the tremor starts, I guess the detonation has been set, I need to time this next part to absolute perfection.

"What the fuck was that!" he exclaims as I grab a tight hold of his sleeve and drag him backwards ever so slightly through time as his words echo back at him in reverse. This is so frigging awesome!

"We must run now, time is upon us," I say coolly as we run together. I pull him back into the past with all the grace and subtlety of God.

MY WONDERFUL FRIEND

I always like being asleep. When you're asleep all your troubles just melt away like a forgotten snowman, never to return in this everlasting state of pure bliss. Unless you're having a nightmare I suppose, then your troubles become your dreams which in turn become your nightmares – which means you're not dreaming any more you're actually nightmaring, which might be a new word. For God's sake Mitch you are just too clever for this world. But hold on a gosh darn minute, if I'm dreaming (or nightmaring) how am I able to come up with clever new words? How am I able to have such an intellectual conversation with me, myself and Mitch? Hmm, once again the plot thickens. Maybe I should open my eyes.

Ow, the sun is burning my bloody retina! Oh no, wait, it's just a light bulb swinging ominously in the centre of what I deduce to be a bathing room. As it swings in my direction, I go blind, when it swings the other way oh say can I see! Probably not the best time to be inwardly singing, best get my detective cap on and find out where in God's name I am. Before that, a point for future reference – I'm going to start wearing hats. There, I've said it, I'm going to be a hat dude. I could have one with detective on it, or FBI, or kiss me, maybe even a big bloody cowboy hat, this is going to be so much fun!

Anyway, enough about hats (for now), where am I? I attempt to scratch my chin for effect, but I seemed to be unable to. Strange, guess I'm tied up, again! Although I have been in a similar situation before so I'm assuming (or hoping) that my best pal Derek has captured me again and wants to have his wicked way with me. Hopefully not in a sexual way though. Actually not in any way to be honest, I just want us to get along, he seems like such a nice chap, when he's not capturing me and tying me up that is.

Back to surveying my surroundings and I'm guessing my friend has found another lair to hide me in, well another room perhaps. And why in God's name am I naked and tied to a bloody toilet! This guy is nuts, and speaking of nuts what is it with people messing about with my bits without my permission all the time! At least they could bloody ask! But wait, that would take all the fun out of it. Wait, what bloody fun? I am not enjoying myself here!

Now now Mitch. Let's just calm ourselves down and look for the positives here. What if you really needed to go pee pee or poo poo in a normal tied up scenario? Wouldn't it be a right kerfuffle? But not now, you could just relieve yourself without any stress or worry. Well, since you put it that way Mitch, I feel a hell of a lot better now, thank you. And with that excellent realisation I have a little wee with a very contented sigh.

"Ah, that's better."

Glancing around the not so spacious bathroom I take in the delights of my buddy's throne room. There's a bath beside me with a floral shower curtain drawn across. Very nice, very Derek. A sink perched upon its ceramic column holds mysteries and wonders for me to gaze at while envy grips my aching heart. Not really, just trying to add a bit of excitement to a boring scene! Damn Mitch, when did you become such an awesome poetic genius? On the left of me is a closet of some sort, guess I have my hiding place all sorted out if I need to disappear. And that's all folks. Oh and a door straight ahead of me, and that light which is still swinging for some reason, now that is weird, must be a draft in here somewhere. Well not in here, a draft isn't a physical entity it's a, well, it's a bloody ghost, I mean it's a wind. Oh screw it you know what I mean!

The only other thing of note is a dense mist hanging in the air, as if someone has just had a shower. I instinctively smell myself and note that I just smell average. Actually I smell a bit whiffy so it definitely wasn't me in the shower, unless Derek just washed my meat and two veg. I try and bend over to smell my special area, but my hands are tied behind the cistern so no joy there.

"Will you shut up in there!" a voice booms from somewhere outside.

Someone's rather grumpy this morning, or evening, or afternoon. Pondering time: if I was wearing a smart watch would it automatically adjust to whatever time I was in? I mean, they do use some form of internet technology, so as long as I was in a time where there was internet surely the watch would simply update the time and date wherever I was. Sounds plausible, right? I need to get myself a smart watch, which wouldn't actually be as smart as Mitch cos he's the smartest guy in town! I reckon in the future they'll be called Mitch Watches and they'll have built in nail checking reminders, how cool would that be? You heard it here first folks!

"Stop mumbling you bloody idiot!" comes another disgruntled shout from another room.

"I'm not mumbling, I'm thinking," I retort coolly, trying to check my nails, which I manage to do while nearly snapping my neck, good job I checked though cos they're bloody awesome.

After a few choice words I hear some clattering and banging, then a loud thump (I'm guessing he fell over, clumsy idiot), a few more words of profanity and then the door is hastily barged open. Derek is revealed in a pair of My Little Pony underpants (didn't know they made them for boys, or men for that matter) looking rather unhappy. Not for long though as the door he hastily barged open rebounds off the bath and smacks him straight in the face, which in turn forces the side of his head against the frame of the door with quite a lot of force. He stares at me for a few moments with a bemused look on his face.

"You OK me old mucker?" I enquire in my best caring loving voice.

"Idiot," he whispers before dropping flat onto his back with a loud thud.

"Hmm," I ponder outwardly. This is a bit of a weird predicament, I ponder inwardly. I guess I could just have a little nap until my mate wakes up. It's not very comfortable in this position though and it's probably best I bugger off in case he wakes up in a horny sort of mood after the nasty bang he has just received on his thick noggin. Wait, has he just received a bang on his head? Kind of sounds like a gift has been given to him, from himself. Maybe he has been given a gift, a gift from God to him, or maybe it was a gift from God to me from Him to Derek. Hmm, kind of doesn't make sense, but then again what does these days!

I suppose I could just jump, but then my very clever brain senses the mist in the air. Guess my buddy was killing two birds with one shower: get clean, stop Mitch from jumping, what a clever little sausage you are my two legged companion. Right, how the hell am I going to escape from this situation? Come on Mitch, get your thinking cap on. Ha! Another form of headed attire I can wear, a bloody thinking cap, this is going to be so much fun! I need to find a hat store, and pronto! Probably should extricate myself from my current scenario first though.

Glancing around I see nothing of use to free myself, where's Batman when you need him? Maybe brute strength would work. I clench my jaw tight, straining every sinew and muscle, my extremely buff six pack and bulging biceps ripple with the exertion. I fart loudly sending an unwelcome aroma up my nostrils which adds a little more power to my movement and then suddenly my binds cleanly sever. I am forced forward right into a face full of My Little Pony crotch.

Well, not exactly the outcome I was expecting but at least I'm free. Retrieving my facial area from the cute little pony (the underpants not the crotch!) I pull myself up into a standing position, checking out my taut muscular frame while examining my perfect nails. I am such an Adonis. If there were ladies here now they'd all be beside themselves with sexual tension. I grab a towel from inside the closet and dry myself off while pondering my next move. I guess clothing should be the first thing I should be looking for.

Heading out of the room I see I am in fact in Derek's lair as I spy his bed before me. Oh how I remember the sweet dreams I had there. Was that when I ended up going to meet my pal Reg? Oh how I loved that guy. I stride over to the cupboard in the corner, not expecting a wardrobe because I'm sure he has one in the other room, but hello! What have we here? Looks like either a fetish or fancy dress closet, have I hit the jackpot here or what? Well, maybe not as I spot a big black dildo with some sort of extension thing on the back staring me right in the face. Is it wrong that I want to smell it to see if it's clean? I stop myself from doing so, Mitch is not that guy, at least I don't think he is!

Snapping myself out of my sexual musings I spot something spectacular: a Wonder Woman outfit complete with a blonde wig, which seems kind of strange as Wonder Woman was a brunette, but who am I to judge a man's taste! Weird thing about the costume though is that it has a crotch, and by that I mean it has an area to accommodate the old wedding tackle. The question is, have I got the balls to try this on? I mean I do literally have balls, so the answer must be yes, but do I?

Rejecting any form of self-sabotage, I hastily dress myself in the costume, giggling like a little girl as I do so. There's no harm in trying out new things, I'm not going to jump anywhere with this on, that would be downright lunacy. I'll just try it on, check myself out in the mirror, then get some proper clothes from the other room. After making sure my bits and bobs are loaded in correctly, I check myself out in the mirror, giving my cape and sexy short skirt a twirl as I do so. What a cool dude I am! Well, I'm actually a dudette at the moment but hey, no harm no foul.

Right, fun's over, best get changed. Wait a minute there's something moving in the mirror. Turning around I head over in the direction of a picture frame hanging on the wall and glance at the person waving his...ah shit!

BASTING THE TURKEY

Watching him run on the spot like a cartoon character fills my brain with pure joy. I see the exertion in his face as it gets redder and redder the more he pushes himself, he resembles a bloody turkey. If only he knew how bloody stupid he looks, his stupid fat gut wobbling grotesquely as his breathing intensifies, he looks on the verge of having a heart attack. I am seriously tempted to just let him die right here and now in this time loop just for the fun of it, but then again that would be too easy. I want him to suffer more. Maybe just five more minutes of running though, just to get rid of some of that chubbiness.

Once again I time my release to perfection and ease us out of our time jog, watching him fall to the floor hacking up the contents of his lungs, what an unfit slob. I stand beside him nonchalantly without an ounce of exertion on my face, probably making him feel very inadequate and fat, which he is.

"How are you not even tired?" he asks while coughing like an asthmatic penguin.

I adopt my stupidest deadpan expression (pretty much imitating the idiot in front of me) and politely exclaim that this is not my time, subtly alluding once more to the aspect of time travel to fry his brain.

"What is it with all this time talk, don't tell me you're from the future, because I don't buy it," he moans like a petulant little brat.

I am so tempted to reply with 'and I'm not selling it' and almost burst out laughing. Before I let my facade fall I proceed in making one cool as hell rotation of my surroundings with all the grace of a sober ballet dancer. I guffaw slightly into my mouth once I am out of his vision and regain my composure once my viewing has finished. It is becoming so hard to keep my grip on this masterful charade, I really do expect a call from the academy after this.

I beckon him to sit down beside me, pretty much commanding him to park his fat ass, which he does without remonstration, good boy, obey your master.

"We're safe now, but we may need to hurry. Time waits for no man," I say softly.

The immortal phrase, uttered for the first time, probably sends chills right through every fibre of his being. I see him staring at me out of the corner of my eye, probably yearning to be as handsome and sexy and cool as I am. Wishing that one day he could be the ultimate personification of excellence which I now possess; well good luck with that one pal, there's only one Gulaxa. Well actually that's not true, but more about that later, or earlier, or maybe I'm just talking about the cat. About which there isn't actually any more of, so no more about that furry dickhead earlier, or later, oh bloody hell!

I adopt my best robotic demeanour and politely demand he listens carefully. He replies that he is all ears, which as we all know is a well-known phrase, but to which I, for some strange reason, reply:

"What a strange turn of phrase, you have only two ears, if you were all ears then your hands and feet and arms and legs would be ears."

I really have no idea where this came from, but I guess it kind of fits into the acting stupid kind of game I'm playing so who gives a shit. I think it might also add a bit of mystery and intrigue into my persona as well, and we all love a bit of that. It seems to get a reaction as well as he gets a little frustrated with his reply.

"For God's sake it's just an expression, please continue I'm listening," he blurts, getting a little red in his stupid face again, excellent.

I then bring out the big guns and bait the thick turkey looking bastard like he's never been basted, I mean baited, before. Have some of this you freaky feathered fowl!

"You are the master of time, in fact we all are, but you are the one who has complete control over it. This place where we are now, you may think that someone else brought us here but in fact it was you. This place is called No-Time for it is in fact not future, not past and not present. It is a place where time itself is obsolete."

"Go on," he smirks.

Not the response I was expecting. I wanted more of a head explosion type of outburst not a smirk as if he was laughing at me. I control my inner rage and channel my Zen mode, don't let him get to you Gulaxa, you're the master and he is the slave. Show him who's boss.

"As you have probably gathered," I politely continue. "We are not getting anywhere when we walk or run in this place. The whole landscape looks exactly the same. This is because without time's construct, when you travel you do not move, simple quantum mechanics actually. Now you may wonder what we are running from, what those shock waves were, well all of that is time. When persons tinker about with time incorrectly, then time has a tinker back, in a bad way."

Have some of that you bloody bastard, prepare to have your mind blown.

"Okay, so far so good," he replies with a massive dose of sarcasm.

I feel like kicking him right in the nuts the cheeky, fat, poultry looking shithead! I've just come up with a very precise and clever explanation about a fictional out of time location while also telling you that you can travel through time and your reply is to smirk at me. You little piss-head! Fuck you and all your four-legged dead friends! Calm down Gulaxa, get a grip will you. I proceed to inform him, in my Oscar winning tone, that we need to head to the glint to fix our mistakes.

"I'll humour you for a bit here pal, how can we get to that glint if we can't actually move from one place to another in this No-Time place?" he says matter-of-factly while finger posing the 'No-Time', cheeky little wanker.

But alas, I see my anger has gotten the better of me, he has a very valid point. Maybe the dumb shit isn't as stupid as he looks, which is kind of hard to believe because he looks like Forrest Gump's less intelligent brother. Quick, think of something clever to say, which I do, obviously, because I am a God damn genius.

"Well that's where you come in. I've been letting you gather your faculties so as you can grasp the enormity of the situation. I do however realise that you may not be taking this situation as seriously as I would like."

Very clever, very cool, just about holding my anger in check.

"No shit detective," he jokes.

Fucking wanker! I'm gonna fry his balls in a vat of acid and then feed them to his stupid deceased hairy dickhead of a cat! Deep breaths, deep breaths, although don't breathe deep or he'll know something is up, just keep a lid on this melting pot. Wanker!

"My point is made," I reply through gritted teeth. "Anyway, for us to proceed forwards, you have to take us. The power of time is in your mind. If we fail to adhere to this simple process, to put it in your basic vocabulary, we are fucked."

Have some of that you thick bastard, how do you like that sarcasm right in your stupid feathered face! I resist the urge to spit in his facial area. I am getting very good at resisting. I am however not getting good at not getting angry, maybe I need to take a chill pill, or just dump this piece of turd onto a farm with his turkey mates.

He then proceeds to call me his two-legged friend which is a: true and b: false. Yes I have two legs, but no I am not your friend you stupid git! I don't hear the rest of his stupid words as the red mist is descending rapidly over my veil of serenity. He does break me from my rage though by jumping up and clicking his heels like Mary Poppins, or was it someone else? Who the hell cares! And then he has the cheek to start laughing like an idiot which just boils my bloody piss!

"You have to remember how you arrived here," I say with all the subtlety of a raving lunatic. "For it wasn't an external force that transported you, it was you and you alone. The power is inside you, you just have to harness that energy."

Let's get this idiot out of here, I've had enough. Come on just jump, it's easy, you can do it. But no, he just stares at me with that same gormless expression.

"Well," he says dumbly. "What now?"

For God's sake I'm really going to lose my shit here pal, just fucking jump!

"Remember what happened when it all went dark," I say calmly and firmly, while gripping my hands tightly and imagining wringing this stupid sod's wrinkly turkey neck!

He closes his eyes, that's it stupid face, you've got it, keep going, keep thinking. You've got five seconds before I smash you right in your horrible face. I pull back my fist ready to strike all my fury into his moronic expression, and when I can't hold on any more and let loose with the wrath of a million slaughtered turkeys he vanishes, sending me face first into the ground. I scream loudly into the earth letting all my emotions explode.

"I'm gonna kill this feathered fucker!".

I then calmly pull myself into a seated position, pat myself down and take a deep breath. God I hate this bastard so much. Once I've regained my cool as hell internal and external composure, I continue on with my quest to torture this stupid sod's life.

WET DREAMS

T orrential rain hammers down on my skimpy attire soaking me within seconds. Sheets of sideways pummelling showers bounce off the surface of the road like pebbles scattered from a fast moving ship, causing miniature explosions on the surface like nuclear detonations. A howling wind shrieks out from all around, incoherent wailing like a screaming banshee, ruffling my sexy skirt and my even sexier hairy legs.

Way to go Mitch, good job, maybe you should invent a time travelling weather forecaster as well before you jump. In Mitch's defence it wasn't a planned jump, it was that stupid picture waving at me. Well not the picture, it was someone inside it, or on it, or in it, or was it actually the picture? I really need to fathom out what all that stuff is about, it's really buggering up my adventure to become the greatest time traveller in the whole wide world. I guess there's a time and a place for everything, and standing here stock still thinking random thoughts while getting soaked dressed as Wonder Woman in a random location is probably not the best time to be pondering. Hey, Pondering Through Time, what a great name for a novel. Shut up Mitch! Get your detective hat on, ah hats, forgot about them. But wait, could I wear a hat while wearing this wig? Saying that, the wig is bloody stuck to my head like an overused mop! Oh that brings back memories, I wonder how my pal MB is doing right now. I miss him. Anyway, once again I digress.

I suppose the best thing to do right now is find some shelter, although it's a bit late as I'm already soaked through. Better late than never though Mitch! The battering rain makes it very difficult to see a bloody thing. I shield my eyes as best as I can and head in the direction of the nearest door which has some sort of sign hanging over the top. I can't make out what it says but I don't really care, shelter is shelter so I reach the entrance and push my way through the thick oak door.

I'm instantly overcome with a coughing fit as the room is filled with smoke that attacks the back of my throat like prying fingers. A cacophony of noise pounds my brain while sending a welcome distraction to my wandering thoughts. Mumbled voices intersect each other in criss-crossing conversations, all amalgamating with all the grace of a talk show host battling incessant callers. A piano plays a soulful melody which reaches my inner core, soothing it like an angel's gently flapping wings. The rain outside has dulled somewhat, but the sound it makes against the window accompanies the soft music perfectly as the patrons in (what I'm guessing) is a pub ignore it to concentrate on their own meaningful chatter.

I close my eyes and sway softly to the angelic noise, forging some sort of connection both inside and outside of my body. Feeling this surge of blissful enlightenment within me, I gather pace with my swaying, seeming to reach the corners of the realms of the known universe one way and then the next. This feels fantastic, it feels as though I'm back in those woods on that other planet, completely at one with everything. Then the chattering and music stops abruptly. All I can hear is the constant drumming of the rain against the glass, probably telling me to get a move on and open my eyes. Which I do, and witness everyone staring at me wide-eyed, full of love and admiration for the beautiful Zen-like human being stood before them. I bet they think I am some sort of angelic God sent down from the heavens to heal their heathen ways. Never fear my children, Mitch is here to save you...

"Who's this fanny?" an abrupt gentleman shouts from the back, sending the whole pub into bursts of raucous laughter and instantly shattering my ego.

"Well that's just rude," I mutter, causing another bout of loud hilarity.

"Nice legs you poofy little wanker!" a nice guy exclaims from somewhere.

"Show us your tits!" another kind person asks from the back once more. Probably the same dickhead as earlier.

Then it dawns on me that I may not be dressed entirely appropriately for this here establishment, or any establishment for that matter. Could I have put myself in any worse a situation? Well, yes, probably, I could be naked, but would that actually be any worse than what I'm wearing right now? That's a tough one to call, as I stare down at my once sexy outfit that made me feel so carefree and now makes me feel ugly and unwanted. I bow my head in shame and disgust at myself for allowing this to happen.

"Oh look, it's going to cry," someone snipes from my right.

This makes me snap with ferocity and explode with fury. I grab him by the neck with the intent of taking him on a journey to the centre of the sun to find out what really makes people cry. Good job I'm soaking wet through as all I get is blood dripping from both my nostrils and a kick in the balls. Not fair, but at least it prevented me from causing death by dangerous jumping and also a possible hint to a room full of people that time travellers do exist.

"Touch me again you little gay boy and I'll feed you your balls, dirty fucking pervert!" My new best friend shouts at me with stinking fag and booze breath, as I rub my nether regions while laid in the foetal position on the floor.

After rubbing and cajoling my two best mates into a happier state of being I stumble to my feet, head still down, shoulders slumped and with another dark cloud looming over my stupid soaking wig. I have no idea of where I am heading but I hear random mutterings of the patrons as I pass them by.

"Cock-boy," one cries.

"Wanker," says a lady from my right, if you can call her a lady using profanity like that.

"Stuffing wanking shitbag," another shouts. I am quite impressed by this, never been called that before. Very clever usage of the English language my friend.

Arriving at a door, I clumsily push myself through, still not bothering to raise my head an inch which would probably be wise, but why bother thinking any more, it just makes things worse. A lady pushes past me tutting disgracefully as she leaves the room, a room which I notice is the ladies' toilet as soon as I lift my gaze, hmm not good. Although maybe not all bad as I have never been in one before. I guess Mitch's life is never a dull one.

Heading over to the huge mirror that adorns the wall I stare at my reflection, and it is not a pretty sight. I bet Wonder

Woman herself would be ashamed of me letting down her costume. I rip off the sodden wig and fling it out an open window, why don't I ever learn from wearing costumes? They don't define me as a person, my actions do. I rip off the rest of the attire and throw it out of the window after the wig. Fuck you Wonder Woman! I mean, I don't mean that, I mean I would, but I don't, oh screw it!

I see a towel draped over a nearby railing and dry myself readying for my next adventure, wherever that may be. I do momentarily wonder why I brought myself here. There's always a reason for everything, isn't there? And then just as I'm stood there completely naked staring into the mirror, my old pal Reg walks into the bathroom.

"Are you alright in..." he begins before stopping mid-sentence and catching my eye (and everything else!) in the mirror.

"You!" he exclaims, pointing in my direction.

"Hi Reg," I say while waving, and then I disappear into the ravages of time.

LOST AND FOUND

Arriving back in the bathroom of my enemy's home, I stand on broken glass. Not a great start! So much for being super stealthy and all that, what's happening to me lately? I seem to have lost all my cool as hell equilibrium. I may need to take something to calm myself a little bit, no harm in accepting a little bit of help now and again from Doctor Laxa. Anyway, where is the bloody idiot? I can't hear any high pitch squealing or squawking. I wonder if he made it to the right place.

I creep into the bedroom and see he's not asleep in his bed so I'm guessing at least one version of him must be lurking about somewhere, this could get interesting. I wander down the stairs in stealth activation mode to the sight of no-one at all – very strange. Well, seeing as though I have the house to myself, I may as well rummage through his medicine cabinet. Off I trundle back upstairs, stealth mode deactivated as I thump up his stupid stairs to head into his bathroom and fling open the drugs cabinet with extreme earnest.

Hmm, what do we have here: plasters, ear buds, paracetamol, ah jackpot! Diazepam, come to papa! Oh 10mg that'll do nicely, down the hatch my little friend, time to get my chill on. I keep a hold of the sleeve in case I need more. You just never know when you might need a little chill pill to take the edge off. I plonk myself down on the toilet seat and await the incoming tide of serenity. As I close my eyes and await the inevitable, I hear a familiar voice call out.

"Oi Gulaxa, where the bloody hell are you?"

I hesitate for a moment before the door is pushed open and I am stood before me. Nothing new here folks, just two versions of the same person in the same place and time.

"I know you're in here I heard you thumping about. Also, I've already been here so show yourself before I kick you in the balls!"

"Alright alright keep your hair on!" I exclaim while making myself visible.

"There you are you lazy bastard, what are you doing? Clean the fucking glass up!" he barks at me like a building site prick.

"Why?" I question innocently.

"Because it's your God damn job, didn't the other guy tell you what you had to do? I bet he's sat on his fat arse as well!"

"If you're on about another version of me, or us, then no, you're the first I've spoken to. Also, if he has a fat arse then so do you, so you're just basically insulting yourself, and me for that matter," I say as I hold my chin in a thoughtful pose.

He looks at me with a very angry expression on his face, I think this guy needs a chill pill too.

"Pass me one then you cheeky bastard!" he replies rudely to my inward question. Very strange, but I decide not to ask how he knew what I was thinking. Best not get involved, especially as I can feel my buzz coming on strong.

I extricate a little blue tablet from the sleeve and hand it to my doppelganger who chucks it down his neck while swallowing loudly.

"Ah that's better!" he exclaims while sitting down on the edge of the bath. "So, how's things?"

"I hate that feathered fucker," I say with soft venom as I feel the enveloping feeling of bliss overcome me.

He laughs heartily. "Yeah, he is a right twat isn't he. I remember the turkey phase so well, wait till you get to...oops sorry, nearly gave away some vital information, can't be doing that now can we? Or I."

"Gulaxa!" someone else shouts, who the hell is this now?

The door opens and there's no-one there, very strange, and then another version of me makes themselves visible. This is getting proper trippy man. I wonder if I've taken LSD and not diazepam, I check the sleeve discreetly to make sure.

"What the hell are you two doing? You should be cleaning the glass up!" He points at me. "And you!" Pointing at the other one. "I actually can't remember what you're supposed to be doing, my head is screwed. Anyone got any diazzies?"

I instinctively retrieve a tablet and hand it over, guess I'm a God damn drug dealer now, oh well all good in the hood I suppose, and I reckon you can't get done for giving yourself drugs. He throws it in his gob and begins munching down on it. Strange, but I suppose it gets into your system quicker, good thinking, I'll remember that for future reference.

"Ah that's better!" he shouts loudly, startling me somewhat from my blissful state of being.

"Right, before this kicks in, let's tidy up the glass you lazy bastards," number 3 orders.

Number 2 chimes in: "Why don't we just sweep it into the corner? I really can't be arsed with doing anything strenuous at the moment, and to be honest no-one will ever know or even care."

He has a very good point, so we all stand up and use our shoes to hastily push the glass into the corner of the room, jostling awkwardly for position. We then push the door almost against the wall.

"See, easy peasy," number 2 says smugly. "By the way, what sort of an idiot has a shower curtain and a glass door? Seems like double standards to me."

"Good point," number 3 agrees. "Maybe he knew this was going to happen, in the past, in the future."

My head hurts, but it also feels nice, I think I need a little nap.

"Wait!" number 3 shouts. "You're meant go and meet dickhead at Derek's! I mean Derek's for the first time, so fuck off!"

"Who, me?" number 2 enquires. "I was going to look for the cat."

"No not you, and yes you're right, you're on cat fucking duty."

We both look at him suspiciously.

Number 3 blushes. "I don't mean you're supposed to go and make love to the cat, or any cats for that matter. I meant, oh piss off! Go and find the cat, and you," he points at me "go see Derek, for the first time!"

"Fine," I say petulantly. "You two are spoiling my buzz any way. Before I go, what cat are you looking for?"

They both look at each other seriously, then burst out laughing. They stop when they see the confused look on my face.

"What, you don't know?" number 2 asks incredulously.

"Obviously not," number 3 retorts. "Look, go and see Derek and you'll find out eventually, go on, fuck off!"

So, I make myself invisible once more and go on my merry way leaving these two idiots to argue amongst themselves. Wait, does that mean I'm an idiot as well?

HEAVEN SENT

This time I planned my jump, which makes a bloody change. I decided to go and pay my grandad a visit to see if he remembers our little encounter all those years ago. The problem is I arrive in the middle of the night, with the strong possibility of waking him up again. Although was he really asleep the last time I saw him at the nursing home? Turns out this time he actually is catching some shut-eye, as the room is in almost complete darkness, guess even experienced time travellers can be sneaked up upon.

Moonlight gazes in through an open curtain, illuminating the silhouette laid in the bed as it rises and falls like a soft flowing wave. Tiny dust particles hang lazily in the air reminding me of a time long ago when I once pondered about dust travelling through time. How much my life has changed since that moment is beyond comprehension. I sit down on the end of the bed, feeling the springs creak like an old man, quite a befitting simile to be honest. Soft droning fills the air as my grandad snores lazily with all the grace of a senile bee.

As a meditative state starts to overcome me once more, I close my eyes and forge another connection with something that is not of this planet, but of all planets, everywhere and everywhen. Somehow, I feel connected to all that ever was and ever will be. Is this what it feels like to be God? Wait, am I a God? Is Mitch God? Mitch Branning: Time traveller, nurse, counsellor, detective, linguistic, God! Can this guy get any cooler? Well, actually no he can't, I think being God is pretty much the pinnacle of everything.

Stopping my runaway thoughts in their tracks I reminisce about my most recent jump. Fancy running into my old pal Reg, what a guy he is, or was. I always knew I'd bump into him again one day. I wonder if he thought the same. Such a shame I didn't have my, sorry, his jumper on me. Oh well, maybe next time, I'm sure our paths are likely to cross again. Maybe I should give it a clean before I return it, but no, that might make him feel bad, so I'll leave it in its natural fragrance of Eau de Reg. We may be bound together by the hands of fate; I seem to have a habit of running into people on more than one occasion. I do however wonder how his mental state may be. I vanished both times now, but worse than that I never said goodbye to him either. What a terrible friend I am.

A noisy trumpet like sound erupts from behind me, startling me from my reverie. What a dirty bugger he is. I imagine I never make such noises while I sleep, I am God after all. Wait, am I the God or am I just a God? Hmm, something to ponder over later. Suddenly I hear the quiet angelic symphony of a classical orchestra. Is this the angels playing their song me for me? Are they calling out to their omnipotent creator? I stand up abruptly creating both a disgruntled creaky sigh from the bed and another tooting noise from its occupant.

"I am here my subjects," I coo softly as I begin to sway and flow to the beautiful voices with my eyes closed.

"Never fear for God is here. I'm always near my darling dears!" I boom loudly while dancing with all the grace of Mick Jagger on acid.

I hear a terrifying scream from the bed. A strange sound to be coming from an ex-soldier, although he did squeal girlishly when I shot him a little bit, many moons ago. I open my eyes to extreme brightness. I'm guessing the angels have opened heaven to receive their Messiah.

"Pervert!" I hear a high pitched voice shout, not really the welcome a God should expect, especially from his loving grandfather.

As my eyes become accustomed to the light, I see a very frightened old lady in my grandads bed with the bed sheets pulled up to her chest. Hmm very strange. Unless, this isn't the right room, shit! Quick Mitch think, say something clever!

"I am God!" I shout profoundly while holding my arms out in exultant fashion.

I realise this isn't the wisest course of action as I still have no clothes on. Good job Mitch. The poor lady screams once more.

"Perverted little wanker!" Nice choice of words you heathen.

Then, right in the nick of time, my grandad flings open the door and storms in like a raging bull. He takes one look at me and shakes his head.

"You are an idiot! Go into my room, I'll calm Doris down, bloody fool!"

Again, not the welcome I was expecting as I trudge out of the room with my head lowered. Why is this guy always such a bastard to me? If only he knew I was God, then he might treat me with a bit more respect. I hear his calming words fading into the distance as the classical music increases in volume. I near my grandad's room, and guess it wasn't the angels after all. Although maybe the angels told grandad to play it? That makes sense to me. Come to think of it why in holy fuckery was my grandad playing music at daft o clock in the morning? Did he know I was coming here? But if he did, why didn't he stop me before I flashed poor old Doris? Hmm, I'll speak to the little bugger when he gets back in here.

As I open the door to his room, the classical music greets me warmly, and loudly, I might add. I'm guessing all the old dears in here are very hard of hearing because if not he'll have the whole building up and awake. Heading over to the ancient stereo system I turn the volume down to a somewhat more appropriate level and sink myself into his favourite chair, hearing it give an unhappy moan at what must be an unfamiliar butt.

"Well sorry," I say petulantly, drawing out the last word for effect.

I start to gaze around the room then stop abruptly. I'm sure there was a picture here before? The one that sent me off on a wild time ride somewhere. I wonder, can the same photo send me to the same place more than once? Would I end up in the same time? Doesn't seem quite logical really, I could just keep coming back and staring at the photo and an infinite number of versions of me would be in the same place and time forever and ever. What if I took the photo with me and just kept staring at it? Would the whole universe blow up or would various versions of myself be vying for position like squabbling geese? Interesting concept, not quite ready for trying it out yet though, maybe later. Let me have a little natter with the bestest grandad first and then we'll see what's what, what? I think I'm losing the God damn plot, I'm whatting at myself now.

I hear my grandad's footsteps thumping down the corridor, what a jovial chap he is, I'm really looking forward to our little chat together. I always get the impression that he really loves me and thinks I am awesome, because well, I am really, aren't I? I mean, I am God, and God is pretty great so that means I am too, and Mitch is, wait, what?

"Stop pondering you idiot!" my grandad booms while giving me an unwelcome tap on the noggin. "And what the devil are you playing at? You've scared Doris half to death, and she was halfway there already."

This stops me in my tracks.

"So, is she dead?" I enquire.

"No she's not bloody dead!" he shouts.

"Hmm, you just said, and I quote, 'you've scared Doris half to death', unquote, re-quote, 'she was half there already'. Half dead plus half dead equals full dead..." I finish my awesome morbid mathematical formula while holding my chin for effect.

He seems to look at me for an age, probably wondering how come he is so lucky to have such a cool and clever grandson.

"You're an idiot," comes his joking reply.

"I love you too grand-papa," I gush while blushing sweetly.

"Get out my chair you fat fool," he asks nicely, which I oblige as the chair wheezes unhappily. And then when my grandad sits down it seems to let out a contented sigh, happy now its favourite butt is nestled in.

"What are you doing here?" he (not the chair) asks coyly. "Wait, before you answer get a towel from the bathroom, you're making me nervous you queer little bugger."

I do as I'm asked and return to sit on the bed facing him as he sighs heavily.

"Why are you wearing the towel like a woman? I can still see your little pecker winking at me!"

"I didn't want you to get jealous of my proper buff six pack grand-papa," I reply sheepishly.

He tuts once more with all the grace of a racist chimpanzee.

"Go and get another bloody towel then, idiot!"

Which I do. Kind of weird wearing two towels but I'm not complaining if it makes my best mate happy. Once more I make my way over to the bed and sit down with a contented sigh.

"Once again, why are you here?"

"I was just wondering if you remembered me coming to see you when you were a young lad? Well youngish, you said you were twenty-five I think. We had a right good old natter, and then a little accident happened."

"Of course I remember you idiot. It might have turned out differently if you had warned me earlier."

I pause, waiting for him to go on, which he doesn't.

"I do not understand, oh wise one," I say, standing up and bowing reverently.

He sighs heavily, I think it's a sign he really likes me.

"Well, when I pulled the trigger, which was an empty chamber by the way, for some reason you only had one bullet in your gun, you vanished. Then five seconds later you appeared behind me wearing exactly what you're wearing now and told me you were God and that I was coming to kill you. Making any sense?"

No, not really, I think.

"No, not really," I say. "But hold on a gosh darn minute, does this really mean I'm God?"

"For God's sake!" he mutters under his breath.

"For my sake don't you mean," I say while standing up proudly. "Bye grand-papa, love you." I say while blowing him a little kiss and buggering off to, well you know where, don't you?

TAG TEAM

Ah Derek, how I miss this brutish idiot. Look at him whistling away without a care in the world washing his pits in the sink. There's a bloody shower not two feet away you stupid sod. I am always amazed by his complete lack of brains, but I guess that's what you get for being a big dumb buffoon. I have to think twice about who I hate more. Is it this stupid rock or the idiotic turkey next door? Who may not be next door yet, but you know what I mean.

"Hello me old pal!" I boom loudly, startling the dumb ape into squirting water everywhere.

"What the fuck?!" he exclaims loudly while spinning around trying to track the sudden outburst. He can't, cos I'm God damn invisible!

I toy with the idea of playing with him for a bit, then realise I need his help for my next charade so make myself visible while leant against the frame of the door like the legend I am.

"Sorry mate, forgot I was invisible, how's tricks?" I enquire nicely.

"How's tricks?" he asks angrily while stepping forward with a hint of venom in his movements. I detect this by the way his giant hands are bunching into fists and thick veins sticking out on his tree trunk sized neck.

"Whoa there cowboy!" I say holding my hands up confidently. "You do know there are more versions of me, don't you? Anything happens to me and you'll be tortured for eternity. Ask yourself, do you really want to mess with us?"

He pauses a foot away from me and I see the terror flicker in his eyes as the anger dissipates like a wilting flower.

"Good boy, get back on that leash, woof woof!" I bark, literally.

"What do you want?" he asks while towelling his pits with all the grace of a preening gorilla.

"I need you to help me mentally torture the idiot that's about to arrive in your rather spacious living room. It won't take too much of your time, then you can go back to being a dumb fucking mutt. You in?"

"Looks like I don't have a choice, do I?" he asks with the slightest hint of dissent.

"No, you don't. Give me ten minutes then grab your biggest gun and come in and start threatening the little wanker. We might have to do a little improvisation, but I'm sure you can manage that."

"Yes, Sir Wankalot," he mutters.

"I heard that!" I say sharply,

I head off into the other room which thankfully is dark due to it obviously being night time. This will make things a little more ominous, but I'm sure I can make the atmosphere way worse! I jump up and rip off the pink lamp shade from the only light in the room, causing it to swing angrily from side to side. I notice a chair in the corner of the room, actually facing the wall for some strange reason. Was this Derek's naughty corner?

Does he put himself there when he is a bad boy?

Anticipating, or rather hoping, that the idiot would pass out again when he arrives, seeing as though it will be his first time making himself jump, I grab the chair and begin searching through some nearby drawers for something to tie the shithead up with. There you go, good old fashioned cable ties, made for one thing and one thing only: tying idiots up.

Just as I'm about to ask if my pal Derek is ready, the idiot appears right in front of me in a cross legged position on the chair. Excellent, saves me picking him up, but then he falls off. Shit! Useless fat tosspot! I attempt to pick him up, but the fat bastard is too heavy.

"Derek!" I shout.

Derek barges into the room.

"Who wants some of this shit?" he shouts while waving around a bright orange super soaker.

I stare at him incredulously.

"What the hell are you doing?" I exclaim.

"You told me to find the biggest gun and start shouting, that's what I'm doing!" he retorts.

"Firstly, you're an idiot. Secondly, I meant a real gun, we want to scare the little wanker not make him laugh his arse off. And last, but definitely not least, thirdly, who wants some of this shit? Threaten the twat, make him shit his stupid little knickers!"

"A: I have learning difficulties. B: I don't own a real gun. And fucking C: I'll try better next time Mr Wankstain!"

I sigh heavily.

"Look, sorry I've been so harsh on you. My diazzy is wearing off a little and this dickhead stresses me out. Come help me lift him up and tie him to this chair I found weirdly placed in the corner."

"Okay," he says sheepishly, avoiding my eyes.

So me and my humongous mate lift up the feathered one, dump him onto the chair and tie him up.

"Good work my friend," I say patting him on the back. "Now, there's a gun behind your sink in the bathroom, go get it and get a feel for it. Come back in here in about five minutes, there's a good little soldier."

I pat his butt for good measure as he trundles away through the door. Just before he does, he lets out the biggest fart I have ever heard, and as he departs the waft of wind created by the door sends the foulest stench my way. What the hell has that buffoon been eating?

"Sorry," he says while opening and closing the door sending more wafts my way. What a wanker! He shuts the door while grinning slyly.

As I am struggling to control my retching, I hear the idiot waking up. I flick the light once more to recreate that ominous swinging effect, then make myself invisible. After checking invisibility has been achieved (with my trusty mirror), I watch the fool come around. This should be fun. With a face the personification of confusion, he gazes around like a little lost puppy, which is quite apt as I just barked at Derek. Guess we're having a dogging session right now, suppose it's better than turkey season. And by dogging I don't mean what you're thinking you dirty bastards!

I can see the utter bewilderment on his face as he takes in his surroundings. I can almost see the cogs turning slowly in his pea sized brain as he asks himself if he has in fact travelled through time. Well, the evidence is right there you idiot, just accept it and move on. But no, that would be too simple for this fool. As he glances around, I see a questioning look on his face. He's probably wondering where I am, time to get my acting guise back on. I walk behind him for effect.

"I am here," I chime up, watching the idiot jump like a little child.

As I'm about to walk in front of him I almost forget to make myself visible which I quickly correct, forgetting about the mirror this time, and just hoping it works. It does because he looks me up and down as if I am imaginary. You wish, bitch!

"How in God's name did you get here?" he enquires incredulously.

"You brought me," I say, finding it impossible to hold in a smirk. Come on Gulaxa get your acting shoes back on!

He doesn't notice my change in demeanour and laughs it off, asking me to untie him so as we can depart. I quickly come up with some bullshit about not being able to interact with anything outside of my own time. How bloody clever am I? I'd better keep up this charade though otherwise he'll know something is up. Saying that, he is as thick as pig shit (or turkey shit for that matter) so probably he won't even notice.

As he is about to reply, probably with something stupid, my old pal Derek booms through the door. Come on pal don't fuck this up! He stands momentarily in the doorway, holding the magnum .44 in one hand. He looks very menacing indeed. He walks slowly over towards us both, not bothering to look at me, and smiles psychotically at the idiot. This guy is in the zone.

"Time and time and time again," he says slowly and lazily. "I catch you; you disappear. Over and over and over again."

Where in holy hell did that come from? This guy was born for this shit. The idiot begins replying with some bullshit before Derek interrupts him with a massive boom.

"Silence yourself!" (This scares the shit out of me). "I've heard all this shit before. I bet your pet is around here somewhere, guiding you with his nonsense." He says this with a supreme air of authority.

The idiot glances at me, then so does Derek, while raising the gun and aiming it at my head, what the hell! As he pulls the trigger, I jump through space and time for a millisecond before arriving just as the bullet passes through where I would have been. Man I bet that looked awesome! Although what isn't awesome is the massive ricocheting sound that attacks my senses, you damn idiot Derek. I stare at him angrily, but he seems lost in some manic state and starts towards me. I time jump again, hoping to judge it to perfection and appear behind the befuddled idiot.

"I see you're suffering from time lag. Good, this will make things a lot easier. I've waited a long, pardon the pun, time for this. Adiós motherfucker," Derek says with that same harsh confidence.

I glare at him to ease off a bit but once again he either chooses not to acknowledge me or is just lost in his own realm of maniacal fantasy. As he aims the gun at the idiot's head I whisper softly into the idiot's ear.

"Remember the dark," and then he disappears.

I snatch the gun from Derek's hand and pistol whip the dumb rock, causing him to fall flat on his face.

"Fucking idiot," I say to his prone form, dropping the gun onto his back. "You'll pay for this."

And then I follow my foolish foe into the past, or the future, I don't even know any more, might be time for another diazepam.

THE WARNING

Appearing into cold air with all the grace of a skydiving chicken I instantly regret not wearing clothes, it's bloody freezing out here! A stab of lightening cracks overhead scaring me half to death (but gladly not to full death like poor Doris, God bless her soul. Or rather, I bless her soul). Rain begins pattering down softly onto my naked shoulders like fingertips playing a damning tune on my soul. I really wish I had thought ahead more. This is the second time in as many jumps that I've got soaked through. Thing is, I knew there was a storm brewing the last time I was here but didn't once think to get dressed properly for the occasion. Maybe one day Mitch will learn to plan ahead. Turning around, I see my grandad holding my gun and clicking the trigger onto empty chambers while muttering angrily.

"Look out grandad!" I shout. "I'm going to kill you! Well, not me, but me. But as for me, the me here now, right now in this very moment, I should probably inform you that I am indeed God. Not really sure if I am the God or just a God, we'll figure that out later."

He turns around to face me, points the gun at my Godlike frame and pulls the trigger again. Instinctively I duck and curse loudly.

"For bloody hell's sake grand-papa! There's no bullets!"

"Then why are you ducking, idiot!" he retorts, while dropping the gun to the ground. The gun happens to have one bullet left, which pings off a lamp post (possibly the same one as earlier) and into his other leg. Hmm, this could be interesting.

"Bloody shit!" he shouts, again in a girlish voice.

I quickly enter nurse Branning mode and help him sit down on the bench while patting his shoulders.

"There there little soldier," I coo softly. "Who's a big boy then?"

I pick up the twice discarded bunch of flowers and lay them on the bench beside him like forgotten soldiers. I begin rubbing his back and then hold him close and start rocking him softly to and fro.

"Rock-a-by grand-papa on the sea shore, when the bullets hit you'll feel a bit sore. But when the rain comes, you will get wet, and then after it all, the pain you will forget." I sing with all the grace of a dying goat. Guess Mitch can add singer to his awesome list of achievements, what a guy.

"Will you get off me you damn idiot!" my grandad booms angrily while pushing me away.

Standing up I hold my hands on my hips in what I hope is a disgruntled granny type pose, whatever that may be. Use your imagination folks.

"Well I never!" I say sternly while pointing one finger at him. "I come here to warn you of your incoming demise and all I get is blasphemous language and a spoilt little brat. Go to your room young man!"

He stares at me with a somewhat bemused expression on his face. All at once his pain is forgotten for the moment as he succumbs to my extreme telling off.

"Who are you?" he asks. "I was just sat here relaxing and then you and your stupid twin disturb my peace, what do you want?"

"Well," I say, standing up straight once more and adjusting my towels while the rain belts down even more heavily. "Now you've calmed your tits down, I am your grandson. The other good-looking gentleman earlier, or later, or when-the-hell-ever, was also your grandson. We are, were, here to save you. Well, I was, he wasn't. Secondly, wait, I think I've already answered that question. We all good now?"

"Oh bugger off!" he shouts, then disappears.

"Hmm," I ponder to no-one in particular. This is all getting a bit weird. If he could already jump why didn't he do it earlier, later, when I pointed the gun at him? Also, it's bloody raining! How can he jump when it's raining? Come to think of it, how come I jumped earlier when it was raining? Something doesn't add up, and I don't mean a broken abacus.

I sit back down on the bench and cross my legs sexily as another jagged fork of lightening lights up the night sky like a nightmarish knife tearing into the very fabric of hell. Instantly a rumble of thunder vibrates violently across the whole world, shattering individual raindrops into smithereens against my unprotected face. Well, one thing is for sure in this hellish landscape, I won't be jumping any time soon unless I find somewhere to dry off. I do have towels on me but of course they are soaked through, so no use there.

In hindsight, which is a wonderful thing. Or is it really? Does it mean you can see your own arse? Is that where the terminology came from? Because you can see your own butt just by turning your head, so really we all have hindsight without even trying, don't we? Maybe there's a better explanation than this somewhere. Anyway, I digress. If I had the benefit of hindsight I could forewarn myself...wait! I've pondered this thought before, or after. I do have hindsight, it's called time travel. Also, I am God so I have knowledge of everything.

"So if I am God," I mutter to myself. "Then why can't I use hindsight to foresee or rather forecast things, like weather and stuff?"

"Because you're an idiot," a familiar voice utters from beside me.

I turn to see no-one. But on closer inspection I see the rain is not quite acting in the way that it should. It seems to be cascading off a man-like object, very odd indeed. I poke the thing at random and hear an exaggerated expletive.

"You just poked me in the eye you bloody fool!" Sounds just like my dear old grandad, but it can't be, can it?

"Grand-papa?" I ask coyly, and then he reappears. "Now this is proper weird. I knew you could time travel, but it seems as though you can turn invisible as well. Can I do that?"

"Wait!" he asks incredulously. "I can time travel?" He grips my arm for good measure.

"Erm, well, you can when you're an old twat, I mean elderly gentlemen. So I kind of assumed you can now, can you not?" I ask hopefully.

"Well, no-one showed me how to time travel," he says. "I just had some weird guy teach me how to become invisible. If

I can travel through time then I could travel back and dodge those bloody bullets you shot me with, idiot!"

"Well, two problems with your statement me old mucker. One: I didn't really shoot you, did I? I mean, I actually shot that lamp post and then it rebounded and hit you. The second time you shot the lamp post and then it hit you, so I ain't taking no blame for any of that shit pal. And two: you can't mess about with time cos it gets a bit angry. Trust me I know about all this shit cos I'm a cool ass dude."

I give my nails a perfunctory glance after my awesome speech. I can already imagine how awestruck he is at my utter coolness.

"What are you doing?" he asks of my perfect composure. "You got shit on your fingers?"

"Grand-papa," I tut loudly. "Not cool! By the way, why didn't you bugger off when you went invisible? Seems a bit weird to be sat there perving on me."

"Because I've been shot in the legs you idiot! Also, I was kind of hoping you would bugger off yourself so I could shout for help, but you just sat there talking to yourself like some raving lunatic."

"Great simile," I say. Wait, have similes even been invented yet? Shit, say something clever. "Sorry, I meant to say smile and added another letter."

Well done Mitch, always knows how to get out of a difficult situation. What a guy.

"Idiot!" he barks. "So why are you still sat here? If you can travel through time, then bugger off! I've had enough of your shenanigans."

"Well, I can't time travel when it's raining grand-papa, that's time travel one-oh-one." I say this with extreme confidence like the time travelling legend that I am. He laughs loudly and then screams girlishly while grabbing his injured legs.

"I've never heard anything so ridiculous!" he bawls in between crying fits.

"He's right," a voice says from behind us.

I turn to see Gulaxa looking dapper as a businessman in what looks like a brand new suit and holding a massive umbrella. Before I have a chance to react, he grabs my arm and takes me away from this rain soaked place.

A FOOL'S ERRAND

Arriving with all the grace of Jesus, I appear standing in the hallway, or landing, of dickhead's home. If my memory serves me right (which it should because I am its master, but which is kind of screwed up right now, but I ain't blaming it on the diazzies), he should be walking out of the door right about now...ish. Hmm, maybe not quite now, which is probably a good thing cos I'm still visible, better rectify that mistake, which I do.

As I make sure invisibility has been restored, I notice that fat bastard cat skulking about downstairs, probably looking for food. I should really report the cruel idiotic moron to the RSPCA for having such an obese moggy, but saying that, the little wanker will be dead soon so who gives a monkeys, or should it be cattys? I think I might be losing my mind more than usual, I wish this idiot would hurry up so I can get on with the show.

As I'm literally wasting time I slump down against the wall and find a comfortable position, reach into my pocket for my favourite friends and pop another pill. I might as well enjoy myself while waiting for the moron. As I wait for the incoming tide of serenity to whisk me away to a calmer place, I remember the other Gulaxas squabbling about the cat. I wonder what they were on about? I mean, he got killed so surely that's it, but they were talking about trying to find it. Did somebody move it? Did it survive? Are we looking at a Pet Sematary type scenario? That book scared the shit out of me!

The opening of the bedroom door startles me from my disturbing reverie as the idiot bundles out looking rather flummoxed. Such a joy to see, although he could have waited a bit longer for my diazzy to kick in properly. Wanker! I stand up slowly and quietly: slowly because I really can't be arsed doing anything, and quietly, well because it's sensible, idiots. Wait, who are the idiots?

I see (and feel) the stupid moggy bound upstairs, almost causing an earthquake with it's enormous bulk, and begin to wrap itself round the idiot's legs. Stupid bloody cat, I really want to kick the little shit, but I don't, because I'm as calm as a Hindu cow right now. And a bloody poet in case you didn't know it! I make myself visible, being careful not to let the cat see me doing so, then introduce myself in the coolest way possible.

"Nice pussy," I exclaim, making him jump like a little girl. We then have a rather stupid conversation arriving from fuck all and fuck where which really has no meaning whatsoever, but gets him riled up so all good in the hood.

"Just tell me what the hell is going on before my mind blows up!" he demands, rather abruptly I might add. Look who's got his pink frilly knickers in a twist.

"You brought us back to your house, when you killed Gulaxa. You need to make sure everything goes exactly as before to prevent further time slips," I say, as though this explains everything, which it does, to be honest.

"Okay, that makes sense, not," he retorts like a dickhead, which he is, so the simile is correct. But is it still a simile if the statement is true? "So where were we before, that stinking room, was that past or future?"

"That was the future, or one of infinite possible futures. You see..." I gaze down and see that the fat pudgy feline has noticed me and is rather bemused, as am I to be honest, my diazzy is kicking in nicely. I wonder if I could just gaze into this fat animal's soul and lose myself in its incoming demise, like a lover lost in an ocean of...

"We need to go!" the idiot cries while grabbing my wrist, spoiling my buzz (what an absolute tosspot) and drags me into the spare room.

I'm kind of lost right now as to what happens next. I'm guessing the cat gets murdered by this callous cretin. Well not this one the other one, you know what I mean! My mind is foggy as hell right now, I feel as though I need to lean next to something, maybe another diazzy might make things better. As I go to reach into my pocket I have a eureka moment.

"The phone call," I drawl slowly, straight into the ear of my companion. We are a bit too close, I thought I was leaning against the wall. Maybe another tablet isn't the wisest course of action as I see him stare into my eyes. Does he know I'm high? Quick, act normal! Shit! How do you act normal again?

"Who was on the phone?" he asks right into my face. "I remembered some yank talking shit, but who was it? And don't say me!"

"I don't know but we need to find out. You have to record the call somehow without being seen. If you are seen, bad things will happen," I reply straight off the top of my head, another Oscar worthy performance or a bumbling ramble, I'm too chilled to even care any more. A shout from the other room ensures this question will never be answered.

Seeing the indecision in the fool's eyes creates a warm feeling in my bones. Or maybe it's just the drugs, I don't know any more. As I stare lazily at him, the previous version of him walks past the bedroom door into the bathroom. This shit is trippy as hell, really need to lay off the hard stuff. Without hesitation the now version of him darts out of the room with all the grace of a, well to be honest, a bloody ninja! Very smooth, I am impressed. This gives me the opportunity to make myself invisible and chill out for a bit as I slide down the wall into a sitting position.

Man this is such hard work, why do I make things so difficult for myself? All I was planning on doing was having a little fun with this fool and then going off on some vacation somewhere. I might need to check myself into a rehab or something, my head is rather screwed right now. At least I have a few moments to contemplate things. I don't think I have anything to do at the moment, think I'll just close my eyes for a little while.

A loud crash awakens me from my incoming slumber as I'm guessing fatso has just been whacked into the shower door. Good night chubs, enjoy your mini kip, you'll soon be dancing with the angels in pussy heaven (not that pussy heaven you dirty bastards!). I suddenly realise I do have a job to do, I need to find some clothes for the other me to dress the other him with in the other place in the other time. Not confusing at all, right? As I hear him whisper goodbye to his furry friend, I suddenly feel a pang of sadness and regret, where in holy hell did that come from? I hate this bastard and his stupid fat companion.

I give my head a shake, stand up grudgingly, and slowly open the cupboard nearest me, almost getting crushed by a blood-soaked duvet. I just about manage to keep it upright and jam the door shut again. Is this guy a serial killer or something? What am I up against here, a bloody psychopath? This must have some relevance here, but I can't quite grasp it at the moment, plenty of time for thinking later, although this has really thrown me and proper blown my buzz.

As I hear the phone ring I hastily open one of the drawers and grab whatever is laid on top. This has all happened before so doesn't really matter if I don't look, right? After the very brief conversation, I decide to follow him into the bathroom and pass on a parting gift to the other me. Shit! The mirror I found in the pocket! I quickly glance around and see no mirror anywhere. That must mean...holy shit! The mirror he gave me is the one I gave him, or give him, now. So this mirror just keeps travelling round and round for all time, how cool. Maybe not cool for the mirror though, what a sad existence, pretty much just a companion for my nether regions, and his, poor thing.

I place the mirror in the pocket and walk into the bathroom to face my other self, making myself visible as I do so, and hand him the clothing. We give each other a little smile and a wink, and they both bugger off. Bon voyage my two legged friends. I snap off a little salute for no reason whatsoever before sitting down on the toilet, which happens to have the toilet seat up. As I stand up to drop the toilet seat my old chum walks in.

"So, I guess I've vamoosed?" he enquires. No shit Sherlock.

"It would seem so," I reply slowly, then decide to utter the immortal words once more. "We have work to do and time waits for n..."

"Yeah yeah, no man," he interrupts, what a fucking prick! How dare he stop me mid flow! Once more I hate this bastard with a passion.

"Just hold on one minute you dodgy twat, why in the bloody hell did you ask me to go down and write down seven God damn words? What are you up to you sneaky git?" He blurts this out in an angry tone, startling me somewhat from my seething hatred.

"I have no idea what you mean," I mumble, momentarily caught off guard.

"You sent me down there to record a pretty much meaningless conversation after disappearing on me. Next thing you're stood in the bathroom just after I, or me, or who-the-hell-ever has just vanished from existence. Looks just a little bit dodgy if you ask me pal," he continues.

If only he knew the truth, that it wasn't me but another version of me which is in actual fact still me. I really feel like telling him but decide to get my acting mode activated again and lure this fool into a fateful oblivion. I drop my gaze somewhat, adopting the manner of submission, before raising my head once more and channelling my inner demon.

"I had no choice, the decision was already made. Time has its rules. I sent you to the No-Time place. I always have and I always will," I blurt out confidently before adopting my usual deadpan expression with a little extra sadness thrown in, because I am such an Oscar worthy performer.

He stares at me for a brief period, probably wishing he was as cool as me, before rudely pushing past and sitting down on the toilet. A rather ponderous expression falls across his face before he looks back up at me.

"Did you put the toilet seat down? Did you know I was going to sit here?" he asks dumbly.

Well, for the first question, yes, I did put the seat down. As for knowing you were going to sit there...actually no. But I nod anyway, and as he holds his head in his hands I grin from ear to ear, got you, you little wanker.

"So, how many times have you done this?" he asks without looking up.

Hmm, not too sure on that one, pick a random number. Erm, two billion sixty hundred and ninety nine trillion...

"Three hundred and thirty-two, not counting this time," I say sensibly, no need to be an idiot like the idiot. That would just be idiotic.

Still with his head in his hands I can actually feel the tension in the air like a physical form of pressure filling the room. It feels kind of awesome.

"We really have travelled through time," he says. "So where's the DeLorean?"

I reply by basically saying he is an idiot believing such nonsense in movies. Which he is, an idiot I mean. As for the movies, well they're just plain awesome, but I'm not going to tell him that. Seeing the cogs whirring inside his head ever more slowly like a toy running out of batteries, I feel joy once more. This is why I am here, to watch the mental torture ruin his mind and soul. Thank you, God, for this opportunity. As he struggles with his questions internally, he tries to fabricate words externally but can't quite find the language.

"When do we come here. I mean, what time do we...shit," he mutters, looking at me with puppy dog eyes, I'm sure I can see tears forming. Awesome, cry you little bitch.

"I don't know, we just have to wait." I say, holding back my pleasure. And, to be honest, I can't remember what happens next.

"Please Master, do elaborate further, I'm sick of asking questions to..." he starts before something happens in his eyes, some kind of spark. I don't like this.

He jumps up and runs out of the door slamming it shut behind him. Prick! As I reopen the door and follow him onto the landing, he hastily plucks the phone handset from the wall. This could get interesting, better play along with my dumb act though.

"What are you doing! This isn't the right way!" I cry.

"If I'm right then if I dial a random number on this phone, I will royally mess up the timeline. If my future's set and I don't have a choice...well, fuck the future!" He exclaims this confidently while dialling furiously on the handset.

Look at him, travels through time twice and he thinks he can change everything. Not that easy pal, prepare to have your world torn apart, because I've just remembered who you call. I see his face falter and his newfound confidence dwindle like a falling star, extinguished in an instant by his own damning voice, how pathetically poetic!

"I..I..." he stutters meekly after listening for a while.

I watch with extreme amusement while hiding my happiness behind a veil of sadness. How the hell did I become such an awesome actor? Maybe I have done this over three hundred times? What, really?

"Hello?" he says, breaking me from my disturbing revelation. "He vamoosed".

"We need to go now!" I exclaim, wanting to get the hell away from here so I can fathom out my newfound information without this fool interrupting my every thought.

I don't know why but I hugged him. I'm guessing because I didn't want him to mess up the jump, nothing more. I hate him, right, I can't stand the bastard.

"This will all be over soon," I say softly into his ear. "I need you to focus now. You need to go back again. You need to go back two hours to this exact point. Trust me, the more you do this, the more natural a process it will become."

I say these words slowly and precisely hoping he gets the gist of my meaning. Just as we're about to jump, another version of me appears behind him and to the left, and then another to the right, the two from earlier, or later. One adopts the universal sign for a wanker while the other coarsely mimics a blowjob action. Pricks!

And then we are gone.

FIRST IMPRESSIONS

Arriving into bright sunshine, I am momentarily blinded as glancing rays of light bounce off a nearby slide straight into my visionary area. Should have brought some sunglasses with me, I muse inwardly. As I gather my awesome eyesight back into some sort of normality, I scan my surroundings and see I am situated in a children's play area surrounded by grass and trees. Thankfully the playground is free of children as I would look a bit suspicious stood here in my two-towel outfit. Don't want a nasty nickname adding onto my cool as hell ones now do I?

As I complete my scanning, I see Gulaxa stood beside me. I'd forgotten he was even here, and with a somewhat cheesy grin on his face. Using my toned and honed instincts, I crouch down and back away cautiously, keeping the sneaky bastard in my sights. As I am coolly inching away, I forget to look behind me and go head over tits over see over saw, and feel sore in my every area, especially my pride. Instantly I jump up into my expert ninja pose expecting my nemesis to be glowering over me with an axe and evil intent. But no. He's still standing in the same place with that stupid look on his face, what the hell is he playing at? I decide it's time for answers. I hitch up my towel, hitch down my other towel, and channel my inner hard man.

"What do you want?" I growl with all the venom I can muster, which to be honest isn't much, I'm too tired.

"Hi," he says while giving me a little wave. "My name is Gulaxa."

Hmm, this is weird, what's his bloody game? Is he toying with me? Well, nobody toys with Mitch except Mitch himself. Wait, that sounded a bit sexual! Oh well, no harm no foul.

"What are you up to you psychopathic bastard? You should be dead," I grumble.

"I'm not dead, I'm alive. My name is Gulaxa," he says like an idiot while giving me another camp as hell wave, what is going on here?

"I know you're not dead because you're stood in front of me, and I know your bloody name. What game are you playing here? I don't have time for your bullshit!" I say, slightly irritated.

His smile never falters, it's as though it has been painted on by some sinister clown, very creepy.

"I am here to help you, do not be afraid," he says. Once again he gives me a little wave, weirdo.

This brings back memories of the first time I met him, but that was ages ago, I think. And the suit he wore then looked old and ravaged, as did the man himself. The guy in front of me is smartly dressed with slicked back hair, the total opposite of our first encounter. Could this be an earlier version of him? Could this be the first time he meets me? Seems a bit far fetched, but then again pretty much every aspect of my life is these days. I'd better be cautious, it could be the old Gulaxa trying to mess with my head. Come on Mitch, detective time.

"Why are you here to help me? In case you didn't know I'm a time travelling legend who needs help from no man," I say, while checking my nails in that cool as hell way.

"Why are you wearing two towels?" he asks, ignoring my super cool gesture while pointing out the obvious: that I may in fact need help, especially of the psychological kind.

"Mitch Branning answers to no man!" I shout for no reason whatsoever.

"Mitch Branning?" he says. "What a lovely name, so cool."

"Well, you know," I blush, giving my nails that cursory glance once more.

"I don't think I've ever met anyone as suave and awesome as you. The way you check your nails just blows me away. If I were a lady, I would be swooning all over you," he says nicely. I think I like this guy.

I stop checking my nails for a while and see he is once again waving at me, very odd chap.

"Erm, what's with the waving me old mucker?" I ask politely, changing tact to a somewhat caring tone, adopting my counsellor role once again.

"Oh sorry," he says with a bemused look on his face, but still with that fixed smile, and lowers his hand. "I forgot what I was doing for a moment, very strange."

"Well, there's nowt as queer as folk I suppose," I say matter-of-factly.

"True," he says blankly, still giving me that creepy as hell smile. This is starting to get a little freaky.

"So, erm, what can I do for you then?" I ask. "As I said I don't really need any help, but you seem a little lost at the moment. Is there anywhere I could take you? Maybe a local hospital?"

"Well, aren't you just the dandiest of chaps?" he says jovially. "To be honest I've kind of forgotten why I came here, wherever here is."

He turns around in a sweeping gesture with his hands as if laying everything out before him. Just then a mother and her two young children enter from a nearby gate, eyeing us suspiciously. Well, maybe eyeing Gulaxa and his maniacal stare suspiciously, not Mitch, Mitch always looks cool. As they walk past us, Gulaxa turns and begins staring at them with that fixed, mad as hell smile etched on his face.

"Why hello children," he says weirdly. "Come to have some fun have we?" and lifts his hand to wave at them.

"Don't mind my friend here," I say. "He's just had a few too many sherbets." I imitate the universal sign for drinking.

"Why is that man wearing two towels Mummy?" one of the children enquires.

"Don't look at him dear. He's a wrong-un, just like his companion," the mother exclaims.

"Well I never!" I retort, pulling up and down my two towelled attire. "Mitch Branning is certainly not a wrong-un! I'll have you know that he is a time travelling legend around these here parts." I sweep my hand around, mimicking Gulaxa's earlier attempt and indicating all around me.

I see Gulaxa copy my expression, still smiling, so I go again with my gesture, and Gulaxa follows suit. And on and on we go, until I get dizzy and need a sit down. I do so on a nearby bench and notice the lady and her children have buggered off. Gulaxa comes to sit beside me, still grinning like a lunatic.

"Well good riddance to bad bastards, I say," I say.

"And not a bloody damn sight too soon, I say," he says.

We sit there for a moment and I take in the beauty of the surrounding area. Sunshine still blazes from high above, warming my skin and thankfully drying my towels. Good job really in case the stuck up mother has a problem with two old friends chilling out together. What if she decides to call the cops and I need to make a quick getaway? Birds chirp in the nearby woods creating a lonely song together as if playing a tune for their only audience; two very disturbed individuals sat together on a park bench. I close my eyes for a moment and take in the serenity of the moment, how peaceful it seems right now just being present here and not worrying about all this time travel shit, or what I might have to do next.

"Ha ha ha!" Gulaxa laughs heartily, snapping me instantly from my peaceful reverie.

"What the...!" I begin, opening my eyes to see him pointing at something off in the distance, still with that crazy grin fixed upon his face.

I follow his gaze but can't see anything. What in holy hell is up with this dude! Then suddenly shadows seem to fall in from every side like Death himself is enveloping us into his impenetrable black hood. The peaceful birds' song now fades away with pain and suffering, like an old record player playing in reverse slow motion.

"Ha ha ha!" Gulaxa once again chortles, this time in a more ominous tone as the world around us breaks apart with all the grace of Armageddon.

What in holy hell is going on? I follow his pointing once more as he raises his finger to the sky.

"Time to wave," Gulaxa says slowly, raising his other hand.

High above the horizon looming over us like a gigantic God is none other than me, seemingly a million feet tall. He gazes down at us with a forlorn expression, like a colossal alien hell-bent on the domination of this planet. If I wasn't such a good looking chap, I'd probably be a little bit scared, but damn I look awesome. But what in holy shitballs is going on? This can't be real, right? This must be some part of a crazy dream, either that or I am having a psychotic episode. I guess my life gets weirder and weirder every day, and I ponder inwardly if this has anything to do with the moving pictures.

I wave back to my God like self and then, darkness.

IT'S A DIRTY JOB

Arriving back in the bedroom and watching him sleep is kind of creepy, especially as we are hugging as well. We look like two right perverted wrong-uns. I hear the birds singing cheerfully outside which kind of has a calming impact on my frayed senses. I can't remember the last time I actually heard such a beautiful sound, or took the time to notice anything apart from my own selfish thought processes. Is this the drugs talking or am I actually having some sort of spiritual experience? I mean, drugs can't be all bad, can they? I could really do with a pick me up right now, but for some reason I just don't have the energy. I could do with a good night's kip to be honest.

We both seem to realise at the same time that we should cut away from our time hug. Wow! Time hug, what a weirdly beautiful concept. We part slightly to stare into each other's eyes. Never really noticed how blue his eyes were, as blue as the deepest ocean and I momentarily lose myself in the vastness of his gaze. What the shit is going on? I snap myself out of this insane trance-like state and wonder if he is at this very moment jealous of how cool and sexy I look. I bet he is.

As he comes to the devastating realisation that he will never look as good as me, he breaks off from our awkward staring contest and surveys our surroundings. Although he probably expected to see himself laid in bed, the look on his face still conveys fear and panic. This kind of brings a little comfort to my overworked imagination and reminds me why I am here. Although a lingering sense of doubt still clings to me like a stubborn plaster.

Fully releasing from our embrace, he walks to stand over his sleeping self, allowing me to sag heavily, put my fist in my mouth and silently scream into my tormented soul. I think I'm falling apart, and I don't know the way out of this chaotic nightmare any more. This cycle I seem to be following blindly feels like falling into a deadly trap that goes on ad infinitum. The thing is, I know how to ease my troubled soul, but I also know this would only be a temporary fix and is quite possibly the reason I am in this mental state right now. Guess I don't have a choice in this any more. I reach into my pocket for my faithful friends and pop another blue bastard into my waiting orifice. I take a deep breath in and sigh silently while closing my eyes. Better get to work. I'm not looking forward to this.

"We have work to do," I whisper as I leave the room. He follows me dutifully, for which I am grateful.

"What now?" he asks quietly after closing the door with all the grace of a loving father.

"We have to set everything up just like it was when you woke up," I whisper again. Don't really know why I am whispering, it's not as though we'll wake him up, is it?

As I see the internal cogs in his mind play through the events of earlier on, I wait until he reaches the moment of extreme dumbness. And, there it is.

"We have to clean the bathroom as well," I say, hoping he thinks I'm a mind reader, which I don't think I am. Then again I did correctly know when to say my previous statement, so maybe I am. Who knows, or who even cares any more.

I walk into the bathroom with my faithful follower hot on my heels to be greeted by death and carnage. What a bloody sight to behold! The look of shock and horror on his face is very evident and he grabs a hold of the door frame to keep himself from fainting. I kind of feel sorry for him again, but this is not how I am supposed to be feeling as another pang of self-loathing taps away at my anxious thoughts like a frantic woodpecker.

After a few moments of taking in the chaos before him, and while his face sinks like that of a heart attack victim, he turns to look at me, a look of utter bewilderment on his sunken face. He opens his mouth in a somewhat comical fish-like manner, and my mind feels locked in turmoil as to whether I should inwardly laugh or cry at his expense. Feeling torn inside by my internal struggles, I instinctively hug him. Again, a bizarre turn of events that further affects my fragmented mind. But I will admit this does feel good, and as he hugs me back, this feels like the right thing to do, and I embrace the moment fully, closing my eyes to appreciate this very second.

"Who is he? Is he that crazy guy from the room earlier?" he blurts out, breaking me from my serenity. I nod softly against his shoulder, still with my eyes closed, not wanting to leave this safe place.

He pulls away from our hug and I reluctantly release fully, gazing at him as he surveys the chaos before us. Following his gaze, I take in poor Derek's prostrate body in the bath. Who could do such a thing to him? And then to dump him here like he's just a piece of trash creates a stabbing feeling within my heart. Was this me? Or have I had an impact on his demise? I did not treat him very nicely earlier, in fact I treated him like a piece of rubbish, just like whoever did this to him. The poor guy definitely didn't deserve this.

"You've done this before, so what's the best and quickest way to get this shit done?" he asks suddenly. Thankfully this has the effect of waking me from what felt like a tidal surge of tears to join the ocean of blood in the bath. To be honest I can't remember what happens next or how we clean it up. Everything feels kind of muddled up right now, I don't even know if I've been here before, maybe another pill would help.

"I don't know," I reply slowly. "The more I do this the more things get muddled up. I seem to gather myself the longer I stay in one time, but when we jump, I become confused." Pretty true statement to be honest, although quite possibly the drugs are having an impact as well.

I feel once again the incoming avalanche of tears and feel like hugging him once more, just to have some sort of connection. What the hell is going on with me? As I look into his eyes, I sense he wants a hug as well. Can he see the pain in my eyes? Can he feel the agony within my tortured soul?

"Okay," he says confidently while taking in a deep breath and exhaling noisily. "Firstly, we need to remove the body. And with any luck that is just blood in there which means moving the body will unblock the plughole and allow most of it to escape. Gulaxa, could we take the body to another time and dump it there? You know, just for safekeeping until we get through this mess. Maybe even to that No-Time place?"

Well, I guess we're doing this! Disposing of a fellow human's body with no regard for who he is or was. No respect at all for the man he used to be or where he came from, or who he has left behind to mourn him. The callousness of this very thought sends a pang of anger through my aching heart, and I struggle to hide my venom.

"I would strongly advise against that," I say through gritted teeth. "For one, when we leave this time and then return to finish off, we run the risk of running into our former selves, or even over-jumping, which would be catastrophic."

"And two...?" he asks, testing my patience to the very limit. I'm starting to hate this bastard once more.

"And two, No-Time is a very unstable place. Any kind of interruption there and time will not be happy. You saw what was happening when we arrived there last time," I reply, once again holding back my festering rage.

Thankfully he doesn't notice and begins staring once more at the morbid scene before us. This gives me a few moments to close my eyes, collect my thoughts, and calm the storm brewing inside of me. As I gather a sliver of serenity to my chaotic mind, he barks an order at me to go into the spare room and get some duvets. Who does this twat think he is? I oblige, however, just so as I can get away for a moment and compose my ever racing mind.

Entering the spare room, I slump against the wall for some sort of moral support. Not that it offers any, but it makes me feel like I'm being held up by something other than my own fractured mind. A multitude of varying emotions zigzag across my ever-changing senses. Fear, resentment, self-loathing, self-pity, all filter through an overwhelming sense of not being good enough. I felt fine not so long back. Why the sudden change in my mood? Maybe another diazzy would fix the problem, always helped me in the past. But, didn't I have one recently? I can't remember. Fuck it, down the hatch, take me away from this horrible place. I reach into the cupboard and grab whatever is nearest because, well, I just don't care any more.

Trudging back into the bathroom I see him checking out Derek's corpse, on his knees as though inspecting the area for clues like some detective. Idiot! He begins ordering me about again and I dutifully follow as I really can't be arsed to argue. I'm just waiting for the drugs to kick in so I can escape into some form of oblivion. As I place one of the duvets on the floor as instructed, we get ready for the lift, I'm not looking forward to this, I can see Derek's eyes judging me, as I suppose so is God.

"...don't pull his fucking head off!" the idiot says after waffling some other shit that I wasn't even listening to.

Then the callous bastard bursts out laughing like some psychopath. What the hell is funny about this situation you sick animal? I control the urge to punch him in the face with all the grace of a flying fish and take a deep cleansing breath. Once his laughing fit has been contained, we begin the lift, with me thankfully holding Derek's shoulders so as I'm not looking into his judgemental eyes. We place him onto the duvet on the floor and cover him with the other one. Once again, the idiot has his supervisor's hat on and decides we should put him in the cupboard where we got the duvets from. A lightbulb pings in my foggy brain as I realise the body that fell on me earlier (later?) was this one, how poetic.

Manoeuvring the body into the cupboard takes a little bit of effort, mainly on his part as I couldn't face squashing and prodding a once known associate of mine. One who I had treated like shit, possibly for a very long time. As we close the door Derek gives me one final sorrowful stare before we leave him all alone in the dark until whatever fate has planned for him next. Following the psychopathic buffoon back into the bathroom with my buzz coming on strong, I feel my mood lift slightly.

"Time to pull the plug on this shit!" he exclaims with a weird grin on his face. What the hell is wrong with this guy? I struggle to hide the disgust on my face.

After literally and figuratively pulling the plug and draining some of the life blood away, he then begins spraying the shower head, attempting to wash away what is left. This is doing nothing, so I start cleaning away with a flannel to get the worst up. I feel like I'd rather get on with it than wait for this fool to drag it out. I really need some alone time right now. Once finished, he surveys the clean bath and looks very pleased with himself. This once more aggravates some anger inside of me.

"How long until I wake u..." he begins to ask, just as I remember that the other versions of us will be incoming momentarily.

"We will arrive soon, we must leave," I say, more because I just want him to piss off and leave me alone for a moment's peace.

I see the cogs in his mind begin whirring again as his overworked brain struggles to decide the next course of action. Grabbing my arm, he drags me downstairs and into the kitchen, which is an absolute shit tip. This guy is just a scruffy bastard through and through, as well as a God damn psychopath. Microwave cartons pretty much adorn the entire kitchen area and there's a full pile of dishes in the sink. What a lazy sod. I'm guessing he doesn't work for a living, another bum sponging off the government. What a waste of space he is.

"Nice kitchen," I say while smirking not only at the area in general, but at his lifestyle as a whole.

After laughing at my statement, he beckons me to hide behind the worktop! This guy is really getting on my tits again. As he turns away to face the other direction, one of the other Gulaxas appears, hands me an envelope, gives me the universal wanker sign with one hand while giving me the universal sign for shushing with the other, then disappears. How weird.

"Shit! The envelope!" the idiots shouts. Ah, now I see. I'm guessing this envelope is quite like the mirror: travelling round and round in a permanent loop of pointlessness. How sad an existence; kind of reminds me of my own.

After fumbling with his own envelope, and ripping a piece of paper from the notepad on the worktop, he orders me to write on the envelope. Stammering for an instant, I initially fake struggling with this request.

"Don't talk just write!" he orders "We don't have much time." Yeah, no shit detective.

I turn my back on him, which he must see as suspicious, swap the envelopes, and expertly place the paper from the worktop into one of them. I hand it back to him.

"Hurry," I urge, as I place it into his waiting hand and watch him bundle up the stairs.

Sagging back against the worktop, I let my head drop into my hands and close my eyes. At least I have a few precious moments to myself. I'm pretty sure that he ends up in the closet again, his favourite place, and then I send him off to somewhere else. Or he sends himself, I don't even know any more. I wonder what I am supposed to do now.

Just as I'm enjoying some me-time, I feel a boot against my leg, then a boot against the other. What the hell! Reluctantly raising my head and opening my eyes, I see the other two Gulaxas grinning down at me.

"Oi, no time for resting," one of them says.

"Yeah dickhead, get up, you have work to do," says the other.

"For God's sake," I moan. "Can't I just have five minutes peace you bloody bastards."

They both look at each then burst out laughing.

"Well actually no, you can't," one of them says. "Because A, we can't find the cat, B you need to help, and fucking C we need some diazzies so cough up!"

"I've only got a few left," I mutter.

"Tough titties," Lefty says. "You'll find more later, trust me, hand 'em over."

I reluctantly pull two from inside my pocket, not wanting to retrieve the sleeve in case they see how many I have left, and hand them over.

"Good boy," Righty says triumphantly.

They then both bizarrely start crunching them while pulling disgusted faces at each other, then in unison they chime "Ah, that's better!" and begin chuckling away.

"Why is the cat so important?" I ask.

They look at each other with a somewhat worrying expression on their faces.

"You'll see," Lefty says.

"Yeah, you'll see" Righty says. "Now piss off and follow him to his old bedroom. Keep on keeping on."

And with that they both disappear. Good, I'm all alone again; I'm just gonna chill here.

"You are not going to chill there," one of them whispers into me ear.

"Fuck off!" one of them says into my other ear.

Bloody hell, no peace anywhere, not even from myself.

"Wankers!" I mutter. I make myself invisible and then off I go.

LOVE AND SUFFERING

"Wake up darling, time to go!" a familiar woman's voice urges.

Why oh why can't I just have a moment's rest from this eternal damnation I seem to be caught in! Just a few hour's gentle shut-eye would be so awesome right now, maybe if I turn over onto my side the incessant ranting of an obviously disturbed female would diminish as I enter the sweet realm of sleep.

"No way mister," she cries again, shaking me violently. "Get your fat butt up!"

"Just leave me alone woman!" I bark aggressively while shrugging petulantly.

A moment's silence occurs, great, she's buggered off. Ha, knew I would win. But wait, the lack of noise seems to have a very ominous edge to it, suddenly I feel a bit nervy.

"Woman!" the female person shouts. "How dare you talk to your mother that way!"

Shit! I open my eyes to see I am back at home and my dear mum is stood over me with her hands on her hips (a lot better than I, or Mitch, was attempting earlier) giving me a thunderous look. I'm in trouble now. Quick Mitch, say something clever.

"Hi Mum, I'm God!" I blurt out, cringing inwardly (and outwardly) at my less than perfect response, get a grip Mitch, you're better than this.

"I don't give two hoots whether you're God, Jesus or the bloody Pope!" she barks. "Get your lazy butt out of bed, you agreed you'd take me shopping and I don't want to get there and all the good stuff is gone!"

Wait, shopping, what bloody year am I in now? Batting my eyelids (but not in a seductive way) I focus on my mother more clearly. She has a bandana around her head and her face seems sunken and drawn like her skull is wearing a too tight mask. Her once full figure seems to have been decimated greatly by an internal decay. The shell of a once fine woman stands before me, my heart breaks slowly and painfully as the sudden realisation dawns on me that my mother is in the last throes of her ravaging disease. Tears sting at the corners of my eyes like pinpricks of sulphuric acid, I ache internally for the loss I will have to endure for a second time.

She must have noticed the change in my expression as she softens her gaze and sits down on the bed, like she has done the countless times before when consoling me, damn she's a fine woman.

"Hey there," she coos softly, stroking my cheek. "It's all going to be OK, the big guy has a plan for us all."

She kisses me on the cheek and gives me a cheeky little slap.

"But unless you're up in the next ten minutes you're going to hell you little bugger, come on, up and at 'em."

And with that loving order she whisks away out of my room with all the grace of a blooming red rose, leaving me to contemplate life and death in the blink of an eye. Also to inwardly wonder how in bloody hell's sake I ended up here. Also, what was going on earlier, or later, or when-the-hell-ever? I mean, was that really Gulaxa meeting me for the first time? Kind of seemed like an earlier version of him so it's a possibility, I don't suppose there's any way of actually knowing if it's true or not, I guess I leave that open to interpretation, good luck with that one whoever the hell is reading this shambles.

Another thing I should probably ponder is that huge good looking chap looming over us, I mean what a guy, so cool and everything, he could probably be a model or something. That has definitely got to be one of the biggest, and bestest, visual experiences I have ever witnessed in my short time on this earth. But one question, in fact a million questions really but no time for that many, lingers in my somewhat overworked brain, was I in a photograph in my previous jump? That really can be the only explanation, although it doesn't really explain how I got there, or why for that matter. Because let's be honest, that's not exactly time travel or jumping, is it? I mean I guess it was sort of time travel as the photograph had to have been taken before I arrived in it, but was the actual place I was in real? My head hurts, lots. A distant jangle interrupts my wayward thoughts, is that Gulaxa?

"Here's the little chubby checker, come here fatty," I hear my mum chime from the next room.

That can only mean one thing: it is Gulaxa, although the furry one not the human one, damn I miss that fat little bugger. Throwing back the covers I am suddenly made aware that I am still wearing two towels. If I was in a western, or a gangster movie, I could be called Johnny Two Towels, what an awesome name. But I already have a name: Mitch Branning, super...

"What the devil are you wearing!" my mum exclaims from the doorway as I'm mid internal ramble.

"Erm," I stammer. "Fancy dress."

"Sometimes I worry about you son," she says smirking. "What do you think chubs?" she says while ruffling Gulaxa's head as he lays lazily in her arms. "Come on, get dressed, I want you in the car

in five minutes or I'll set fatty bum bum onto you."

As she says this she gently puts Gulaxa down and goes downstairs. Meanwhile, Gulaxa sits on his butt and eyes me suspiciously.

"Hello old friend," I say softly while doing the universal kissy noises you do with cats while crouching down as a rather disturbing moment of deja vu passes over me. "Missed you."

No response from my former feline companion, very odd, he was always my bestest buddy in the whole wide word. So I inch nearer to him, cooing softly as I do.

"Who's a lovely little checker, who's got a lovely big fat belly, who's..."

Just as I am about to ruffle his chunky little head he hisses violently and claws at my outstretched hand. What a little wanker! What did I ever to do him? Well, apart from snap his neck in the future, but that hasn't happened yet, and he can't possibly predict the future, can he? As he thunders away I quickly dismiss the disturbing idea and decide I had better get dressed, don't want to upset mum as well as my cat, that would be down right disastrous.

Opening the nearby wardrobe, double checking to make sure I am not hiding in there, weird statement but I'm sure you understand, I quickly grab some jeans, an old Arsenal football shirt, and my favoured black Eminem hoody with the red backwards E and hastily dress myself. Once dressed in proper clothing for the first time in like forever I instantly feel a lot better about myself. As I leave the bedroom and descend the stairs I pause momentarily as I see Gulaxa staring at me from the landing, I wonder what the little bugger is thinking. I go to reach for him again, and the little bastard disappears. And by disappear I don't mean he darts away quickly, he actually vanishes, like invisibility vanishes, or time travel vanishes, what the hell!

"Come on," my mum calls. "Chop chop!"

"But..." I say as I begin pointing at basically nothing.

"No buts, let's go!" she urges, grabbing my arm and placing my black trainers in my arms.

Clumsily climbing into my footwear, which seems like quite a strange verb to use, but no stranger than a disappearing cat, my mum throws the car keys at me without any warning. Having little time to react as I'm still traversing my footwear, the keys clunk against the side of my head and fall noisily to the ground.

"Sorry honey," my mums smirks. "Better luck next time."

"Hmm," I mutter. "A little heads up would have been nice."

"Oh who's a little grumpy stumpy," she jokes while grabbing my cheeks and forcing them into a smile.

"Mum," I blush. "Stop it."

As she leaves the house and heads to the car I watch her depart with utmost love and affection. It never ceases to amaze me how strong this woman is; in what she probably knows is the final throes of her life she still oozes class, she still has that same wicked sense of humour, she is still the best mum a son could ever wish for. Damn I love this woman with all my heart, I would literally die for her if given the chance.

Locking the door I head after her, rushing ahead so as I can open the door with all the grace of a dutiful son, allowing her to enter and thank me sweetly. As I close the door I happen to glance up and see Gulaxa stood at the window glaring down at me, I thought the little sod disappeared earlier. Was that time travel or invisibility? My grandad could do it, but a cat having this ability seems a little far fetched for my liking. As I raise my hand to wave at him, because who doesn't wave goodbye to their pets, his little neck seems to twist at an impossible angle as a blinding light shimmers off a nearby window, and he disappears once more. What the holy shit is going on?

"Come on dear, who are you staring at?" my mum asks.

"Nothing mum," I reply.

Jumping into the car I shrug off the surrealness of the day thus far, maybe my mind is playing tricks on me. Wouldn't be too surprising to be honest, how I'm managing to cope with my new found life is staggering. Guess this shows how resilient Mitch is, what a guy.

"Who's Mitch?" my mum asks innocently.

I stare at her incredulously, wondering if she can mind my read, then recall how she learned to read my lips.

"Just a friend mum," I reply. "Probably the only friend I have in this world."

"I'm your friend," she says, looking at me with that look of complete love, making my heart shatter a little more.

Yes mum, you are, but not for much longer.

"I know mum, thank you. Shall we get going?"

"About bloody time," she says jovially. "I can't wait to see what offers we can find."

I press the button to start the engine and nothing happens, shit. I try again numerous times but to no avail. Guess God has a different plan for us today. Only one thing for it.

"Shall we go the old fashioned way?" I ask, raising one eye in comical fashion while smirking cheekily.

"I don't understand what you mean darling," she says softly with a look of complete sincerity.

Wait, she thinks I'm the other version of me, the younger one, the one who doesn't know. Speaking of him, I wonder where I am, he is. Screw it! Don't care.

"Mum, I know, I met you at Chino's, when I had the overalls on..." I say, leaving my statement unfinished.

The sudden realisation flashes up on her face.

"Oh hello Hank, but which version are you?" she enquires.

"Which version?" I exclaim. "How many have you met?"

"Oh never mind," she says dropping her head. "But I'm feeling kind of weak today, not sure if I can manage it."

"One last trip, for old time's sake. Don't worry, I'll be the guide," I say, lifting her chin.

She looks me straight in the eye while that steely look and that cheeky glint emerges victorious.

"Oh bugger it!" she laughs. "Let's do it."

I take her soft hands in mine and mother and son embark on a beautiful journey with all the grace of boundless love.

A NOVEL IDEA

Arriving into the past with all the grace of a burning hamster my throat is instantly attacked by an acrid tang that claws away like daggers of steel. Before I have a chance to instinctively cough I see my nemesis wearing some sort of oversized jumper glaring dumbly at a can of polish. Surely he didn't just spray himself with that, did he? He can't be that dumb. As he heads out the door with a look of extreme concentration on his stupid face I wait until he is a good enough distance away before violently coughing into my arm. Good job there's some sort of muffled cheering going on outside to mask my ravenous retching.

First things first though, I'm guessing I'm not in his younger self's bedroom because a: this is some sort of cleaning cupboard judging by all the various items in here, and b: he's wearing different clothing, or rather just wearing a jumper, with no trousers, or footwear, and probably no underwear the dirty bastard. I'm guessing I have jumped to a different time and location entirely. Funny thing is I have jumped to the same place he is, or was, in the past, or the future. I'm wondering if we have some sort of internal connection with each other, maybe a tenuous link throughout space and time that binds us together. To be honest that sounds pretty shitty! I want my own story, I don't want to be tied to this fool's errand until the end of time.

I could probably just bugger off right now to be honest, he doesn't know I'm here and I'm supposed to be somewhere else anyway. But, I do feel kind of intrigued to know where we are or, more importantly, why I am here. God has a reason for everything, doesn't he? I'm also quite shocked at my many references recently to God, never believed in anything like this before, maybe this is my new way of life. Guess it's good to have faith in something, why not a higher power? So, my decision was made, time to follow the oversized jumper wearing idiot and see where this journey takes us.

Seeing him walk along the corridor I follow behind him at a safe distance, mainly because of not being seen, but also as there is a very nasty smell of body odour slightly masked by polish emanating from up ahead, and I'm guessing it's him. What the bloody hell has he been doing to get that stinky? It's absolutely revolting and I struggle to stifle another coughing fit. I'm not sure why he thought polish would make the smell better, or even why he thought that was a good idea at all. If anything it seems to have added a layer of pain into the smell, that's if smell can cause pain. Knowing him he didn't read the label, I mean only idiots don't read labels, right?

Passing rows of books, which leads me to believe this is a library, he pauses momentarily at one and begins perusing the cover. A look of shock falls across his face, I wonder what basic vocabulary has stimulated his tiny brain, can't wait to see. Just as I edge nearer, while holding my breath to escape the sickly stench, he walks away with the book under his arm, wanker! As he opens the door out into what looks like a stairwell, I glance at the books from where he procured his from, just World War 1 stuff as far as I can see. How could something like this have caused such a reaction in him? I'm guessing it was a children's pop-up book left there by mistake that took his fancy, makes more sense.

Following literally in his footsteps I see he has headed up to the next floor, about time he got some exercise the lazy sod. When he reaches the next floor he bends over and starts panting, you've got to be kidding me! He's only walked up one flight of stairs and he's out of breath, that's what you get for having a poor diet you fat bastard! As I get a little closer I see what looks like shit on his feet, what the hell is wrong with this guy? He's certainly gone downhill since I last saw him, come to think of it, where am I? I mean I know I'm here, well I don't know where here is, but I know I'm here. I mean, where's the other me? Better be careful I might be invisible, I mean I am invisible, I mean, oh screw it!

I'm sick of trying to explain my sensible inward workings to a bunch of morons! God I need a diazzy right now, so I retrieve one from the sleeve and chomp it down. And by chomp I mean chew, bloody thing tastes like shit to be honest, why those guys do it I'll never know. Well I actually will, but that's besides the point.

As I'm gathering my insane thoughts my oh so clever best friend stares out the window, why didn't I think of that? Might give me an idea of where we are right now, I guess this fool might have some brains after all. I take in the area below and see some sort of carnival atmosphere, seems very old fashioned, very sixties if I'm not mistaken. I bet he didn't realise that the dumb fool. I see plenty of American flags being waved and a seemingly jovial atmosphere playing out, maybe this is something to do with the moon landing, very interesting.

Hearing the creak of a door from above I see he has buggered off the sneaky bastard, so I dutifully follow. Not because I am duty bound to him, I have free will. I am only following him because I want to, screw all this fate bullshit, I don't believe in it. Taking the steps two at a time (because I'm not an overweight wanker) I reach the next floor and follow in his wake. This is quite easy because his wake smells like a dead rat's arsehole, and that's being polite.

I see him tip-toe around the side of a bunch of lonely cardboard boxes as the baying crowd's noise reaches my ears from a nearby open window, I presume, because I'm awesome. As I creep slowly after him like a stalking cat I see his intended target, a guy with a rifle aimed out the window, deep in concentration. Wait a minute! That's...no, it can't be! Is this the book depository store? Am I about to witness history in the making? What is my nemesis' game here? Surely he doesn't think he can change such a massive event in history, not that easy pal. But hey, go ahead, I'm gonna stand here and watch the show.

Leaning against the wall with all the grace of Cool Hand Luke, I watch on as the idiot suddenly realises he doesn't have a gun but just a bloody book. As he reaches back his arm to throw the paper-bound projectile the first shot rings out, too late pal. Two more shots in quick succession follow before the book clonks Mr Oswald on the side of the head. Good shot sir! Probably too late though as I think three shots were fired, so I'm guessing Mr President won't be having any more birthday singing shenanigans any time soon.

Ozzie swings his rifle round with practised precision and fires off a single round that just misses the fool's stupid head, that would have been interesting. Imagine if he had died here, wouldn't that be poetic. The man who actually killed Kennedy was a dumb idiot wearing a stinky jumper and shit on his feet. Probably would have made the whole thing more interesting, and more believable to be honest. As he runs away like a coward, Lee Harvey sprints past and bounds down the stairs. Funnily enough the idiot doesn't follow him. I bet he internally justifies this in some way rather than accepting the truth: that he is a fat, shitty footed tosspot who couldn't catch a cold if he lived in a freezer for forty flaming years!

As he heads over to the window I follow him closely behind, seeing the book on the floor by the window and hoping on hope he doesn't pick it up. That shit is mine. For some reason he starts staring out of the window, why in holy shitballs did he think that would be a good idea?! This guy really is mentally retarded. As the people (and the many, many police officers) look up in his direction pointing and shouting, he raises his hands in submission, probably showing the world his tiny pecker. And then he vanishes. God, how have you made such an imbecile as this and given him the wondrous gift of time travel? Sometimes I marvel at your creations.

But, now he has gone, time to have a look at the book. Picking it up I am astounded at the front cover: it's a picture of me smoking a cigarette in what looks like military clothing, very odd. As far as I am aware I have never been to war, is this what my future holds? Or my past? Well, I always considered myself as a legend of sorts, why not a hero as well, sounds good to me. I read the title of the book: Time Waits For No Man – A Story Of The Great Gulaxa. Holy fucking shit! What a great name for a: me, and b: a book. Someone certainly had their head screwed on while coming up with this title, good work. Wait, is that me? Am I the author in this scenario? It is a first person narrative so...maybe.

I flick through the pages at random and read (on page 107) 'I flicked through the pages at random and read (on page 107)'. What the shit! Very weird. I go back slightly and read a passage at random again, it reads 'Bloody hell, no peace anywhere, not even from myself...' and then goes on to call the other Gulaxa's wankers. As I flick back further I see most of the story is what has happened to me recently, and the rest, well the rest is from some other guy. Wait, that's him! He's the other guy! As I flick forward I see the rest of the book has blank pages, but what I'm thinking right now is being written as I think it. Holy bloody shitting hell!

Right, close the book, nothing to see here. I'm just going to think random stuff just to prove this is not happening right now. I like things that are nice, I like elephants and seals and meals on wheels. I like coconuts and jam on toast, blah blah blah with all the grace of a Lampoon's vacation! Right, surely all that can't be in there. I open the book hesitantly, flick through the blank pages at the back and...shit!! It's all there, this is literally witchcraft! I fling the book to the floor. I'm done, I'm out of here. I'm not doing this any more, no more drugs for me, no more messing with the idiot, I am finished with this shit.

"No you're not," Gulaxa says from beside me, making me fart unexpectedly.

"Yeah, what he said," Gulaxa number two says from the other side.

"How is this real?" I exclaim at my visible other selves while pointing at the book with extreme wonder.

"This is just the beginning," Lefty says. "Shit is about to get even weirder than this, we just found the cat!"

"Yeah," Righty chimes in. "We founded car car, broom broom."

"Yeah..." Lefty says, before pausing and looking at Righty confusingly. "What is wrong with you?"

"Yeah, what's wrong with you?" Righty says while looking at Lefty confusingly and then sniffing the air and wrinkling his nose.

Well, this is getting weird, these two are obviously very disturbed right now. I wonder if it's the side effects of the drugs? As I hear footsteps and shouting from the stairs I decide to take matters into my own hands, because to be honest these two are not capable right now.

"Come on chaps," I say while holding onto my two doppelgangers. "Best get vamoosing."

As I whisk them away I wonder if the fart I left in that room will be smelled by the first officer who walks in, and who he will blame for the smell. Time travelling farts, I love it!

A BRIEF MOMENT IN TIME

Arriving at our destination holding my mother's hands is such a beautiful experience. It reminds me of the first time we travelled together in what seems like a different lifetime. Her eyes are closed and I study her features intently; the outline of her face, the deep set look of her eyes, the faint wisps of hair still clinging on for dear life while trying to escape the confinement of her bandana. A sad metaphor that describes her predicament in immaculate detail. How is this fair? How can God allow someone so beautiful to go through such torment and pain? There must be some overriding purpose for all of this, some defining point He is trying to make. But, right now, I can't see it, and I hate Him for making her suffer like this.

As she opens her eyes the spark in them rekindles her features, transforming a once sullen expression into one of pure beauty. She smiles softly, melting my heart once more and the pang of anger at God diminishes in an instant to be replaced by pure love. I feel my eyes welling up with tears of sadness and of joy as my loving mother brushes away a single tear that tries to escape from the prison of my soul.

"It's going to be OK," she says softly, releasing my hands and hugging me warmly.

Struggling to hold back my emotions I sob uncontrollably against her fragile frame and succumb to her warm embrace. I let go of everything. I let go of Gulaxa, of my dad, of everything that has happened to me over these mad few days? Months? Years? I let go and accept that I cannot change that my mother is going to die, it happens to us all, right? Aren't we the people we are because of our mortality? Isn't this what it means to truly be human? To accept that one day we will die and so will everyone we know and love. That is why we owe it to ourselves to live our best life, to be the person God wants us to be. To be humble, honest and true.

As I control my sobbing we release from our hug. She strokes my cheek softly and gives me a soft peck on the cheek.

"I love you son."

"I love you too mum," I reply through a snot filled nose.

She hands me a tissue and I blow into it with all the grace of a rasping snake and try to hand it back to her.

"No thanks," she replies while laughing. "You can keep that."

I stuff the snot filled tissue into my pocket and survey our surroundings. For once I seem to have arrived in the destination I had planned, that makes a bloody change! I wonder if it's the right time though? We're sat on a bench overlooking the deep, blue sea as waves crash nosily against jagged rocks. Huge clouds loom overhead like floating jellyfish, their tendrils whisking this way and that, as a soft breeze breaks their momentum briefly to allow golden sunshine to break through and strike the sea with a beam of fire. Gulls caw lazily in the air, calling out in a language of their own, never to be understood by anyone but their fellow brethren.

I sigh heavily as I take in the serenity of our environment. My mum leans her head on my shoulder and we both stay present in this precious moment for what feels like an eternity. As I concede to the moment, I am acutely aware of God's presence and I am suddenly struck by a provoking thought. Because of the incoming death of my loving mother, this moment is all the more special. Without the presence of loss, without the absolute certainty that our loved ones will leave us, then how can we appreciate them fully? It seems only when they depart do we truly realise how important they were, how much they meant to us. Is this my gift? I know that my mother is going to die, I've seen it. That is what makes this time we are spending together a moment of supreme bliss, and one which I could not appreciate without prior knowledge of her impending demise.

I'm broken out of my inward pondering as the gulls suddenly cease their own ramblings. Waves cease to crash against the rocks. The clouds above us fall silent and still. Even the air around us stops abruptly. Silence seems to have come upon the whole world. That is apart from the soft breathing of the woman beside me. I watch her closely. The gentle rise and fall of her frame. The tiny strands of hair that flow and ebb with her breath with all the grace of angelic love. Carefully I brush away a strand from her face and she moans softly against my touch.

"Bill..." she mutters softly, before resuming her peaceful breathing.

Don't worry mum, you'll be together soon. As I embrace this moment fully, I close my eyes and thank God for allowing me to appreciate this time we have together. For showing me the true purpose of what it is like to be a friend. To be a son. To love and be loved. After all, is that not what we are all on this earth for? Yes we all suffer in one way or another, some more than others. But if we can find love somewhere, anywhere, even in the darkest crevices of our existence, then surely there is hope for us all.

With this beautiful revelation time once again starts up. As if by a magical switch the gulls start their incessant warbling, the waves once more bash their unyielding foes like swords against shields. The clouds once more resume their onward ambling towards never-ness. A breeze softly blows a kiss against the side of my mother's face as she opens her eyes.

"Sorry my dear," she says softly. "I guess I'm more tired than I thought."

"That's OK mum, would you like to go home?"

She nods softly against my shoulder.

"No problem, just one more breath here and then we'll go."

"OK dear."

We both look out at the sea for a final time. Mother and son breathing in unison. As the beauty before us fuels our soul, the love inside us mends our hearts. This is love, pure and simple, and no-one can ever take this away. And then, we jump home, together.

Arriving back home with my loving mum laid against my shoulder life suddenly takes on a fresh new meaning, I feel rejuvenated once more to fight another day. As we sit together on the edge of her bed I once more take in the beauty of the moment I have with her, and of the precious time we have just spent together. I guess love can conquer everything and anything. I stand up slowly and lay my mum down gently.

She opens her eyes briefly and gives me a little smile before succumbing to the sumptuous pillow.

Although it pains me to remove myself from this beautiful situation, I really do need to urinate. Nature calls and all that. As I go to exit her bedroom I am suddenly aware of a shift in my equilibrium, as though something or someone has entered my stream of consciousness. Wait, what day is this? I step back into the bedroom to check the clock: 5th March 2013. Shit! I'm guessing I'm in the other room right now.

I stealthily peak around the door frame using my ninja like skills and yeah, there I am, sat on the bed looking miserable as shit, preparing to jump to the centre of the sun as my depression takes a grip of my tortured soul. Sitting back down on my mum's bed I gently rub her shoulder, she looks so damn peaceful and I really don't want to wake her. But she is the only one who can stop the incoming darkness from the other room. Opening her eyes drowsily she must sense the urgency in my strained face.

"I'm in the other room," I whisper. "I need you."

Without any hesitation, without any doubt, with the sickening disease about to take her from this life to the next, she drags herself up into a sitting position. She strokes my face softly before standing up on unsteady legs, teetering briefly. Before I have a chance to catch her, she stands firm in the face of her ravaging adversary and steps out of the room to prevent her son from joining his father into an early grave.

I close my eyes for a brief moment, awaiting her incoming return, awaiting her oncoming death. My hands and feet tremble. I'm not strong enough for this. I can't watch her leave this place. I need to leave. I can't cope with this right now. How can anyone manage a situation like this, especially with prior knowledge? I remember the beach. I remember the stillness. I remember the presence of God. I feel a surge of love inside me. I feel strength. This is an honourable moment to be a part of. I can do this.

I feel the bed soften beside me as my loving mother lays back down. Opening my eyes I watch her loving head gently swallowed by the perfect, pink pillow. Before she closes her eyes for the final time on this earth she looks straight into my soul. She sees me for the person I am, the person she always wanted me to be, the son she deserved all this time. She reaches out a hand and strokes my face once more, one final time.

"I love you son," she whispers. "I'm proud of you my darling, and your father would be as well."

I cover her hand with mine, unable to speak, and kiss it gently. She closes her eyes. A single tear rolls down her cheek. Her breathing slows. It slows. It slows. And then, it stops. Silence. My lips tremble. My heart breaks. My tears fall noiselessly like liquid prayers. I kiss her hand once more and lay it upon her chest.

"I love you mum," I whisper as I kiss her head gently.

Standing up I take in the deepest breath I have ever taken. I take one last look at the angel laid before me. Goodbye mum, until we meet again. And then I jump.

BABYSITTING

Arriving once more into the bedroom of my shitted footed frenemy I let go of my two doppelgangers. If I've timed this correctly then no-one should be arriving here any time soon. In fact, it should be the day after all the chaos that ensued before, or after, or later. As I gaze at the two disturbed individuals I can see a gradual decline between the two. Lefty (I'm calling him that for obvious reasons) seems a little dishevelled, suit is a bit more tatty than mine, strands of hair are coming loose from the awesome pony tail, bags under the eyes. But Righty, well, he looks fucked to be honest. Pony tail pretty much a matted blob of horse's arse, suit ripped to pieces as if he has been dragged through a hedge backwards, twice! And the bags under his eyes, well it's quite impossible to see where the bags begin and his eyes end, what a mess. He also seems to have developed some sort of nervous twitch. Is this what my future holds?

"We found meow meow, broom broom!" Righty exclaims while turning a pretend steering wheel and hissing erratically.

Lefty stares at him incredulously.

"What is wrong with you?" he cries. "Please God, don't let me end up like him!" he falls to his knees and begins praying pathetically into his hands.

"Hmm," I ponder to myself. "Now then chaps, let's just all have a little natter shall we."

"Broom meow broom!" Righty chimes in.

"OK," I say, slowly dragging out the two syllables.

Lefty grabs my trousers and starts muttering incoherently into my crotch area, very disturbing. More mentally harrowing though is the image I have of myself pleasuring myself, and I am for some reason not adverse to this. Is this normal? Probably not, but what is normal these days! I gently pull him up and place him on the bed, soothing him like a little child as I do so. As I turn around to grab Righty, he seems to have buggered off.

"Oi, Righty, where have you vamoosed off to!" I shout, and turning to Lefty I say. "You just stay here me old mucker, everything's going to be peachy," I give his chops a little jiggle for good measure, which has him grinning somewhat sheepishly.

As I head out of the bedroom in search of the vanishing lunatic I hear distant car and cat sounds, at least it shouldn't be too hard to fathom out where the little bugger has, well, buggered off to. I always wondered why that terminology was used. Doesn't buggered mean anal sex? So I am basically asking where this bummer has gone to do more bumming, very weird. What would be more weird was if I found him doing some bumming, then the statement would in fact not be weird, and nor would this entire narrative. Although if I found him doing some anal shenanigans right now, then it wouldn't be that strange as he is a little bit messed up at the moment, but it also would be out of the ordinary because there shouldn't be anyone here. That is unless he has time travelled to a random location, picked up a random person and brought them back here for some back door action. Anyway, instead of standing here fantasising about bullet hole activities, I should probably find him.

As I come to the landing I hear increased activity in the spare room. By activity I mean more motor vehicle and feline falsettos, this guy is so easy to trace, I kind of like him, seems like a decent enough dude.

"I'm coming to get you my two-legged friend," I say jovially.

As I peek around the wardrobe my eyes take a double take, a double blink, as my brain struggles to take in the scene before me. Righty is comically dressed in a woman's pink flowery summer dress while also wearing a huge Stetson cowboy hat, and by huge I mean bloody massive! To top off this somewhat bizarre attire he's also wearing a high heeled shoe on his left foot and one steel toe-capped boot on his right.

"What do we have here me old twitching bugger?" I enquire while holding my chin for effect. "A bit of the old fancy dress, me likey likey."

"Broom meow broom!" he booms excitedly, twitching randomly to add more comedy to the scene.

"Yes, broom meow broom," I repeat. "You found cat car, well done," I clap enthusiastically.

For some reason the clapping stops him from his incessant ramblings. He looks me deep in the eyes, as if seeing me for the first time in ages. A sorrowful expression fills his whole face.

"Help me," he mutters pitifully, then vanishes.

"Shit!" I exclaim.

Now what the hell am I supposed to do?! It seems as though there is a possible future version of me travelling through time, but wait! Maybe he's just invisible. I shut the door quickly and run about the room grabbing at basically nothing like an utter lunatic.

"Double shit!" I exclaim again.

He has indeed time travelled, this is going to get messy. How in the holy mother of fuckery am I supposed to find him? He's obviously very unpredictable, so trying to forecast where he has vamoosed off to is virtual impossible. I'd better go ask Lefty to see if he has any idea. So I head off back into the bedroom, but that bastard has departed as well!

"Bloody triple shit shitting shit!" I once more exclaim.

This is just great, two time travelling vanishing and very disturbed individuals who look exactly like me are roaming around the universe causing God knows what mischief. I sit down heavily on the bed, reach into my pocket for another blue villain, and pop it into my ever waiting gob. As I crunch it down with all the grace of a gurning pill head I ponder my next move. I guess the best thing to do is to do what I was supposed to do in the first place. So off I got to...well, you know, don't you?

SUITS YOU SIR

Arriving back on the bench where I was previously sat with my mum, I let my tears flow freely. Seemingly the same gulls soar overhead, echoing my outpouring emotions with their lonely cries as we sob in unison at the desolation of our tormented souls. As I hold my head in my hands, trying to come to terms with the unenviable loss of my dear mother, I feel a presence sit down beside me.

"There there, dear," a woman's voice says.

It can't be, can it? I turn around to face the familiar tone. It's her, it's my mum, but not exactly her, something is different, and I can't quite place it.

"Mum?" I whisper.

"Yes dear?" she enquires softly with that sweet smile.

"Is that really you?"

"Why of course dear, who else did you expect?"

"W-well," I stammer. "Didn't really expect you to be honest, you do know you've just passed on, right?"

She looks at me, and for the briefest moment a sign of confusion wanders across her beautiful face, before vanishing into the highway of her soul.

"Of course dear," she replies. "But the people we lose are never really gone, they are always with us, love never dies."

So this isn't my mum, or any other version of her, this is, what, an apparition? A ghost? A memory? Not really sure how to fathom this one out, come on Mitch get your vocabulary sorted out.

"I'm neither of those things dear," she continues. "And why the need for understanding everything? Just know I am always here, always. I will never leave your side my darling son."

These words strike a chord deep within the very fibre of my being, igniting some form of burning embers, stoking the flames of love to blow away the depressing thoughts of loss with a fiery kiss.

"And one more thing," she whispers into my ear. "Just around the corner is a fancy dress store, I think you'd like it in there. I love you." And then, she wisps away on the wings of love with all the grace of a rose scented breeze.

So, I guess I've just been visited by the memory of my mother, call it what you will, I call it a messenger of love. A reminder that although our loved ones leave us in physical form, they are never truly gone. They stay with us every single moment of our mortal lives, until we pass from this world onto the next to join them in everlasting peace. My heart is filled with such joy right now, I feel on top of the world. And what better way to cap of this supreme moment than to take my mother's advice and head to the fancy dress shop, might even find myself a nice hat, I'm sure I was pondering about them earlier, later. Departing from the bench of hope I take one last look out at the beautiful scene before me, salute the ever noisy gulls, because why the hell not, and head off around the corner onto the busy high street.

As I turn into the incessant noise of enigmatic engines and bustling shoppers I am dragged instantly back into the reality of life. Such a far cry from the blissful serenity I was recently cocooned in, it's like I've been awoken from a beautiful dream into a rapacious nightmare. I have half a mind to abandon my adventure to great hatness when I catch a glimpse of the aforementioned shop. Wow! In the window is the biggest Stetson I have ever seen. I mean, pardon my French, but it's fucking huge! This could be interesting.

As I hustle my way through the bumbling crowd I get jostled this way and that like a pinball on a spasmodic journey heading nowhere in particular. After seemingly working every muscle to gain access to my destination I finally arrive. Hatson's Hat Shop is emblazoned above the window in huge sprawling letters, interesting name for a fancy dress shop, I wonder who came up with that ingenious title, probably some special character who shall forever remained unnamed. Another line of writing in the far corner of the window explains my previous musings: Welcome to the realm of Sir Stephen Hatson – Legendary Creator of Fine Wares. Sounds like a reasonable chap, although if he called himself a legend rather than being crowned one, then I doubt his credentials, can't wait to meet this guy and enquire about his apparent status.

Walking into the shop a high pitched jingle grabs my attention, igniting memories of a friend long since forgotten, bringing back the pain of his loss at my own hand. Even though he did turn into a psychopath, I actually miss the guy, well miss the man he was before whatever or whoever turned him into the monster he became. Maybe our paths will cross again some day, who knows, I guess only time will tell. I stare up solemnly at the bell above the door and close my eyes, trying to recapture a moment in time. I then stupidly remember that I can time travel by thought alone and this may not be the wisest course of action.

"Ahem," a voice behind me coughs.

I turn around to see a rather tall gentlemen, well don't actually know if he is a gentle man, but I'll give him the benefit of the doubt, for now. He seems to have a Viking-like appearance with a narrow face complete with a salt and pepper goatee beard. The eyes gleam with a creative intelligence I have not seen in many men, I believe this man is destined for great things. I think we're going to get along rather well. I then watch as he begins checking his nails in probably what he believes is a cool as hell way, good luck with that one pal. So I proceed to check mine in an even cooler way, because nobody does this better than me, I am Mitch Branning – the coolest guy on earth. Watch as the ladies swoon at my suaveness, watch as their knees quiver at my awesome demeanour. See the men cower and whimper in their caves as jealousy breaks apart their trembling souls.

"Ahem," the vicious Viking coughs once more, interrupting me from my awesome inner dialogue, I'm starting to dislike this guy.

"Well ahem to you too!" I retort, flicking my nails this way and that with precision perfection, have some of that you twat!

The bastard then begins mimicking my movements, or rather tries to, what an absolute prick! As if he thinks he could match the pinnacle of my greatness with his shit gestures. So I step it up a notch and begin gyrating and dancing around with all the grace of Bambi on ice on magic mushrooms, have some of this you Viking wanker! As I spiral into pirouettes, warrior poses and everything in between, my nails seem to glide through the air slicing each individual atom like sharpened steel. I am a legend at this! Bow to my knees peasant!

"Ahem!" he coughs loudly, breaking me from my dazzling dance.

I try to catch my breath while bending over and resting on my aching thighs.

"Have...some...of...that...twat," I blurt out through deep lungfuls of air.

"My name is Sir Stephen Hatson, welcome to my store," he says proudly, seemingly ignoring both my coolness and my insult.

I hold my hand up in the universal sign for 'give me a second here pal, I'm dying' while I bring my breathing (and my heart rate) down to a somewhat steady rhythm. Damn I am an unfit dude, but maybe I just need a nap or something, I have been rather busy of late. But wait a gosh darn minute, didn't I just have a kip at mums? Did I actually sleep? Or did I just wake up in bed? Can you sleep while travelling through time? Can you time travel while dreaming into other dreams or nightmares? Hmm, maybe something to ponder over later, or earlier.

"A-fucking-hem!" Mr Hatson rudely interrupts.

"Alright pal!" I reply curtly. "I was just having a little think about stuff, no need to be a dick about it."

I walk coolly over to the counter he is stood behind, stifling the odd coughing fit as I do so.

"So, Mr Hatson sir, what wares have you available for my expert perusal?"

"It's actually Sir Hatson, if you don't mind," my new found friend bluntly exclaims.

"OK, Sir!" I retort, snapping off a sharp salute as I do so.

He shakes his head slowly.

"No, no, no," he says. "I'm not that kind of Sir, I'm just a knighted Sir."

I ponder this for a moment before replying confidently.

"Well, knights were soldiers of some sort, probably higher up than pawns I'm guessing. So my salute stands, Sir," I snap off a little salute to confirm my statement.

"Very well," he sighs. "So what brings you to my fine establishment?" he asks while sweeping his arm across in, well, a sweeping gesture, a bit like me and the other Gulaxa did, earlier, or later. I'm tempted to mimic his comical attempts at servility, but I refrain, I might need this guy's help.

"Well, I am rather partial to dressing up in different clothings me old mucker. You wouldn't believe some of the awesome stuff I've been gallivanting around in, proper cool as hell."

I await his inquisitiveness about my previous wearing, but he just stares at me with a slight smirk on his face, is he mocking me?

"No, I'm not," he says, smirking less subtly than is needed.

"What?" I ask.

"I'm not mocking you, do please go on sir, I have a lot of other customers to attend to."

I may need to hold a hand over my mouth when I'm thinking, this bastard can read my lips as well, sneaky git.

"Firstly, you know what, screw firstly, I think I already know the answer. Secondly, which I suppose is actually firstly now, but never mind, there's no-one else here!" I exclaim confusingly while copying his stupid sweeping gesture earlier on, dickhead! "And thirdly, which as we both know is actually secondly, you just called me sir so we're both sirs now, Sir!" I salute sternly, once more emphasising my awesome statement.

He sighs, shakes his head, and then rubs his temples.

"Sir...Mr, I had a feeling when you walked in that you may not be a full shilling, and that a conversation with you would probably be hard bloody work, I was not wrong. But, to be blunt, and not to be rude, how may I assist you?"

"Well now, you're a right bloody git aren't you?!" I enquire/exclaim. "A fine outstanding member of the public enters your humble place of shoppings, simply to browse your tit for tats, and you rudely upset my equilibrium. Well how bloody dare you? I have a right mind to report you to somebody!"

"And who might you report me to, Mr Sir?"

He has me there the little devil, but he has me all hot tempered and flustered. Let's just calm ourselves down and try and have a decent conversation with this so called Hatson. And what type of idiot is called Hatson without wearing a bloody hat! Doesn't make sense to me. I take in a deep breath and relax.

"I think we got off on the wrong foot here. My name is Mitch, Mitch Branning," I check my nails in that cool as hell way, anticipating his confidence dropping instantly.

"Mitch Branning you say?" he enquires with extreme earnest while raising one eyebrow.

"What? Have you heard of me?" I reply with probably a bit too much eagerness.

"No," he smirks. Wanker!

"Then why..." I begin. "Look, doesn't matter, can I buy that Stetson in the window?"

"Of course Mr Branning, that'll be £500."

"Five hundred bloody smackeroonies? You're having a giraffe ain't ya?" I blurt out in a somewhat cockney-ish accent, don't know where that came from.

Mr Sir No-Hatson sighs once more.

"That hat, Mr Branning, was once worn by none other than Billy the Kid. Hence the inflated price tag. Now if you don't mind I have other business to attend to, do you want the hat or not?"

"Can I ponder over this for a wee while laddie?" I enquire, this time in a perfect Scottish accent, guess Mitch is getting rather adept at his linguistic talents, what a guy.

"Yes," he says curtly. "And just so you know mimicking a Pakistani accent could be considered racist. Let that be a warning to you, Sir!"

"But..." I begin.

"No more conversing," he cuts in. "I'm going to do some stock taking, if you want the hat bring it to me and I will package it expertly for you. I have no more time for nonsense."

And with that abrupt outburst he turns around and begins counting some stupid leather wallets behind him.

"Dick!" I mutter under my breath.

"What was that?" he shouts while turning back around.

"I said I feel sick," I said.

"Hmm," he replies suspiciously, once more turning around to survey his obviously more important task.

Well, screw you Hatson! I back away with very large strides towards the door. As I reach the exit I quickly glance around and eye the position of the hat, then quickly turn back around. Great, he's too busy counting his stupid things. I deftly pluck the Stetson and plonk it on my head. Awesome. Now I could just walk out the shop, but that wouldn't be as much fun. I think I'll wind this dickhead up.

"Oi, Stephen!" I shout.

He turns around, sees the hat on my head as I watch on in amusement as his face turns a thunderous shade of crimson.

"Cheers for the hat, Mr Sir No-Hatson!" I shout as I check my nails coolly, stick up a middle finger to my new best friend, then bugger off.

DOUBLE TROUBLE

Entering into another time and place, with a whole raft of new problems to deal with, I am overcome instantly with jealousy. There lies the fat git all tucked up in bed without a care in the world, what a lazy twat! But what a lovely bedroom adorned with beautiful women on posters, Pamela Anderson always did it for me, can't fault his taste, even though he is an irritating arsehole. As he stirs in his cocooned state I feel like giving him a little scare to wind him up. There is a little bell attached to a bracelet on the floor beside his bed. I pick it up with the intention of giving it a little shake, before noticing in the mirror that I am still visible, almost messed up big time there. These bloody blue buggers are maybe starting to have an impact on my actions. I place the bracelet on the bed and rectify my mistake, just as a knock at the door startles both me and my nemesis.

"Are you getting up lazy bones?" a kind woman's voice asks, this could get interesting.

The figure in the bed opens his eyes sharply, instantly pulled from his blissful state into acute alertness. I bet this is one hell of a wake up call and I can't help but feel some light hearted relief at this, just what I needed. The door is pushed open and a very beautiful woman enters. This can't be his mother, surely. How in the hell could this perfect creature give birth to such a moronic imbecile? Once again God I somehow doubt your credentials, maybe you messed up on this one.

"Come on sleepy head, we're going to visit grandad's grave today," the lovely woman says to the petrified soul hiding under the sheets as she sits on his bed, this is way too much fun.

I cross my arms across my chest and enjoy the moment, also feeling the blessed relief of my recently taken blue friend, as his mother pats his shoulder lightly. I seriously wonder how broken his brain must be right now, I'd need a bloody diazepam after all this if I was him. Maybe I could get him hooked on them, then watch him suffer the pain of withdrawal like a psychopathic drug dealer. Something to think about for the future, I suppose. The nice lady stands back up and heads towards the door.

"Okay lazy bones, ten more minutes then up and at 'em. I love you son," she says just before she closes the door.

Wow, that has actually had an impact on me in some way. The look in her eyes as she said those last three words was one of complete devotion. Kind of brings another pang of jealousy to my resentful being, but also brings a sense of loss to my soul along with pinpricks of tears that threaten to bubble to the surface. Not today though, I have work to do.

Lazy Bones finally plucks up the courage to leave the sanctuary of his warm habitat and peaks over his covers like a frightened squirrel. Guess I'd better get in position and make myself known. As his gaze moves around the room I sneak out of his eyeline and make myself visible. Time to say hi.

"Nice bedroom," I chime in, making him jump a little which not surprisingly pleases me somewhat, and also causes him to pull the covers up to his chin in a childish way.

"Will you stop scaring me you weirdo, you always put the shits up me when you appear. I'm gonna have to find you a bell or something as an early warning system," he remonstrates, someone's woke up grumpy.

He then notices the bracelet on the bedside table, hmm, I guess I put that there for a reason, another bloody paradox enters my overworked brain: if I hadn't of picked it up he wouldn't have noticed it. But I don't think a stupid bracelet will have any impact on any future shenanigans, right? As I'm thinking this thought I hear movement outside the window. I turn to see a gangly figure preparing to pull back the net curtain and climb in. Before I have a chance to do anything I am grabbed hastily by the arm and dragged into the wardrobe, what is it with this guy and tight spaces?

It's very dark in here, the only visible form of light is a thin sliver that slices along where the two edges of the door almost meet like lost lovers, never to touch one another again. To be honest it's kind of comforting in here, I very much enjoy the darkness, I feel at peace for a moment. I close my eyes and take in the serenity that the blackness invokes on my troubled soul. I could stay here forever, but alas no, we have work to do. To be honest I don't really know what to do next, maybe he knows or will take us to a random location.

As I go to question him I hear a thump from outside the room. I reach out for my closeted companion but he is nowhere to be seen, or felt for that matter. Where the bloody hell has he vanished off to? I gaze out through the narrow gap and can't see anyone there, very odd indeed. I attempt to push open the the doors but something seems to be blocking the way, a quite heavy something. Has he gone out there and collapsed? I doubt that very much, I would have heard him, that leaves only one explanation: he has looked himself in the eyes and caused himself to randomly jump, and the other him to simply collapse. Well now this is going to get interesting, how am I supposed to find him now?

I hear footsteps enter the room and a woman's voice give a disheartening cry. I can see slightly through the gap as she bends down and tries to awaken the young idiot.

"Hey G, wake up, no time for rest sleepy head," she coos softly as she lifts him up to a sitting position. "Mark, quick come here and help, your brother has passed out."

A brother? This idiot has a brother, I always assumed he was an only child, this could get interesting, I wonder if he's as stupid as his sibling. And then he walks in, oh my God! He's his bloody twin, and by that I mean they're actually twins, although this one looks lot more tidier. Less of the long hair and more a close cropped military style buzz cut, seems to be a bit more athletic as well, has a good build on him.

"What's he done now?" Mark exclaims. "Probably been out on that wacky backy again, he's nowt but a waste of space mum."

"He's still your brother darling, come on, let's get him up and take him next door to see the doc."

"By the doc, do you mean our resident psychiatrist who loves next door," Mark sarcastically replies. "To be honest, that's probably what he needs."

As they lift him up and attempt to manhandle him out of the room I breathe out a sigh of relief, probably a bit too loudly. Shit!

"Did you hear that?" Mark asks.

"Yes dear I did, it seemed to come from the wardrobe."

I hear the bed springs creak softly and I'm guessing they have placed the skinny sod on his bed. Time to get my invisibility on, I have no way of checking just got to hope it works. Just before they both fling open a door each I squash myself into a corner with all the grace of a flapping fish, hoping against hope that I'm not leaving some sort of visionary imprint somewhere. They both stare at hopefully nothing until Mark seems to gaze right into my eyes, he can't see me, right? I mean I'm bloody invisible, I hope. Just as he's about to open his mouth to speak I hear a little moan from the bed.

"He's waking up, come on, let's get him next door," the mother says.

Mark gives me one last look, winks straight at me, then closes the doors. Well that was weird! Is his brother in on this as well? Is he part of the time travelling saga? Maybe they're all travellers of some sort, which is not as far fetched as it actually sounds, stranger things have happened. As they bustle him downstairs I hear them leave and close the door behind them. Allowing me to sigh once more, this time in peace. I really need another pick me up right now, my head is swimming with anxious thoughts.

Opening the doors to let some light in I breathe in a huge lungful of air and let it out with a long whooshing sound. What now, I internally ask myself. I have no idea where he has gone. I have no idea where the other two Gulaxa's have gone. And I think I'm running out of pills. I retrieve the sleeve from my pocket and see I have two blue friends left, shit! Going to need a new stash soon. I wonder if there are any in this time, so I head off into the bathroom to check the medicine cupboard, seems like the most likely place. Walking out of the bedroom a familiar tone stops me in my tracks.

"Broom meow, broom broom," I hear from the spare room.

No prizes for guessing who this crazy person is, I have to try not to startle him though. This loony is randomly jumping all over the place, there's no telling what chaos he may have caused. But he also might know where both the idiot and the other me have vamoosed off to. If I can just grab a hold of him I could follow him to his next location. But saying that, the psychopathic bastard could jump to the middle of the ocean for all I know. I guess it's worth the risk.

I creep into the spare room and fortunately he's facing the wall seemingly oblivious to my entrance. Still wearing his flowery dress, which seems to ripped in all sorts of places, and his huge Stetson hat, he looks the personification of insanity. Stealthily inching closer his movements become ever more erratic, as does his disturbing ramblings.

"Meow, broom, meow meow broom," he chunters with a nice bit of rhyming rhythm. "Meow, broom, I know you're in the room!" he booms, turning around to face me with a demonic stare, this guy has lost the God damn plot!

Only one thing for it, grab him. My being invisible makes the leap towards him that little bit easier. I just about sense the shift in my equilibrium before he jumps as I grab a hold of his hand. Then we disappear off to...God only knows.

BRICKS AND TREES

R ight, this time no crazy shenanigans, no wind-up merchants like Mr Hatson, basically just a chilled out time. I think I deserve it after all the mayhem before me, or after me, and probably what lays ahead of me, or behind me. Bloody hell, it's so confusing even trying to get the terminology right, I guess this is what makes my life so much fun, I think. So, where do I decide to jump to catch a bit of R and R? None other than my own home...only kidding! Although my humble abode is rather nice, I fear running into previous versions of myself, and I really need a break from all of that bollocks, so screw that for a game of sausages. But hang about, maybe my home might not be such a bad location to jump to...a thousand years into the future!

This may be the trickiest jump I have ever attempted because, well, how do you jump to a place that doesn't even exist yet? Most of my previous excursions, barring the random ones, have been places I have seen in newspapers or online, so traversing to those locations was quite straight forward to be honest. But saying that, when I jumped to the alleyway just before 9/11 I'd never actually seen that place before, I just used my awesome imagination. So, what, it's just my imagination that gets me there? No specific need for prior knowledge is required to make a jump? If so, then surely jumping to the future can't be that hard, just use my IQ of 72, set my awesome hat straight upon my perfect noggin, check my nails in that cool as hell way, then blast off to a time conjured up in my totally stable mind.

Hmm, bit dusty in here, I think as I cough noisily. Shit, better be quiet there might be some versions of me lurking around ready to pounce and cause me untold suffering. Stifling my hacking lungs into my sleeve with all the grace of a box of frogs I survey my surroundings. Which is kind of difficult as part of my arm is covering my vision. Hold on folks, let me get my coughing fit under control before I continue my smooth as hell virtual tour. Wait, is it a virtual tour if I am physically here? I mean, you aren't, but I am, so is it virtual for you and physical for me? Wait, am I talking to readers of my own internal dialogue, or am I a character in a book I have written? Am I a work of fiction or...screw it! Enough inward rambling as my lungs are now content with the odd graceful tickle.

Gazing around the room like a star struck lover I am somewhat bemused, which is very unlike me, I'm usually very much on the ball. Apart from a shitload of dust everywhere my bedroom seems pretty much like it was the last time I was here. Well, I say pretty much the same, the bed has collapsed, and the wardrobe, and the ceiling has caved in a bit, and it's damp everywhere. But apart from that it's pretty much the same. You know what, it's not the same, I lied, I was trying to make you feel better, or me feel better, or Mitch.

Stumbling over some masonry, I'm guessing from the ceiling due to the gaping hole from above, I head out onto the landing to survey the area. Ah, there's my old computer chair with the missing arm, oh how I miss her disgruntled sighs, what a discontented bitch she was. She seems to have fallen through a huge gap and landed in a heap on the floor, have some of that you moaning cow. I give her bruised butt a little kick for old time's sake, causing a nostalgic trump to emit from her saggy seat. I love you too old girl, now shut up and rest in peace, or in pieces, as the case may be.

Entering the other rooms on this floor seems very improbable as the way is blocked by a multitude of different sized rubble, all precariously balanced on top on one another like a visible challenged crack-head's attempts at Jenga. Now, I am an expert ninja, which in turn most likely makes me a top notch mountain climber, but I see no reason to showcase my skills here. Heading to the top of the stairs I see the way down is only slightly encumbered by fallen debris. I reckon if I wall ran for a couple of steps, twisted into a somersault, and executed a perfect backflip, I would land on my feet in an awesome finisher pose while checking my nails. I mean I could do that if I wanted to, but, I kind of have a bad leg so... oh to hell with it, let's do it, pity there's no-one here to witness my special skills.

I take in a breath. I compose my inner being. I check my nails (which are awesome). I straighten my hat. I close my eyes. Then off I go, spiralling and spinning like a ballet dancer on amphetamine as I perform my preplanned ritual of excellence to the roar of a deafening crowd. Well, not quite. I've got to be honest, it didn't go as planned. The mistake I made was not opening my eyes after I closed them. Instead of executing my expected range of talents, I tripped over the first step and bounced down the stairs on my butt with all the grace of a tyrannosaurus rex swimming in jelly. Needless to say I landed at the bottom on my bottom and did a little swear.

"Shit!" I swore.

I stand up and dust myself off, both literally and metaphorically, and gaze around the room. First thing I notice is my hat is on the floor and not on my head. I rectify this unfortunate incident immediately and instantly feel better about myself. Back to my gazing and it is very evident that there are no windows. I know this because a: I can't see them, and b: there's a big tree sat in the living room (can trees sit? is that personification? I really don't care any more!) and the once firm glass is laid about like shattered memories. The rest of the room is pretty knackered to be honest, old father time along with mother nature's elements has pretty much ground everything away to dust. A once great home decimated by the ravages of the ages. But the memories of my time spent here will forever hold a place dear in my heart.

Itching to see what the world looks like a thousand years into the future, I try and judge whether to climb over or crouch under the fallen tree. Using my expert knowledge I decide to walk around it instead, good old Mitch, never one to pass up a good opportunity to use his top rated IQ. After traversing many fallen objects, and also many foreign items blown in by the winds of time, I make my way onto what used to be a garden complete with an artificial lawn. Not any more though, all that lays before me is desolation of the highest order. All around lay trees of all different sizes seemingly intertwined with each other, as if even in their final resting places they couldn't bear to be alone.

As the horizon looms off far away, I am struck by the fact that all the houses that used to surround my home are gone, or reduced to rubble, which is pretty much the same thing, I suppose. This beautiful home of my mine (not sure if it is legally still my property!) is literally the last house standing for miles and miles. In fact, it seems to be the only building of any sort for as far as the eye can see, a testament to the love that bound my life together, that still clings on with sheer, stubborn will.

Turning my gaze towards the sky I am overcome by a sense of foreboding. A heavy mist fills the sky with a vice-like grip, sucking the light from the world. The dimming sun hangs lazily in the centre of the earth, as if it is being held up by invisible hands like a peace offering to a lost humanity. Occasional wisps of solar activity threaten to ignite the sullen mist embroiled around the life-giving fireball, only to be sent back into it's cauldron to simmer and smoulder within. The world seems to have fallen, maybe man has fallen as well. I take off my hat, hold it to my chest and bow my head in mourning. God bless this once beautiful planet, I guess He has forsaken us all.

Well, at least I know what a thousand years in the future looks like. Pretty bloody depressing if you ask me, but at least I know now that I can travel forward as well as back. Might be time to go back to a somewhat cheerier time, this place is putting me on a proper downer. As I place my hat back upon my head in a cool as hell way, I prepare for my next adventure.

"Broom meow broom," a voice chimes up in a very odd tone to add a bit of cheer to this darkened world.

Turning around I see no-one, just the lonely building before me with it's new lodger, the fallen tree. Hmm, very strange, did I just imagine it? Wouldn't put it past me to start creating false people in this never-ending craziness I seem to be living with these days.

"Meow broom broom broom!" the voice chimes in again, this time with more gusto and really revving his engine.

"Who goes there?" I holler.

Silence.

"Hmm," I ponder while holding my chin for effect. "Come on Mitch, detective time, how can I entice this bugger out."

Aha! I exclaim inwardly. I pluck the hat from my head and place it on a nearby tree, this should interest whoever is screwing with my sanity. I know it would grab my attention, and my intelligence is of quite a high ranking, so this imbecile should certainly be cajoled into action. I walk back into my home and crouch behind the fallen tree.

"Meow broom?" the voice enquires, maybe I have stoked his attention after all.

After waiting a few minutes, while feeling my own attention beginning to waver, I decide to take back my hat and go home, home to real home not future home, which will actually be past home, I think. But when I leave here, which is future home, and go back to past home, then this future home will be past home, because I was here earlier, later. Hmm, my head hurts. Just as I'm about to leave my hiding place a very disturbed looking individual appears out of thin air wearing a pink summer dress, which looks a lot like the one my mum used to wear. What do have here then?

"Hello me old mucker," I greet him warmly. "What's with the blooming dress? There ain't no blooming sun."

The man, I think it's a man, does not turn around. He seems to be overly interested in my hat while twitching nervously.

This guy may need to see a good old fashioned quack. I head towards him with my hands held out in a friendly manner.

"Let's just have a little natter, shall we old chum," I jovially comment. "No need to be getting our tits in a tether now is there."

"Meow, broom," he innocently announces.

"Yes, meow broom. Good grasp of the English language. Who's a clever little boy then?"

This seems to momentarily halt his twitching. Ever so slowly he picks up my Stetson, places it on his head and turns around.

"We found the cat, he isn't dead, I'm wearing your hat, upon my head!" he booms.

It's Gulaxa! Or rather a very freaky looking Gulaxa, but it's still him.

"You little..." before I have chance to finish my outburst he vanishes. Why of all the bloody fucking shitting bastards! Now I'm mad! He took my bastard hat! I'm gonna kill the twat! But, how do I find him? Wait, I know who might have an idea, do you?

AN UNFORTUNATE INCIDENT

Arriving somewhere without prior knowledge is one hell of a wake-up call. It reminds me of my early days of time travelling where I had many a near miss and numerous startling encounters. Maybe I should write a book about them. Who knows, maybe in the future, once I have time to write and not be chasing throughout the ages on the tail of a messed up version of me. Come to think of it, where in the hell are we? More importantly, where is he?

One thing which is an absolute blessing is that it's pissing down, no more random jumps for this little sod. But also, rather unnervingly, none for me. Dark clouds loom overhead like a depressing blanket, smothering the world with doom and dismay. Although the rain isn't heavy yet as it patters down upon my well worn suit, the horizon threatens more persistent pours in the near future. I am always struck by how cool the rain looks as it hits my invisibility and just runs off. The thing is it doesn't run off, most of it soaks into my clothing and into my skin, but the illusion creates a completely different experience to the onlooker. Quite magical actually, I'd love to tell you how it works, but I simply don't have a clue – just like I can't explain time travel to you.

Anyway, back to where the hell I am. As I gaze around I see we are at a beach, a spiralling vertical pier adorns the sky in the distance, what a seemingly waste of an idea. Surely a pier would be of better use horizontally so as the public could walk along out to sea, or maybe, I don't know, fish! It is the sea after all, what will these ever so clever architects think of next, maybe a diagonal swimming pool, although that does not really make any sense at all, but neither does a vertical pier, so there! I really need to stop digressing all the time, I didn't use to be like this you know, I used to...there I go again! Right! Back to the story.

As the weather is pretty shitty the beach is somewhat deserted, apart from a few lonely dog walkers scattered around like random thoughts, each with their own personal journey towards endless destinations. It doesn't take me long to notice a kerfuffle in the distance just along the promenade, as a man seems to be having an altercation with a lady in a dress wearing a cowboy hat. Guess that's my cue to get my arse in gear. I check my surroundings, all clear, make myself visible while checking in a nearby window that this has been achieved, then off I go.

"What is your problem buddy?" I hear the man cry as I draw nearer.

"Meow meow?" the other me (who I shall now refer to as Catlaxa for obvious reasons) enquires in quite a serious tone complete with a curious look on his face.

"I know not of what you speak!" the guy replies innocently while holding his arms out. "Are you asking if I have a cat? Are you pretending to be a cat? I can't help me if you don't speak-a-de-English!"

"Hey there me old pal," I say softly as I approach. "Where did you vamoose off to? We need to get you back home, we don't want you catching your death in this rain."

I take him by the shoulders in my most caring manner, making him flinch against me.

"Sorry about this," I say turning to the confused man. "We lost the family cat a while back and it really hit him hard. Sometimes he gets flashbacks and goes a little loopy," I finish off by using the universal sign for 'this guy's nuts'.

"Hey no problem buddy," he says, with a hint of worry on his face at Catlaxa's nervousness around me. "You should take better care of him, maybe buy him a new cat or something, or at least some proper clothes."

"Really?" I say, feeling a surge of anger rising in my frayed state of being. "Well, how about you fuck off! Twat!"

"Well there's no need for that now is there, I have a right mind to call the cops. Your brother is obviously very disturbed and seems petrified of you, what are you doing to him?"

"Whoa there cowgirl," I say slowly. "No need to get your knickers in a twist, we're all cool here. Look, how about I buy you an ice cream and we'll forget all about our little rendezvous, capiche?"

Capiche? Where the hell did that come from? Last time I checked I wasn't an Italian mobster.

"You know what," my new found enemy replies. "I'm calling the po po, there's something amiss here and I don't like it one iota," he says, as he reaches for his mobile phone, this could spell trouble.

I suppose we could just run away, I mean he doesn't know our names or anything, and a far as I am aware we are not from this time (wherever this time may be). But Catlaxa is definitely not in the right attire for running, especially his footwear, a steel toe capped boot and a high heeled shoe, I mean come on!

Just as I am about to remonstrate further with the man, Catlaxa breaks free from my grip and sticks the nut on him.

"Meow!" he screams into his face. I watch helplessly as his eyes roll back into his head and he plonks to the concrete with a dull thud.

OK, not the decision I would have made, but at least he made a decision, good for you.

"Good for you," I say to Catlaxa.

"Meow?" he enquires.

"Yes, meow, good meow."

So, what the do we do meow, I mean now? We have a guy unconscious on the promenade, we can't jump anywhere at the moment to escape our predicament. How about we just sweep it, metaphorically, under the carpet. Glancing around I see no-one looking at us, so I bend down and simply roll him over the edge of the small wall onto the sand. Excellent. People will just think he is drunk or something. Catlaxa and I lean on the edge of the railing to watch the man, who hasn't hit the sand but has landed on a slope of concrete, to slowly roll down the stony driveway towards the sea, shit! Screw it, someone will save him, there's plenty of dog walkers about. I'm sure he'll be fine.

"Meow!" Catlaxa shouts pointing at the man.

"Shh," I shush him. "Yes, meow, dead meow."

He turns to look at me with a sullen expression on his face. He takes the hat off his head and holds it to his heart.

"Dead meow," he says quietly and begins sobbing.

I pull him to my chest and hug him closely.

"There there," I coo. "All good meows dead dead some day."

No idea what the hell that might mean, but it seems to soothe him somewhat. He breaks apart from our hug and hands me his Stetson.

"For me?" I ask as if speaking to a small child.

He nods enthusiastically and plonks it on my head before I have a chance to refuse.

"Why thank you kind sir, always wanted to be a cowboy. I'm going to go check myself out in the mirror, come on."

The rain has stopped now, and as a warm sun breaks through the once darkened clouds a feeling of hope overcomes me, everything is going to be OK. As I near a shop window I gaze at my reflection, wow don't I look awesome! All I need now is the rest of the attire and I will look damn fantastic. A glimpse in the reflection catches my eye as I see Catlaxa stripping off all his clothes. This could get weird, even weirder than it already is. As I turn around he grabs a blanket off a nearby bench and begins drying himself furiously. Shit! Before I have a chance to go after him a hand grabs me by the scruff of the neck.

"I believe that hat is mine," he shouts into my ear. "Always knew I would catch you you little thieving idiot."

He flings me around easily and I am faced by a bearded Viking looking dude.

"Wait," he says. "You're not him, where did you get that hat?"

Before he has a chance to take my hat I kick him in the balls and make myself invisible.

"Have some of that you twat!" I say instinctively as I turn around and run toward Catlaxa.

Shit, he's gone, not a-fucking-gain! I quickly take off all of my clothes and begin running around screaming blue murder.

"Shit! Fuck! Twatting shit!"

I grab another blanket from a nearby bench and rigorously dry myself. Not forgetting to straighten my new hat perfectly upon my head. Staring back at the Viking prick I see him looking very bemused, this pleases me somewhat, because for some deep centred reason I really dislike this guy.

"Adios Mr No Hat!" I bark, and go on another mission to who knows where.

SOUL MATES

W hen will I ever learn not to jump while enraged, it never gets me anywhere. Well, that's not literally true, it always gets me somewhere, but not where I actually want to go. Anger is definitely not a friend of a time traveller, especially one as cool as me, and I really must learn to count to 72 in order to calm my tits down. What a silly billy I am. But I am passed the point of remonstrating with myself and putting myself down, that type of negative self-talk gets me nowhere, apart from in a world of hurt. So, in God's beautiful English language, where the bloody hell am I?

I seem to have arrived in a random person's house in a very nice spacious living room. OK, this is a bit different. A TV that seems too large for the room sits atop a shiny black stand, underneath is a gleaming white PlayStation console – I like this person already. Strangely enough there is another TV in the far corner of the room on top of a writing table, seems a bit odd having another television in the same room, but I won't judge this person too much just yet. Gazing out of the windows I see a row of houses that are loomed over by towering trees, what a wonderful view to have out of one's own front room.

As I turn my gaze further into the room I nearly shit my knickers. There's a guy sat on a poo coloured sofa typing away on a laptop, seemingly lost in his own narrative while I just happen to be lurking just out of his eyeline. He seems like a very focussed individual with a beautifully big nose, I bet that runs in the family. I kind of like him already, but I thought the same about that bastard Hatson, and he turned out to be a right dick. I will not allow my quick judgements to run away with me this time, don't judge a book by it's cover and all that. Speaking of books, I wonder what he is writing. I sidestep stealthily to my right and peer over his shoulder.

"What do you want?" the guy enquires as he quickly closes his laptop.

I fart a little at his sudden movement and feel somewhat embarrassed, quick Mitch say something cool.

"Creaky floorboards I see, what?" Well done Mitch, what a guy.

"Hmm," comes the non-amused reply, please don't be a dick like Hatson. "I'm not a dick. I am however concerned as to why you are here..."

He leaves the question (or statement) lingering in the air like a forgotten song.

"To be honest, I don't know why I'm here either, so that makes two of us."

A silence falls upon the moment as we stare at each other. But the moment isn't tense, it's kind of awesome, like two lost souls have found each other through sheer will. I feel some sort of connection with this guy, as if he is a part of me. Something deep and meaningful is happening here, something I do not know the true purpose of. What I do know is that I'm not going to speak first, I will never break, I am Mitch Branning, master of the known universe, time travelling legend...

"Hi, I'm Mitch Branning!" I blurt out while reaching out my hand, so much for not breaking first.

He shakes my hand firmly, good grip, a slight charge of static seems to develop between our connection.

"Hey Mitch, I'm Ali Round, please to meet you."

For some reason that name sparks a chord within my mind, it has a deep meaning in some way, why can't I grasp what our connection means? Time to get some answers.

"Please to meet you Roundy," I say while getting an eyebrow raised look from my new friend. "So, what you working on? Anything exciting?"

He glances back at the laptop, seemingly forgetting my calling him an unwelcome and maybe too personal nickname.

"Oh, nothing much, just a story about a very disturbed individual who thinks he is clever and funny."

He smirks when he says this, as if he thinks I might get some internal joke. Wait, is he talking about me? No way, that would literally be insane, wouldn't it? I'm not even going to entertain that idea, my life is already crazy as it is without more nonsense adding to it.

"Erm, nice place you have here," I say, changing the subject away from something I really don't want to try to comprehend.

"Thanks. So, if you don't mind me asking, why are you standing in my living room?"

Shit! He's got me there, how do I get out of this one. Quick Mitch, think, you always know what to say in awkward situations.

"You've got a big nose!" I blurt out. For God's sake Mitch! Why in holy shitballs would you say that?

"Thanks, it runs in the family, it's commonly referred to as the Round nose. It helps sniff out the bullshit from, well, the bullshitters."

Great reply, I'm starting to like this dude.

"Great reply me old mucker, put it there."

We go for a high five, but as our hands crack together a surge of electricity reverberates through what feels like the entire universe. Time stops as cascading versions of him roll backwards across the room and off into the blackness that has now appeared all around us. The floor falls away, as does the whole world, as we are suspended in dark space while glimmering stars pulsate brightly in the distance. I turn around and see an infinite number of me are back-folding across the depths of space the same as my new companion. As I turn around to face him, our hands still touching, he winks with a knowing smile, then our hands release and the world falls back into it's normal rhythm.

"Nice to finally meet you Mitch," he says slowly. "Now piss off, I need to write all this down or I'll forget it."

"OK," I say, still stuck in a sort of limbo and not really having a clue what the hell is going on, and what he has to write down. This whole encounter has really thrown me.

I'm not normally stuck for words, but this guy has me absolutely flummoxed, he sure is something else, and definitely not a dick like Hatson. Maybe we'll meet again some day, I guess only time will tell. One last look at the beautiful room around me and then off I go.

DARK INTENTIONS

R ight, you know what, I'm leaving that Catlaxa to fend for himself, I'll never be able to predict where he ends up anyway. I'm sure he won't cause too much trouble. Although saying that, he has just headbutted someone for pretty much no reason whatsoever. What if he ends up as a time travelling serial killer or something? Oh well, not my problem. But wait, if he ends up a serial killer, does that mean I do too? I guess there's worse things to end up as, as least I'll be remembered for something.

So I cuts my ties with the disturbed one, ignore where the other one went to, and carry on with my hellish journey. I do recall previously that the idiot had a conversation with himself two hours into the future which, to be brutally honest, is total bullshit. I can comprehend the fact that time travel and invisibility are things, but a normal mobile phone reaching through time to make a call, not buying it one bit. So I'm guessing that so called future version of himself was in fact somewhere in his house, most likely place would be the attic, so that's where I went, and there's no-one here, shit!

But maybe I've just timed things wrong, and to be honest I do need some clothes first as I am completely naked. Although you wouldn't be able to tell cos I'm invisible, so I rectify that little mishap first, checking to make sure in the nearby mirror, which just happens to be there. Right, clothes, but most importantly, a black suit that fits me, can't be meeting him in different attire. Even though he is an idiot, he will surely know something is amiss if I turn up wearing a completely different outfit.

I start rummaging through various boxes while stumbling over a fallen Christmas tree searching for my prize. I pick up a one armed computer chair, that has obviously seen better days, and stumble face first onto the seat, causing a trumpeting like sound. Bloody hell it stinks! It smells like a thousand butts! I can actually taste past aromas caressing down my throat like a slithering shit stained snake. I retch involuntarily at the unwelcome invasion. What a horrible piece of furniture, I give it a massive punch to vent my anger, letting out another moan and another waft of faecal ferocity into my waiting mouth. For fuck's sake! Calming myself down I continue on my quest, but find nothing, double shit!

And then I notice something dark hanging down the bottom of the mirror. Hello.

"Hello," I say.

Walking slowly over I reach around the rear of the mirror and lift a hanger off the back. Guess what folks, a black suit. Now, this was either put here on purpose, or maybe it was just fate. Who the hell cares?! I put it on with all the grace of a warbling thrush and check myself out in the mirror, cool as ice. Just as I'm realising how cool I am I feel a shift in the air, he's on his way. Better make myself invisible, but first hide my hat somewhere, somewhere safe, oh screw it, just chuck it. Which I do and it lands on the corner of the mirror, what an awesome shot. Just in time as well as the idiot appears out of thin air sat on what I'm guessing was his favourite chair. The vile stench that violated my nasal passage earlier was most likely from him, my anger towards him surfaces once more.

"Nice attic," I murmur, making him jump and twirl around like the swivelling idiot he is.

"For God's sake!" he cries. "You are a sneaky Pete aren't you. And before you say it, I know you're not called Pete. Here, let me put this on your wrist, it can be your early warning system so you don't put the shits up me every time you appear!"

The cheeky wanker then attaches his old cat's collar to my wrist, how dare he! I'm not his pet that he can command and look after like a little lost puppy. This really enrages me. But then I see a change of look on his face as he stares at my wrists, is he falling in love with me? I mean, I wouldn't blame him, I am bloody gorgeous after all. He stares at me and begins to say my name before something in his pocket attracts his attention, phew, that could have been awkward.

Another look of confusion falls across his already bemused looking face as he stares at the screen. If it's the call from himself he had better take it, otherwise the space time continuum will be in a world of shit. He turns the phone to me and I see a reminder of the screen saying 'make the call'. Hmm, very weird. I wonder who set that? I mean, it can't have been him, the now version of him, and it definitely wasn't me, the now version of me. Oh screw it, who the hell cares. I simply play dumb, which to be honest is accurate as I have no bloody clue who set it. I do however know what it means, but why tell him this, let him do some brain work for a change.

"Gulaxa, I can't remember what I said, I only kind of recall sounding like a cocky bastard," not sure if that is a question or a statement, prick.

"I cannot remember what you said either, just be yourself," I reply in a weak little voice which seems to cause him some inward moodiness, good.

"When do I make the call then? Hang on, this has already happened, so whenever I actually choose to make the call is going to be the right time isn't it? I ain't being ruled by time any more, I'm going to chillax for a bit and make the call when I want to." He says this like a spoilt little brat, but for some strange reason this worries me, because if he chooses not to make the call then previous events will not happen, and that could be bad shit.

He lets his seat down, closes his eyes, lets out a huge sigh and says it's time to chill out. This is serious shit you time travelling amateur, you have no idea what's at stake do you! I feel like kicking him right in the nuts. Thankfully I resist my urges as the phone rings with a melody I kind of like, good choice in music. Also, I guess I may have judged him harshly, this version of him didn't have to make the call, I'll let him off, this time.

He then begins having a conversation with himself in what he believes is two hours in the past, I mean what a stupid sod! How can such an idiot believe such nonsense? Oh yeah, because he's as dumb as a stupid dumbo. At one point he starts laughing like a psychopath, wow this guy is losing the plot, keep it together pal. I adopt my most worried expression, which actually isn't too far from the truth, his maniacal chuckling scares me a little. Well you know what, lets see who likes being scared shall we.

The conversation seems to be going on a lot longer than the previous one, which means if I time this right then I can have a little fun with him. As his attention and gaze are not on me any more I step out of view and make myself invisible. Let's mess this guy up!

CHAOS AND MAYHEM

So much for taking it easy for a while. My last two jumps have been a thousand years into the future, which I suppose was quite relaxing until that bastard Gulaxa stole my hat, and then a very surreal moment in some guy's house. I'm really trying not to address the elephant in the room with that whole scenario, it's too much of a head fuck, maybe I'll let you guys and gals infer the meaning behind that weird encounter. Needless to say I felt some sort of universal connection with him, some deep rooted bond between us that binds us together to whatever universes we both may traverse. I have a strong feeling that we will meet again some day.

One good thing that came out of my most recent charade was a calming presence over me, which makes me no longer want to chase after Gulaxa and get my hat back. There's plenty more hats in the sea, I mean the stores. I could even go back and visit Hatson if I wanted to, but he kind of irritated me, so screw him, I'm sure I'll find another hat store somewhere along my journey. Thinking of Gulaxa, that didn't seem like the old him. He seemed kind of messed up in some way as though time travel had really screwed with him, I wonder if that is what changed him into the psychopath he turned into. Moreover, the bastard was meant to be dead, I pretty much watched him get obliterated by that bomb. So, was that a different version of him? If so, how many versions of him are there? Which brings me to my next devastating realisation: how many different version of me are there? Mum dropped a little bombshell not so long back about other versions of me, and then quickly changed the subject, this could get very messy.

Predicting my next jump with what I hope is perfection I decide on a little experiment. You may be thinking this a little unwise, but let me tell you something, I am a time travelling legend (certification pending), and my unique experience allows me to pretty much do whatever the God damn hell I want, so that's exactly what I intend on doing. Because like everything in life, sometimes we have to take a little risk to enjoy what is beautiful in this world.

So I arrive at my destination with all the grace of a time travelling ghost smack bang in the middle of hopefully a lot of chaos, this will be fun, I hope. As far as I am reasonably aware no-one (and that includes me) entered into my mum's old room amongst the mayhem of that weird and wonderful day, so that's where I vamoosed off to. As I am just an absolute genius at my craft now, I appear out of thin air (why not fat air? Seems a bit discriminatory against obese air molecules to me!) laid on my back under the main double bed, good job Mitch. Now, have I judged the time correctly?

Then, right on cue, I hear the shattering of glass as my soon to be deceased friend has a very close encounter with an unnecessary shower glass. I always wondered why I had a glass door and a shower curtain, guess this was why. Does this mean I always knew this was going to happen? Or did a previous version of me coerce me into buying both? Enough shit to deal with without worrying if more of me were having an impact on my spending habits (although would make sense with some of the useless junk I have purchased in the past!).

Slowly rolling onto my side, I slightly lift up the veil like a peeping tom and see Gulaxa laid prone on the glass strewn floor, poor little bastard, at least you'll be at peace soon. I have time to ponder who the hell cleaned up the glass, I'm pretty damn sure it wasn't there when I came back previous/later times, and as far as I'm aware I don't have a cleaner. Oh how the plot continues to thicken, I have a feeling shit is about to get insane.

"Sorry my little baby," I hear myself mutter.

Watching on like some perverted psychopath as I murder my beloved pet, I am overcome with a disturbing sense of deja vu. This is a very surreal moment in my once peaceful life, I am effectively reliving a perfect re-enactment of a once fractured version of my past. Somehow we forget or stuff down hard to deal with events, causing them to distort somewhat into a more palatable scenario. Not here though. As he/I snapped the neck of my beloved pet I could actually feel the bones break inside my mind, I could once again feel the sense of loss that I felt at the time, it was like it was happening all over again. And in a weird way it was, right before my very eyes.

Lowering the veil slowly I roll onto my back and close my eyes. Why did I return here? This is so painful to see and my heart bleeds with sorrow and loss once more, reminding me of my most recent experience watching my own mother pass away. Familiar feelings of darkness threaten to claw their way through my fragile soul like friendly hands, prying open each misfiring synapse with practised ease. Just as they are about to drag me down into an awful oblivion a phone rings, startling me back into my unwanted reality.

I remember this call, some guy with an American accent, I still don't know who it was, I wonder if I'll ever find out. Also, not long after this I disappear to No-Time, I never did find out why this happened, maybe now I will, this could get interesting. So screw you dark depressing shit, I haven't got time to entertain you right now, although I'm sure you'll creep in some time later you conniving bastard.

Reaching for my veil of secrecy, I slowly lift her up an inch to get a little view into the bathroom like a teenage pervert. I've just hung up the phone so should be entering the bathroom soon, there I am. Still no clothes on, but what an absolute Adonis I am, so adorably sexy. If I was gay I would definitely do me, which would be weird, and would it actually be gay? I mean masturbating isn't gay, so would having sex with yourself be gay? Hmm, something to either ponder over later, or quite simply forget as it's a very disturbing thought.

As he/I opens the blinds, Gulaxa appears out of nowhere holding the clothes I was wearing when I arrived at No-Time. He then hands them to, well, actually no-one, they just sort of hover in the air, and then they and I/me vanishes. Then Gulaxa sits down on the toilet, before standing back up to drop the seat, then in I walk, the other me, damn this is confusing the shit out of me! Then both of us/them begin conversing a well known conversation which I really can't be arsed narrating again because my head is falling off.

I head back into the safety behind the veil to ponder. Firstly, who took me to No-Time? It can't have been Gulaxa because he's here/there. Although he handed something or someone some clothes, but how in the hell did they just levitate? Oh shit!

Didn't grandad mention something about invisibility earlier/ later? Has grandad been screwing with me all this time (not in a sexual way!)? I'll have a word with that sneaky bastard later/earlier. Secondly, Gulaxa must have had a part in this somehow as he handed over the clothes, was he being a sneaky Pete from the start? I always thought there was something fishy about him from the first time I met him, and I don't mean his aroma, that was kind of nice, but again not in a sexual away. And thirdly, in fact there might not be a third issue, well not one I can think of right now.

Hearing a commotion outside of my comforting veilness startles me from my incessant inward chattering. Pulling the screen of serenity back slightly I can't see around the corner, I can however gaze across at the mirrors on the wardrobes opposite and see the bottom half of Gulaxa and me/I. I've obviously just made the call to myself and am a bit perplexed, Gulaxa informs me that we have to go and I remember where to now, the literal bloodbath, I'm definitely not following them back there again, it's too bloody bloody for my liking. As I see our bottom halves draw closer I presume we are entering our time hug, I remember this well, always felt like such a beautiful moment. Then another pair of legs, matching Gulaxa's exactly barring a few rips here and there, appear out of thin air, then me/I and Gulaxa vanish. What the shit is going on here? And who are these wankers?

"Right," one of them says. "Find the cat."

"Sir yes sir," the other mocks. "Must find meowing machine."

"Stop being a dick, give me a diazzy."

I can just about make out one of them pulling a plastic sleeve from his pocket with blue tablets inside, he breaks a couple loose and replaces the sleeve. I then actually verbally hear them both crunching down on the prescription pills furiously.

"Ah, that's better!" they both chime in, and then being laughing like nutters.

As they both exit the reflection in the mirrors I turn my gaze back to the bathroom to follow my prey like some stalking predator. Who are these guys? Holy bloody bollocks! It's Gulaxa, and Gulaxa! Two bloody Gulaxa's! What the shitting hell is going on?!

"Shit," the left one says. "The bloody cat's gone, we're too late."

"Meow gone?" Righty chimes in a sarcastic but familiar tone, is that the hat stealing bastard?

Coming somewhat back to my senses they are indeed correct, Gulaxa (the cat) has vamoosed. Where in the shit has he buggered off to? I mean, he/I broke his neck, right? I felt it, I was there, twice, there's no way he could have survived it. Unless...no, sorry, I'm not going to entertain it. I am not even going to mention it. I'm not even going to try and wrap my head around it. But wait, isn't it plausible? I mean, there's more versions of me, more versions of Gulaxa, so in a sense does that mean there are more versions of the cat? Might explain what I saw when the feline Gulaxa vanished earlier, later. Oh how the plot thickens. First things first, go and remonstrate with these sneaky bastards first. Dragging myself from beneath the veil I prepare my wrath.

"Right you two doppel-ganging wankers, where in holy fuckery is my pussy!" I blurt out.

OK, so no-one is here, where have they buggered off to? Not really any way of finding out either, shit! I crouch down where my loving companion had laid and met his untimely demise, a soft indent still bears witness to his soft round belly. I close my eyes and try to come to terms with my new found insane scenario. So, the cat has miraculously disappeared, there seems to be a few versions of Gulaxa mooching about causing mayhem including stealing hats, and quite possibly grandad might have a say in it all with all this invisibility crap. Guess there's only one thing for it, go have a stern word with my ever so loving grand-papa. Maybe this time I'll try and not scare some old dear, good job I have clothes on, that's a great start. Could really do with a hat though, I wonder if there's any in my mum's old wardrobe.

Dancing my way over to the wardrobe door like Fred Astaire on six pints of whiskey I fling the door open. And there, staring right at me, is a black ladies sun hat complete with a cute little bow and a huge white feather sticking out the top. Screw it, you only live once. I plonk it on my head, slam the door shut, and check myself out in the mirror. Awesome. Wait, before I go, better check the nails, then I check myself out checking my nails out in the mirror. Two versions of me doing a cool as hell nail checking scenario, life doesn't get any better, Well it would if someone held a mirror up behind me, but better not wish for shit like that to happen.

Screw it, off I go. Grand-papa, here I come you invisible bastard!

DARK TIMES

O nce a time traveller has reached legendary status (certification approved and validated) they have certain skills bestowed upon them. But these new powers are to be used sparingly and never for ones own personal gain. One such perk of this awesome ability is to suspend any individual in a stasis field where time and space do not exist. Obviously this is only to be used in extreme circumstances, but sometimes, like now, a legend's discretion can be applied. Time to have some fun with the idiot.

Having this awesome control in my hands is so very empowering, I feel more like a God than a mere mortal right now. I watch as the fear falls across his face like a veil of darkness, cocooning him inside his own chaotic thoughts. Is this what omnipotence feels like? To have someone trapped in their own version of hell fills me with a sense of overwhelming satisfaction. For now my blue bastard friends are forgotten as this moment becomes the reason I am alive, the reason for my whole existence.

I watch on in perverted amusement as his eyes flicker and dart around like a spasmodic action man, searching endlessly for some glimmer of light, some beacon of hope. None to be found here my idiotic friend, you are my prisoner now, I decide when you leave. I alone decide how long you will endure this mental torture. Trying desperately to open his mouth and speak he resembles a lonely fish swimming around and around, lost in a cycle of pitying despair. If I could have one more ability it would be to read his mind right now, to feel his fear. But it is pretty evident on his face and that will suffice. Closing his eyes to likely attempt to rationalise what is happening, a moment of calmness envelops his features, this is not what I expected. But it doesn't last long as another bout of terror comes across his face. He opens his mouth as wide as a dark yawning sea, seeming to attempt to swallow the blackness that is sucking the life from every fibre of his mortal being.

Then something very surreal happens: the bell he had attached onto my wrist starts jangling, seemingly all by itself, as if some external force was willing it to move on its own. Surely it can't be him, can it? He's in God damn time jail! He's not supposed to be able to do anything apart from go insane. And then, as if by magic, the irritating jangling stops. But a deep meditative state seems to fall over his face, like a yoga master accepting some sort of serenity, this isn't supposed to be like this. Almost at once the stupid bell begins it's chirpy chiming again, what the hell is going on?!

I grab at the irritating instrument on my wrist to cease it's chattering, hoping that the darkness will suck him back down again into loneliness and pain. Quite the opposite happens. A look of steely resolve comes across him. I watch on as he clenches his fists together, summoning whatever strength he has inside him to overcome his inward turmoil. Even though I am holding the bell it moves slightly against my grip, damn this guy is strong. Maybe I underestimated him. Gathering some resolve of my own, I attempt to completely shut off the bell. Then a powerful internal shock wave seems to pulsate through my brain as I hear him shout inside my head.

"I SUMMON GULAXA TO BE IN FRONT OF ME RIGHT NOW!"

Fucking holy shitting hell! This has never happened before. I don't want to admit it, but this guy is something else, maybe he is actually the master of time. Maybe time will wait for him because he isn't even a man. He's something greater. I had better tread carefully. To be honest I kind of feel in awe of this guy now, but also a little scared at what he may be able to do. I instinctively hug him to try and suppress whatever powers he may have awoken, what I may have awoken.

"Gulaxa," he says into my mind, which is such a surreal experience. "Is that you?"

I reply in the affirmative using a soft reassuring tone, not wanting to aggravate him any more.

"Where are we? I...am...frightened," he whispers into my mind with both fear and relief.

"We are somewhere outside of time, a bit like No-Time, but darker," I reply in my usual monotone voice, keep it simple stupid.

"Yeah, no shit," he replies, as I feel rather than see his sarcastic smirk. "So next question, tell me how in holy hell do we get out of here?" I feel once more a spark of fury within his soul, but can't resist with a little sarcasm of my own.

"Quite simple really."

"Well then kind sir," he reacts. "Do please enlighten me as to how to get out of our untimely predicament, at your earliest convenience of course."

At this point I release him from his stasis and allow him to take us away to wherever his overreaching mind desires. For the first time in what seems like an eternity I feel fear. I crave one of my blue friends to take some of the unfamiliar feelings away, and the dawning realisation that I left them in the old suit crushes my tortured soul.

LOVE AND DEATH

Before I jumped I was not sure when to go and meet my grand-papa. Do I go back to the nursing home? Or to when he was younger when we had our little incidents? I decided against the latter as I recall a couple of versions of me had previously had near misses there, better not complicate an already over complicated scenario. Nope, I'm going back to the nursing home, this time with the intention of only meeting him and no-one else. I will not be responsible for another's innocent bystanders half death. And to be fair, I always found a sense of warmth from my ever loving grand-papa whilst we conversed in his favourite place, he always seemed so pleased to see me.

Arriving with all the grace of a drunken sailor, I crash and bang my way into pots and pans to sprawl ungracefully onto a bleach smelling floor like a dying kipper. Good job Mitch, way to be subtle. Standing up and straightening my awesome hat I check my surroundings. This proves difficult because it's pitch black, but this welcoming realisation calms my dented ego somewhat at my less than ninja-like entrance. As I attempt to head off into whatever direction I am facing, hastily kicking the once quiet but now noisy pots and pans, I am filled with a sense of extreme jubilation of meeting my grand-papa.

"Grand-papa! Grand-papa!" I cry out shrilly. "Where for art thou Grand-papa?"

As I clumsily kick the forgotten pans and pots, a cacophony of noise reverberates off the walls like a constant attack on the old ear drums, this is not going as expected. Maybe if I slowed down and took baby steps while exclaiming quietly, instead of allowing my eager anticipation to get the better of me, then my noise may be limited somewhat. But my childlike giddiness knows no bounds as I skip along in the darkness like, well, a child skipping to be honest. I do however regret not searching for a source of illumination as I plough head first into something immovable, probably a wall.

"Ow!" I cry. "That bloody hurt my noggin!" I cry again.

I have a brief moment to ponder about the condition of my awesome hat when I receive a clout around the back of the other head, or rather the other side of my head, which sends the other side, that being the previous side, once again into the hard wall like surface.

"Double bloody ow!" I wail. "Who is attacking my lovely headed area?"

As the room is still pitch black, I have no alternative but to curl into a ball on the clean smelling floor and hope the bastard buggers off. However, my assailant (is it my assailant? do I own this person?) seems very adept at attacking people and goes to work on my legged area, what an absolute bastard. I once again worry about my hatted friend and feel a slight surge of anger.

"You may take my freedom, but you will never harm my headed garment, you heathen!" I boom in Braveheart like fashion.

As I emit this explicit outburst, I strike my foot into what I hope may be a crotch and hear a very high pitched squeal, very much like a woman's, shit! Although best not jump to conclusions, my adorable grand-papa has previously emitted pitches of the highest note while under situations of duress. But I really do not want him to be the recipient of my kick as I may need his help, so I do rather hope I have kicked someone else, just hopefully not a female someone else. Whomever I have just booted falls atop of me very ungracefully while also seemingly trying to bite me. But not with teeth, more like with gums, this is very disconcerting. A flash of illumination brightens the room to my joy.

"What the blazes are you doing?" a familiar voice booms.

"Grand-papa!" I cry jubilantly. "Help! I'm being molested by a thing!"

"That's not a thing you idiot, it's bloody Doris!"

As I turn my gaze towards the writhing figure on top of me, I recognise instantly the half/full dead woman I flashed earlier/later. Her wriggling ceases as she flops to the side of me struggling for breath. I feel a slight pang of guilt at her predicament, but this is quickly dissolved as I remember my glorious hat and hope that it is not battered and bruised. Relief quickly overcomes me as I see it within my reach in all its glory. As I reach for the headed garment my ever-loving grand-papa bundles past, kicking it across the pan strewn floor, what a bastard!

"Oi grand-papa!" I shout. "Watch the blooming hat me old mucker!"

I hastily push old Doris away from me and jump to my feet with all the grace of a sack of shit to trundle towards my headed companion. Retrieving my friend I place it on top of my head and breathe a huge sigh of relief.

"Ah, that's better," I sigh, prompting me to remember the other Gulaxa's sighing this same phrase in unison, time to have a good old natter with my grand-papa.

"Grand-papa..." I begin.

"Go into my room you idiot," he rudely interrupts. "Once again you have frightened the life out of old Doris."

Feeling somewhat belittled, I trudge out of what I now see is a kitchen and head towards the old man's sleeping area. As I make my way along the corridor I see various heads peeping out of doorways, probably admiring my cool as hell hat. I guess a nail checking scenario would be the cherry on the cake for these old dears. So I duly oblige with expert suaveness, even chucking in a little twirl as I do so. Damn Mitch, you are one cool son of a bitch.

"Pervert," I hear a lady mutter as I walk by, charming.

"Tiny todger Thomas," another woman incorrectly chimes in.

"Fucking prick!" a gentlemen shouts.

I get the sense I am not really welcome here, and I have no idea why. Do they not know of whom I am? Of whence I came? I am Mitch Branning – Time Travelling Legend (certification in the post). Ye should all kneel before me, for I am a God. I turn around to belt these words out to my lowly peasants before my loving grand-papa takes me by the arm and pulls me into his room, slamming the door behind us. He seems a little perturbed for some reason, I bet I can cheer him up.

"Sit down!" he shouts.

I go to sit on his favourite butt chair before he hastily shoves me onto the bed.

"Not my chair, the bed you bloody idiot!" he barks.

I do as requested, seeing as though he was so polite in his wording. This guy really does love me, and I can see why, I am probably the best grandson in the whole wide world. As he sits down in his stinky chair, he breathes out an exasperated sigh.

"Poor Doris, you can't keep doing this to her. You've scared her to death."

I ponder for a moment before replying.

"I'm kind of concerned that Doris may be a zombie, or maybe even a vampire," I begin. "I apparently scared her half to death before and you said she was halfway there already. So, in my humble opinion, she was actually dead. Then earlier/later you said I had, and I quote 'frightened the life out of her' unquote. And now, without quoting, you said I've scared her to death. So in the space of however bloody long it has been, she has died three times, something is amiss here. Maybe we should stake her..."

I leave the question lingering in the air like a rose coloured balloon. He stares at me for a little while, probably a little while longer than is needed, before sighing loudly.

"What is wrong with you?" he asks softly. "I mean, well done this time for arriving wearing clothing, but why are you wearing your mother's hat? I seriously think you may be losing the plot a little. Look, you're my grandson, I love you and I always will. And I know sometimes I may be a little tough on you, but you're an idiot, and idiots need pushing. So, on that note, what are you doing here?"

I really don't know what to say. This isn't the first time he has showed me compassion, always knew he liked me. My tears well up momentarily as I gaze into his well worn features. This guy fought in the war like a true hero. Yet here he is stuck in this God forsaken place whittling away his existence until his day of reckoning comes. Maybe I can make him proud of me for once in his life. But first I need answers. I wipe the tears threatening to evacuate my soul and prepare my well thought out narrative.

"Firstly, I'm doing tickety boo. In fact I'm downright awesome. Secondly, this hat is awesome so, pardon my French, you can suck my balls, not literally, obviously. And thirdly, have you been spying on me in my own home? I went back to observe some shenanigans going on and someone invisible seems to be causing some mayhem. Also, there's at least three versions of Gulaxa. Also, the cat Gulaxa, my furry little friend, seems to have vanished, but I saw him earlier/later and it was weird. Help!"

He stares me straight in the eyes and deep into my tormented soul.

"I have not been watching you, it's Gulaxa, it's been him all along, toying with you, stringing you along in his twisted little game. This guy has been doing this longer than you can possible imagine, he is one of the first. But he has lost his way, he has strayed from the path of righteousness onto the road of darkness. Only you can stop him now. But to do this you have to find the cat, he is the key to all of this."

Wow, don't think this guy has ever talked so much in all of the time I have known him. I watch as he leans back into his chair and closes his eyes slowly.

"I wish you well on your journey, for mine ends here. I always knew you would be here for my final breath, just as you were for your mother's. Take care grandson, time waits for no man."

And with this he breathes out a slow rasping breath and falls silent. The air in the room all of a sudden takes on a feeling of heaviness, as if the sword of destiny has fallen at my feet. It is at this point I realise I am actually alone. My mother has gone, my father, my grandfather. I feel like a tiny speck of loneliness on the sea of the barren universe. I let my tears flow for a few moments before pulling myself back into the reality that is life. Time to make this awesome man proud.

I stand up and plant a soft kiss on his still warm cheek.

"Love you grandad, sleep tight soldier, until we meet again."

I snap off a sharp salute, then push onward towards my ongoing quest for answers.

A DOG'S LIFE

Arriving to a view of pure beauty I struggle to accept my surroundings. As I have mostly been the person who decides my destination, I feel it very disorientating travelling with someone else as the navigator. A sense of fear always plays a factor, because if the person guiding is very inexperienced (and this guy certainly is) then we could literally end up anywhere. God help us when he learns that there really are no limits to where or when he can travel to.

As soon as we arrive I take a step back out of view, forgetting my invisibility for now, doesn't really seem any need as he is too busy gazing out at the vast ocean that lays before us. It certainly is a beautiful place he has brought us to, seems a lot like paradise. Although the surrounding area is one of serenity, I can't help but feel a sense of anxiety begin to claw at my frayed senses. What happened back then was something that I have never witnessed before. How could he have managed that? To mentally break himself from the stasis he was held within demonstrated some supreme power that I don't even possess. Speaking of possession, he was actually inside my head, literally a voice within my mind shouting words throughout my brain like a loudspeaker, this worries me.

As the feelings of fear intensify, I once again crave one of my blue friends to take the edge off the incoming tirade of mental torture. Instinctively I reach into my pocket, knowing full well it is empty, but hoping against hope that maybe I am wrong. I dig deeper and deeper, with the fear and anticipation growing stronger and stronger, threatening to overwhelm my breaking mind. Realising that I will not find any form of release here I reluctantly pull my hand from the pocket, noticing that a tremor has started, which causes the irritating bell to begin chiming.

"Here Gulaxa, here boy," my travelling companion crudely mocks.

Who the hell does he think he is? I'm not his fucking lap dog! This degrading comment once again fuels the fire within me, stoking the flames of hatred that has festered somewhat over recent times. I must however curb my angry enthusiasm, I don't know what more this guy may be capable of. Play it cool.

"Nice beach," I utter, completely disregarding his derogatory statement.

"So nice of you to join us Mr Laxa," he says while pretend stroking an invisible cat on his lap. Does he think he is some sort of Bond villain or something? Looks like a damn fool to me.

I wonder if he can sense my anxiety as he pretty much orders me to lighten up and chillax. That's the second time he's used that word, such an irritating phrase which grates at my already tender soul. This feeling is abated somewhat as he attempts a cool toke on his cigarette and ends up coughing like a virgin smoker, making me smile inwardly.

"Smoking is bad for you," I say sarcastically while adopting my usual deadpan demeanour.

"No shit Sherlock," he smirks. "And yes, I know you're not called Sherlock before you chastise me! So, that dark place, what is it, and how in the hell did we end up there?"

For God's sake, am I going to have to explain every little detail to him? This is getting rather irritating now. But I do, in lazy fashion, while keeping my cool, insinuating that Dark-Time is actually the opposite of No-Time and that they cannot exist without each other, which actually makes some sort of sense. Check me out making shit up on the spot. But only an idiot would believe this nonsense, right? I'm not getting at whoever is reading this obviously. In fact, reading what? These are just my inward thoughts, no-one will end up reading my thoughts, will they? But shit, that book, in the JFK place. I wonder if it's still continuing, I seriously doubt it, I mean it was probably just a dream, right?

"You know that makes no sense, right?" he exclaims, breaking me momentarily from my inward monologue.

"I'm not here to make sense. You asked me a question and I'm giving you an answer," I reply, a bit more aggressively than I intended, keep your cool Gulaxa. "As for the second part of your question, we ended up there because of you. Remember, you are the master of time, you control where you go, and where you go, I will always follow."

Now I think that last statement is bullshit, but I've seen stuff like this happen before. A bond sort of strikes up between two travellers that is pretty much unbreakable. I really hope this hasn't happened between us. I was meant to be the one playing him, but if he ends up dragging me along with him on his future escapades then his here boy jibe earlier will become quite apt.

As he seems to sink into some sort of inward daydream, I take a look around and wonder where in the hell we are. It certainly is a beautiful beach, with not a cloud in the sky, seems a lot like perfection. The temperature is just lovely, not too warm, not too cold, just right. Goldilocks temperature. What are the odds that he randomly jumps to a place that is quite simply perfect, and with only being a novice as well? I think this guy is something very special indeed. Wait, am I developing admiration for him?

"So every time we travel," he interrupts my worrying revelation. "It is me who initiates the jump? Even if I don't mean to, which the majority of the time I don't, it is always me? Not some external force?"

"It is always you," I say softly. "When you are not actively meaning to travel, we jump to random locations and times based on whatever is currently in your subconscious. What were you thinking about before we came here?"

Time to try and get to the bottom of how he managed to jump to such a sublime location in pretty much a blink of an eye, this should be interesting. I hope for some intellectual stimulus into the brain of what could be the most powerful traveller I have ever encountered.

"I wished I was sat by the beach smoking and drinking," he says.

Wow, mind-blowing or what! Knew I should never build him up to be something he obviously is not. "So let me get this straight," he continues. "I can not only travel through time, I can also travel to anywhere? Does that mean anywhere on the planet? Can I travel to another planet? What are the limitations here?" His voice went up a couple of octaves at this moment, as did my heart rate, shit, he's learning too fast, have to try and curb this.

"Yes, yes, don't know, don't know," I reply monotonously. Not the greatest deflection, come on Gulaxa get with it. His sarcastic thanks mimics my terrible reply.

"So how do we know where we are and what time we're in?" he enquires.

For God's sake, can't you do anything yourself? It's like having a little child around asking stupid questions. Use your bloody brain man!

"Use GPS and look at a clock," I reply abruptly, adding a somewhat playful smirk at the end hoping he doesn't notice my act dropping slightly.

He reacts by slow clapping me and mock laughing, before asking if I'm actually serious, which to be honest, I think I am.

"How do time travellers in your very clever movies know where they are?" I ask smugly.

I see his brow furrow as he begins back-pedalling throughout his life, most likely reminiscing over the many nights he sat on his own eating rubbish food and watching old movies. No wonder he ended up a fat twat sitting on his arse all the time, immersing himself in his own stench. I bet his settee stinks of farts. I retch slightly at the thought, thankfully he doesn't notice as I see him patting his pockets for something, What is he...ah, his phone. He looks at me for affirmation.

"If you were holding something when you travel and you picture holding something different when you arrive, the item you are holding will be replaced by the new item," I say, as though it made perfect sense. Which in actual fact it does, if you're a time travelling legend (certification signed, sealed and delivered) like myself here.

"So let me get another thing straight..." he begins, making me remember that I have to continue to try and play the idiot card.

"Why does everything have to be straight?" I ask dumbly, trying not to smirk.

"It's a figure of speech numb nuts, and yeah I know your nuts aren't numb. Well I don't actually know but...kind of figure they aren't. Anyway, I can travel through time, I can travel to any location, AND I can conjure up various items? How complex can the item be? Could I summon a nuclear bomb?"

This stops me in my tracks. Does he know? Is this another version of him from the past? Surely not, I'd be able to tell. But why the hell has he mentioned nuclear bomb? It has to be just a random thought. I mean, if you were to be asked what item to magically appear while you travelled through time, everyone would say nuclear bomb, right?

"Please, do not even joke about that," I say quietly, hoping he doesn't see the fear in my eyes.

"Sorry," he replies. "I didn't mean to upset you. Does something like that happen in the future?"

"I can't remember," I say solemnly, staring out at the view before me to avoid his gaze.

"I think it's time for a test," he announces triumphantly. "Might as well try out my newfound skills, and there's no way to know exactly where we are right now, so let's try somewhere I know."

Shit, where in the hell are we gallivanting off to now? I reach out too late to grab a hold of him as he vanishes off to God only knows where. I have no way of finding his destination, he could literally be anywhere in the known universe. Although more than likely just somewhere on earth, which narrows it down to anywhere on the planet! I guess we'll see now if we have any sort of bond going on, if we do then I'll join him soon, won't I? I hold out my hand and watch the tremor ebb and flow along with the ocean. I make myself invisible (I hope) just in case I need to make a quick getaway. Damn! I could really do with a...

TEA TIME

Searching for answers like the last guardian searches for glory I arrive back at Chino's. Now you (or whoever is reading this nonsense) may be wondering why. The thing is, I'm bloody famished, and I need fuel to continue on my journey towards hope and redemption. Well, not really hope, but maybe redemption, I'm not sure any more what most words mean, I think I may be losing my marbles a wee bit. See, I think I'm bloody Scottish now, och aye the bloody noo me hearties. Shit, now I'm a dastardly Scottish pirate. This is what happens when you let yourself go and lay off the rejuvenating food. Hence why I came here. See, I'm not as daft as you all thought I was.

As for why I chose here, well why the hell not. Nobody seems to notice anything, all the waiters and patrons are as blind as bats, so I decided it would be quite safe in this here establishment. I probably could have picked any other time than when previous versions of me are here, but why be a boring sod? We have to make life interesting for ourselves otherwise we become lesser people in this unforgiving world, and you never know I might find out the cause of that explosion earlier/later. But this time I decide to pick a table right at the back, right by the fire escape so a: I could see everyone, and b: I could make a quick exit if needed. Although I can just jump anywhere at any time so probably really didn't need b. But saying that, it is also near the urination station as well, so that'll do me fine.

Arriving with all the grace of a one-legged horse I land perfectly on a seat, with a pint in front of me and a great big steak, awesome. Seems a bit fortunate this outcome, but may as well get stuck in. Maybe another version of me came here earlier/later and ordered this for me, so as when I arrived I could get stuck in, what a guy he/I is/am. My brains hurts. If I'm talking about myself in the third person in both past and present tense, is that now talking about myself in the third and fourth person? But there's only two of me, so who are the third and fourth? I guess I'll never know the answers to these mind-bending questions. Screw it, enough time for intellectual musings later, it's food time.

Before I begin my munching you may be thinking that I have taken the death of my grandfather lightly. This is not really the case. You see, and I think I mentioned this earlier, I can go and see him any time I want. Although the death of my mother was extremely painful to see, mainly because I knew it was going to happen, that experience alone seems to have roughed up a few edges. Death no longer seems final, and I'm kind of OK with that. Let's be honest, my loving grand-papa would love a steak and a pint right now, so I'm actually giving him a lovely little send off. As I come to this beautiful realisation I raise the glass in salutation and take a big gulp.

"To you grand-papa," I shout unnecessarily, causing various patrons to turn around, one of them being my mother, who waves lovingly at me.

I wave back wondering if the other two versions of me are any the wiser. There's a big pillar in the way so my view is blocked somewhat, which is probably a good thing, don't want the universe to blow up or anything, not before I've eaten my steak. Speaking of steak, better get tucked in. I reach for the knife and fork, cut a nice big chunk, stack some chips on the fork, and ram it into my gob. Bloody delicious.

"Oi, that's my bloody steak you cheeky twat!" a rude individual exclaims as he enters from the toilet area, this could get interesting.

The guy is of quite a stocky build with tight black leather pants and a white tank top bearing the slogan 'bite me I might bite back', interesting attire, even more interesting slogan. Closely cropped black hair gives the instant impression of Tom Cruise; but taller, fatter, dorkier, and not as good looking, so not really like him at all, if truth be told. He seems a little red faced for some reason, I wonder if he's had a little play with his pecker in the toilet. Time for answers.

"You been playing with your todger in there son?" I enquire, while picking up a chunky chip and pointing it in his general direction like a judgemental stick.

He blushes slightly before replying.

"No, I just had a wee."

"I think differently my two-legged friend, take a seat, let's get you a drink and talk all about it, shall we?"

I stand up and usher him into what was most likely his seat, while stealthily pushing the plate and pint over to the other side of the table. I pull the chair back for the red-faced one and allow him to sit like a gentleman seating a lady. I hustle over to the other side and accidentally cough all over the food.

"Oh bugger," I mutter. "Might as well finish now. Hello, Mr waiter man?" I shout, hoping against hope it isn't the same waiter that served me earlier/later.

As the same bloody waiter strolls over I curse inwardly at my follies. Time to activate ninja stealth mode. I pull the hat over my eyes and pull my hoody tight around my face.

"Yes...sir?" he says, drawing the sir out over a longer than necessary time.

"Yeah, my mate here wants a steak and a pint, same shit I have here, thanks."

"OK," comes his slow reply. "Is this correct sir?" he asks the man, shit don't even know his name.

"I suppose so," he replies meekly, good lad not making scene, I kind of like him.

"OK," the waiter once again slowly speaks. "Are you gentlemen OK? You look kind of familiar, do I know you?" he says to me.

"Yeah, I'm your dad. Now sod off and get my mate his scran, what?"

"What?" the waiter asks.

"What?" my mate asks.

"Never mind, quick, he's got diphtheria, or dementia, or something, he needs to eat quick or he'll croak."

"I believe you mean diabetes, sir," the waiter says matter-of-factly.

"Whoa, check out the doctor in the house," I reply in a very sarcastic tone. "Quick, food, or he dies."

"Very well, sir," he mutters, and walks away with that same metaphorical chip on his shoulder like before, I really don't like his attitude.

I decide to throw a chip at him to join the not real one on his shoulder, but I misjudge the distance and it lands on the floor miles away. He does however turn around and gives me a little glare. I give him the universal sign for 'chop chop' and he pulls a tutting face in my general direction. As he wanders away I pull my hoody back down and re-adjust my beautiful hat, making sure the feather is all nice and pointy.

"So," I begin, while abandoning the knife and fork and picking up the steak with my fingers. "What's your name me old chum?"

"Christopher Johnson, with a T," he confusingly replies.

"With a T what? A T bone steak? A cup of T? A T shirt? Which is it me old mucker?" I ask through bouts of less than civil like eating behaviour.

"No, the T in Johnson, there is one."

"Ah I see, or rather I T," I await a laugh, none arrives, don't really like the cut of this guy's jib any more. "Hang on, you said Johnson not Johnston, so there isn't a T. So, like, what in holy shit?"

"There is, it's just silent," he says, as though this makes all the sense in the world.

"Hmm," I mutter while shovelling a handful of chips into my ravenous gob. "So, let me get this straight me old mucker. When you introduce yourself you make a point that your surname has a T, but neglect to inform your audience that the T is silent, which in actual fact makes it completely obsolete. So your last name is actually not Johnston it's Johnson. You get me bruv?" guess my cockney accent is making an unwelcome return.

"No, no, no," he replies. "Think of the word psycho, the P is silent. Like in my name, the T is silent, it's very clever."

"Pardon my French, but it's fucking stupid!" I reply, while bursting out laughing and spitting half eaten chips everywhere. "You sir, are a bit of nutter."

"Says you wearing a ladies hat and eating someone else's food."

"Now then, no need to be a twat. I thought I had brought myself this food earlier/later, like a premeditated meal from the other side of the cosmos. As for the hat, it's bloody awesome, so screw you Johnston!" I emphasis the T in Johnston to what I hope is comical effect.

"Ah, that's better!" I hear from somewhere behind me, shit that's me from not earlier, not later, but actually now.

My new mate looks across the room at me/I, then gazes back in my direction with a somewhat bemused expression on his face.

"Look," I say. "We're twins, but that's not important. What is important is I ate your food and I drank you pint," I gulp the last of his drink down before burping elegantly. "But wait, that's not important. What is of vital importance is that you are really weird. And after my doppelganger utters his next words, I reckon this whole place is going to go up in smoke, any last words Johnny Boy?"

"Oh right!" he/I continues from afar. "I exclaim loudly and everyone notices, but when two people disappear into thin air no-one bats an eyeball! Idiots!" Love this guy's humour.

Johnny looks me square in the eyes, looking as determined as he probably ever has in his whole life, preparing some epic speech that will inspire millions of people to keep an unwanted and pointless letter in their name. He takes in a deep breath.

"Too late," I mutter just as the explosion begins, sending the other me hurtling past my head causing us for the briefest moments to make eye contact, shit!

GROUND ZERO

"**L**-Look, this isn't what it looks like," I hear him stammer weakly. I see him confronted by two well built police officers with their guns drawn, where in holy hell are we?

I gaze around at my surroundings and we seem to be in an alleyway of some sort, cocooned on all sides by huge skyscrapers that reach up into the heavens like prying fingers. The noise that attacks my senses is very much different to the peaceful beach of before; a multitude of beeping horns coupled with varying shouts of anger play a less than melodic tune, threatening to overload my already anxiously warped sense of being. Gazing out of the alleyway while ignoring the gun-toting cops (they can't see me, I hope!), I see many a yellow taxi cab which reminds me of an alien invasion for some reason, bit of a strange analogy I know. But then again, I am in a weird sort of situation right now, I apologise for any future miscommunications.

"I need you to lay your weapon down on the ground," one of the cops says in the unmistakable accent of a New Yorker. "Slowly and carefully."

What weapon is he on about? Oh for God's sake! Why in holy hell did he think it would be a good idea to arrive in the USA holding a bloody gun? Doesn't he know the police here all have firearms, I mean how stupid can you get! And why oh why a magnum? Them things are bloody heavy, I'd have gone with a Berretta 9mm, be all bad ass Die Hard. As I watch on in amusement, he goes to lay down a bunch of flowers instead of the gun, very odd. You know, this guy really confuses me some times. He has just learned that he can picture arriving with an item, any item he can possible imagine with no limits whatsoever, and he picks a heavy bloody gun and a really shit bouquet of flowers. I mean, come on!

"The gun, sir!" the cop booms, making me jump somewhat.

This guy is certainly not messing around, I wonder inwardly if they both saw him arrive, that would be interesting. As my bonded frenemy apologises and places the actual weapon on the ground, I smirk at the look of relief on his face, and the little twist of his wrist as he releases the gun, bloody wimp, think more cleverly next time, wanker! I mimic the universal sign for my latest insult, causing the blasted chiming to make an unwelcome appearance. I see his eyes flicker slightly, but he doesn't turn to face me, hopefully the cops are too busy with their dimwitted subject to notice. At least I must be invisible as they haven't clocked me.

"Turn around and place your hands on your head," the cop barks.

Yeah that's right, give this bastard some orders. He's so used to ordering other people about (namely yours truly) it would be nice to see him told what to do for a change.

"What about the flowers?" he bizarrely asks.

Seriously! He's stood in a foreign country, possible arriving into thin air like some deranged terrorist, with angry cops pointing death weapons at him, and he's asking what he should do with the flowers! This guy should stop saying everything that pops into his head, what a nutter. The cop simply booms at him to drop them instantly, which he does without hesitation. Look who's a little scaredy cat now!

He interlocks his hands behind his head, or rather he attempts to, probably copying all the movies he has pigged out to, but can't decide which way to adjust his fingers and ends up simply holding them, idiot. He gazes up at the skyscrapers above him and I follow his gaze. Oh shitting fucking hell! Are those the twin towers? Surely he hasn't brought us here to witness the planes hitting? I mean, that's just God damn insane! But, to be fair to him, if you're going to experiment with time travel, go big or go home, and he's certainly gone big.

"Why have you brought us here?" I say as he stares wide-eyed at me. "This is extremely dangerous."

"It's OK," he replies. "I got the time wrong."

Once again he stares right at me, right fucking at me! Can this guy see me? The cops obviously can't, but he can. Oh how the plot thickens, this can't be happening! How is this even possible? First he breaks out of a super strong stasis, now he can see me, this guy is really starting to worry me now.

"Radio for back-up, we've got an escaped lunatic here," one of the cops barks into his radio, startling me from my inward reverie. "Sir, who are you talking to?"

This definitely confirms that he can see me and they can't, but does nothing whatsoever to calm my overworked thought processes. I really need some time to mull this over. As my chaotic mind tries to come to terms with this devastating realisation, a massive boom thunders throughout the entire planet, causing the ground to rock and tremble like it is cowering from the Lord above. Followed hot on it's heels is a searing shock wave that pummels my weakened core like God's vengeful wrath, decimating anything and anyone who dare stand up to the untethered rage, forcing all four of us inconsequential minions to fall to our knees as if we're praying for forgiveness. Managing somehow to raise my head, I see a huge ball of fire erupting from the side of one of the buildings, like a dragon breathing flames of hell onto an unsuspecting world.

As the noise dissipates somewhat, screams begin filling the air, it feels contagious and I succumb to the terror of this whole Godforsaken place. Screw it, I'm out of here, he can fend for himself. And off I go, anywhere. Please God, take me away from this nightmare. I close my eyes and pray for the sweet blessed relief of a serenity filled beach. But nothing happens, what the actual fuck! I try again, nothing. Has this guy broken me? Am I destined to die here? An unnamed civilian burnt to a crisp to live out his next life as ashes floating about in a never-ending sea of despair? No! My time is not now, only one thing for it, I need his help.

"We have to go, NOW!" I scream into his ear.

He just stares up into the sky, as if revelling in this entire moment as I cling tightly to his arm like a needy child. As he closes his eyes, a feeling of utmost serenity falls across his face. Is he accepting his fate here, or is he praying? Either way, get us the fu...

A NEW FRIEND

C oming to my senses on a rolling road that seems
to continue unabated into the distance, I give my
head a little shake, which makes me realise I am no
longer wearing my lovely hat, shit! Must have came off in
the explosion, oh well, I'm sure I can find other hatted attire
somewhere along the line. Random jumps truly are a head
screwing experience, and one that I really do not care for any
more. Saying that, I didn't really enjoy them previously, but
before I had this awesome power in my hands they were all a
part of the learning curve of time travelling. Now I am officially
a master of my craft, sporadic jumping really messes with the
old equilibrium, and not in a good way. But come on Mitch,
let's turn back into Positive Peter and kick nasty Negative
Nancy into touch shall we. This is a perfect opportunity to
showcase our detective skills, while probably meeting some
very interesting individuals.

Standing up from the dusty road I survey my new
surroundings with extreme earnest. Not really, I just kind of
casually look around with all the grace of a stoned out hippie,
far out man! The rolling road seems to morph into the horizon

like a joining of differing worlds. Looking both left and right they both seem to mimic each other, a seemingly identical view in both directions. Lifeless trees adorn both sides of the road, their gnarled branches resembling an amalgamation of a million crows feet perched haphazardly on top of each like stacked murder. A light fog blankets the furthest reaches of my vision, seeming to surround me like a fortress of grey steel.

This place is eerily silent, I can almost hear the sound of my own heartbeat. I must say it is rather ominous indeed, but you probably got that from my amazing descriptive narrative. I'm getting quite good as this, I might take up writing after I hang up my time travelling cape, I think I might make a good author. I may even make a memoir of my escapades, that would be fun. I wonder if people would read it? Just think of it, people actually seeing inside my warped imagination, good luck with that boys and girls, welcome to the lunatic asylum!

Dragging myself back into the present moment I hear a chuntering voice aimlessly babbling some form of nonsense from somewhere nearby.

"Bala, balala," the voice echoes.

Hmm, very oddly made sentences from this chap, but I will not judge this guy yet. I'm sick of making quick decisions on people before I actually get to know them. I mean, check Hatson out, I thought he was alright at first, but he turned out to be a right dick! And the less said about old Johnny Boy the better. Let's just see what this gentleman has to offer before I inwardly chastise him. Then, as if right on cue, a figure emerges from up ahead, as if walking out of a veil of smoke into the limelight of an arena.

"Bala, bala," he chirps away as he saunters ever closer.

His walking seems to mimic his incessant rambling as he takes a step forward on one syllable and then another on the next, before pausing briefly and repeating the same routine each time he speaks. As he draws nearer I gather this gentlemen is a postman, judging by his royal uniform and red mail bag. Thing is, there's no bloody houses in either direction, as far I can see. So what in holy Jesus is this dude doing way out here? He notices me when he's about two trees away (that's about 25 metres in old money) and stops to appraise me with a cheeky looking face.

"Bala?" he enquires.

Does this chap know any other words? Maybe he is a bit on the slow side, although he must have some grasp of English as he has asked me a question, albeit in his own distorted made up language. Better get my top notch linguistic skills back out.

"How's tricks me old mucker?" I ask in my best friendly voice.

"Bala, bala," he says, while rocking one hand to and throe in the universal sign for 'so so'.

"OK," I reply. "Good stuff. So are you a bloody postie then or what?"

Bit of a stupid question to be honest, because clearly he is.

"Bala," he replies while once again using his hand rocking gesture.

Hmm, not really the greatest reply. So he's sort of a postman, or he doesn't know if he is or not. Come on Mitch, work this guy out, you are highly likely the cleverest person on the planet, get a grip!

"Yeah, nice," I dumbly state.

Way to go Mitch! You've just nailed the art of conversation in two words, pat yourself on the back why don't you. I mean, how can you claim to be the greatest time traveller and detective in the known universe if you can't work out some simple dude with a made up language? Must try harder. Maybe if I approach him a tad then we could converse in a more civilised manner, and I could also get a good look at him, see what makes him tick. I mean, he actually makes himself tick with his balaring, but you know what I mean. Hey, have I just come up with another new word? Balaring? How awesome am I! My skills just never seem to cease.

Taking a couple of steps closer, my new friend mimics my movements, but in the opposite direction. Hmm, this could get interesting. I hold my hands up, showing him I mean no harm.

"Whoa there cowboy," I say softly. "Me good, no fear. I nice man, no want sucky sucky, just friendly man."

I inch a little closer, but once again he moves the same distance backwards. This could go on for some time. I try a different tactic and point my hand in the sky.

"Look, a massive bala!" I shout.

He instantly snaps his attention to where I'm pointing giving me the opportunity to rush him, damn I'm so clever, and so clumsy it seems, as I take one massive stride with my head bowed down like an Olympic sprinter and trip over a massive tiny twig, causing me to stumble with all the grace of a one armed octopus straight into the nearest tree.

"Ow!" I shout quietly, as I roll onto my back and gaze up at the sky with my pride and ego dented like a sixteen car pile-up.

If only my physical prowess could match my superior intellect, then I would most likely be the complete human being. But sadly this is not the case, and I fear my new found friend has probably buggered off and I won't ever get to see him again, which is a damn shame, as he seemed like an alright dude. Just as I am apart to jump to another location a face appears right above me with very cheeky looking features accompanied by a wide Cheshire cat like grin. I'm guessing the extreme happiness in his face is because of my less then cool tumble. At least my misfortunes please someone, good old Mitch, always knows how to turn a bad situation into something awesome.

"Bala!" the cheeky character exclaims, his grin widening further.

"Yes," I say with a resigned tone. "Bala."

He offers me his hand, of which I accept gratefully, and he pulls me up onto my feet, bloody strong this guy is. As I face him I study his features closely and I'm amazed at the colour of his eyes. The left one is emerald green and the other one is blazing blue, which is as blue as the deepest ocean, what a contrasting image to be presented with. Somehow I manage to pull myself away from his penetrating gaze to take in the rest of his appearance. An oval like face sits atop a well built frame, this guy definitely works out, although probably nowhere near as buff as old Mitch. I being pretty much the Adonis of man, a pinnacle of physical perfection. A closely cut crop of blonde hair sits atop his young face, reminding me instantly of none other than Sir Slim of Shady. I like this guy more and more.

"Cheers me old pal," I say in jovial tone, our hands still clasped together.

"Bala," he says in a 'you're welcome' tone.

I think I am beginning to understand this guy now. Most of his balas you can manage to interpret by the inflection of his voice, and also his hand gestures. Don't know how I'll get his name though, suppose it's worth a try.

"Me Mitch," I say slowly while pointing to myself. "Who you?" I point to him with my other hand.

He tilts his head to the side in a confused manner, this could be harder than I thought. Come on Mitch, think! As my brain searches every synapse like a stoned sloth, he scares the shit out of me.

"I'm Jamie La Bamba!" he shouts.

"What in holy fuckery!" I squeal in a slightly high-pitched voice. "You can speak?"

"Bala?" he says while staring blankly at me.

What in holy shit is this guy on? I'm starting to feel somewhat exasperated right now, is this guy messing with me? He'd better not be another Hatson trying to take a lend of my good character. I'll kick him in the nuts if he is. But as I stare once more into his dazzling eyes I see no malice, no dark humour, just a gentle inquisitiveness that endears me to him. This guy is alright. Maybe he is trapped in some sort of balaring loop but still remembers his name, makes sense, right? I mean, stranger things have happened in this crazy universe, so why not this? He releases his grip on my hand and bows purposely. Not sure how to respond to this so I, for some bizarre unknown reason, decide the best reaction would be to curtsey. This seems to be the appropriate decision as he rises from his bow as I reach the top of my cool as hell curtsey in perfect unison, like two ballerinas finishing their routine.

Straightening his satchel on his back he snaps me a sharp salute, turns around, and heads off the way he came from. I have a brief moment to wonder if he has any mail in that bag, before his gentle voice warms my heart.

"Bala, bala," he chirps away as he glides down the road like a gentle breeze.

"Stay safe my balaring friend," I say softly after him. "May God keep you safe you beautiful soul."

With his soft chirping voice echoing in my soul, I decide it's about time I made a concerted effort on my never-ending endeavours. Time to find the cat! But where can I find my furry friend? If I go back to before I prematurely ended his beautiful life, then I run the risk of causing untold chaos, while quite possibly causing my current self to be eradicated from existence. Only one thing for it, best get my ninja mode fully activated and go all super duper stealth-like. This could be interesting, hope I can judge it right...

A DEATHLY ENCOUNTER

Holy shitting fucking hell! My head wobbles and shakes at the terror that has just happened, how is this all possible? As we arrive at a moody graveyard, I deftly remove my grip from his arm and slink around the back of a nearby gravestone, while he gazes forlornly around on his butt. I need some time alone. But it seems to me that alone is something I may be craving for a long time, I may just be stuck with this psychopath for the foreseeable future. How in the hell has he broken me? I am unable, for the first time in many a year, to travel, this can't be happening, can't be real, and I struggle to hold onto my frayed sanity.

I succumb to the cold and unrelenting granite behind me as I slide down it's rough surface, feeling it's sturdiness hold my back, giving me the rock solid support I need right now. Oh how I would do anything for the sweet relief from one of my blue friends at this very moment. I'm shaking both inside and out, as I hold out my hand it vibrates like a jack-hammer causing a slight jangle from my stupid bell, which I manage just about to stave off before being noticed, could this situation get any worse? Well actually yes it could as a light drizzle dampens my already darkened mood. I suppose one good thing is that we won't be able to jump at the moment, might make things a little more bearable if we stay in one place.

As I gather my senses slightly, I still have no idea what is going on! Not so long back, in fact before I had him in stasis, I could jump to any place and any time. The stories I could tell would quite simply blow everything he has done out of the ocean. The trails I have blazed make his silly day trips pale into insignificance. I have visited the deepest oceans and the highest peaks. I have fought alongside kings and have had meals with presidents. I have conquered that which is unconquerable. I've even danced with dinosaurs in a terrific game of cat and mouse. Yet now all that seems so far away as my beautiful gift has been taken from me by a bloody novice. A newbie he may be, but damn he has got some power!

My breathing steadies somewhat as I regain some sort of composure, although my heart-rate still hammers harshly inside my hollow feeling chest. A light perspiration develops on my brow, allowing my anxiety to increase slightly. Am I suffering from some form of withdrawals? Or is just the extreme stress of the situation making me feel this way? I'm sure it will pass in due course, I am the Great Gulaxa after all, I've overcome worse trials in my well-lived life.

All seems quiet from the other side of the gravestone, so I risk a sneaky peak around the side to see what he is up to. Still adopting a prone position he seems to be gazing off into space with that usual stupid look on his face. His lips are moving incessantly, as if he is having some sort of inner dialogue with himself, this guy is certainly not normal. Saying that, how do you define normal? Isn't each individuals normal different from the next persons? I guess it all comes down to perspective. He stands up suddenly and I quickly disappear back behind my stony shield. Maybe he might disappear off on another adventure, allowing me to depart somewhere on my own. Maybe, if I put enough distance between us, my powers might come back. That brings a sense of hope to my downtrodden heart. As for distance, I'm thinking a different time and location entirely. But with this drizzle hanging in the air this is not going to be possible, and while he is stood gazing about like an idiot this will not be achieved any time soon. Only way he can possibly jump is with a paradox, but they aren't exactly easy to fabricate. Time to show my face and see what I can come up with.

Sneaking around the other side of the gravestone so I can walk behind him, I follow his gaze across the vast expanse of deathly rows. He seems to be somewhat transfixed on a woman and child not to far away staring forlornly at a gravestone. On closer inspection I see the woman is most definitely his mother (I'd recognise her beauty anywhere). So, is that him? Looks like a fat little git, so I'm guessing yes, this could get interesting. If I could get him to stare himself down, then all my problems may be solved. Damn I'm such a clever, devious bastard.

As I come to terms with my awesomeness, I glance at the inscription on the gravestone, it reads:

Here lies an unnamed soldier,
Died in the Battle of the Somme,
Fighting bravely among his comrades
Until time came upon him.

"We have no time to waste, for time is what is giving us chase," The Great Gulaxa.

What the holy shitting shit?! As I stifle the incoming scream from my wide open mouth, a slight jangle alerts my companion to my presence. Quick, say something clever.

"You can't keep doing this," I say softly. "You're going to get us into a lot of trouble."

He sighs heavily. "I know, I'm just confused. Is that...is that me? And my dear Mum?"

"Yes, this isn't doing you any good."

That's it, play the guilt trip on him, get him riled up so as he does something rash. But he just hangs his head a bit and begins his inward musing while moving his lips like a ventriloquist's dummy. What a damn fool! The paradox is over there you moron, not inside your own stupid mind! How can I get him to look over there without making it too obvious? I can't let him get too suspicious, he's way too powerful for me to mess with. Without powers of my own he could quite literally burn me alive on a blazing hot sun. Oh how the tides have turned, the predator has now become the prey, how poetic! Or should that be pathetic? Because that is exactly how I feel right now.

"Am I the only one who can travel through time? Are there more like me?" he blurts, startling me from my own inward chastising.

I try to avoid eye contact, I really don't want him to see the fear and confused look in my eyes.

"I don't know," I reply dumbly, that'll do.

This seems to satisfy him somewhat as he turns back around to stare off at his mum and younger self. That's a start, at least he's looking over in their direction. But they have their backs turned focusing on the grave before them, I can't stand here waiting forever for them to turn this way. What if they don't turn around and just simply go the other way? I need a distraction, I need something to get a reaction out of him, what can I use? Ah, shit! The gravestone! I nearly screamed when I saw it, so I'm sure his reaction will be ten times worse than mine.

I realise I am stood in front of it, so I ever so coolly do a big not at all exaggerated stretch and step to the side. He doesn't notice as he too busy gazing at his former self. Come on idiot, turn, look, fuck off! I need you to leave so I can live. Turn around you God damn fool! Then, as if by magic, he turns to look at the gravestone. I see his eyes widen as he reads the last line. That's it, he's going to pop, don't let me down now.

"What the holy fucking shitballs!?" he exclaims loudly.

Bingo! I gaze over at mother and son, who dutifully turn around at the sudden expletive outburst from behind them. Then, right on cue, the idiot disappears, and the boy collapses. Awesome! My dastardly plan has worked out perfectly.

As I'm inwardly congratulating myself, I was just about to take a little bow and wave at my adoring fans when I saw a familiar figure peering around the side of a gravestone not too far away. Wait, is that him? What the hell is going on? Has he just randomly jumped over there? That really doesn't seem likely. In fact, no it isn't, I can see he's wearing different clothes, looks like an army uniform. What, so he thinks he's a soldier now? Idiot! It seems as though I just can't get rid of him. Am I supposed to go over there and spend time with him? Don't really want to, but I might not have a choice in the matter. I don't know what version of himself he is, or how powerful, or come to think of it, how much he knows. Better play this safe.

I wave my hand jovially and prepare to walk over to meet hi...

A SNAP DECISION

Arriving with all the grace of a deranged butterfly I hug myself into the wall as best I can. Which is kind of difficult as there's a shower protruding against my butted area, along with some taps pressing against my calves. Not the best idea I have ever had, but as long as I keep quiet then everything should be fine and dandy. I wonder if I've judged the time right, it seems awfully peaceful. Just as I'm about to leave my safe place I hear some choice swear words from the other room, I'm guessing I've just been bitten. This could get very interesting, or very messed up, most likely both.

I should be entering the bathroom in a bit to run my hand under the tap. Good thing is I can't see the doorway, so that means anyone who enters will be unable to see me too, I reckon I'm safe here, I hope. Hearing footsteps draw nearer I hold my breath and close my eyes. When I hear the tap begin running, for some bizarre reason I exhale noisily like a runaway train, what the shit am I doing?! Compose yourself Mitch, you're better than this. Hearing the tap stop it's persistent rushing (which makes me glad because it was making me need a wee wee), I hear a slight creaking noise. Is that someone coming up the stairs and walking on the infamous creaking step?

As I'm trying to recall who is where and how many versions there are of me and Gulaxa, I hear a snarling sound. I'm guessing this is my beloved pet, which sounds more like a rabid dog than a cute little pussy cat. I ponder inwardly how many times I have witnessed this event, or how many times this has happened. I mean, it's only happened once, surely each event in time can only happen the one time, but I've witnessed it (or been in the same vicinity) many times. So does that make this a continuation of the same event and time? Or a completely different one altogether because I am here? Does this whole scenario count as another strand of time I have created just by being present, even though I am not involved? Hmm, a lot of mind-boggling shit to ponder over.

A massive crash against the shower door literally scares the shit out of me as I let out a little fart at the point of impact. Don't think he/I will notice though, he/I has bigger fish, I mean cats, to fry right now. I do however notice a slight whiffy aroma entering my nasal area though, must be that steak I ate earlier/later. I can't remember if I ever noticed the smell of shit while I murdered my cat. Come to think of it, I probably had bigger things on my plate, and I don't mean fish. Wait, what?

"Sorry my little baby," I hear myself mutter for the second time in quick succession

A huge sense of deja vu attacks my overloaded brain. I instantly recall my previous self peaking from underneath the veil of secrecy to witness the upcoming sickening act. I try to close off my mind for what happens, but it is no good. I still hear the heart wrenching snap of my furry friend's neck as I end his beautiful little life and send him off to pussy heaven (again, not that one!).

Before the incoming tide of depression can set in I steady myself for the most pivotal stage of my dastardly plan. I will only get one shot at this, have to time it to perfection. Right on cue the phone rings, and as I hear myself pick up the receiver to answer I jump ungracefully out of the bathroom and scoop up my still warm loving companion. Deciding to recede back into my hiding place to prepare my next jump, I make the mistake of knocking the shower head slightly which begins dripping water onto my head and down my arms. Shit! Reaching round I attempt to shut off the incessant drip and get a massive squirt of water right in the kisser. Double shit! Guess I'm not jumping anywhere now, I'll have to just ride out whatever happens next.

I gaze down at my beautiful furry angel and rock him from side to side like a little baby. How I wish I could just get the hell out of here right now, there may be a chance to save him, he's still warm, maybe it's not too late. But alas I just have to bide my time, dry myself off when everyone's gone, then disappear. I close my eyes and listen to myself walk back into the room and open the blinds. Guess I'm about to go bye byes. I hear the toilet seat drop, guess that's Gulaxa doing his sneaky shit. It's at this point I feel a massive urge to go and hug him, I could really do with some close contact right now, even from the double-crossing bastard. How I miss those early days of travelling when it was just me and him traversing the space time continuum.

The other me enters and plonks down on the seat. We have that same conversation about toilet seats, favourite numbers, and pretty much confusion of the highest order. I remember how insane all this was at first and trying to comprehend it all. Until that is I had a brainwave to dial a random number, which just happened to be me. So in actual fact I just rang my own phone, not really very random, was it? Although I never actually memorised my own number, I never could. But I guess I was always meant to call myself, it was inevitable. Does that mean that what I am doing now is the same? Am I once again caught in a stupid bloody time loop like that proverbial puppet on a string? As I hear myself storm out of the room and slam the door, I feel the same intense feeling of rebellion at my predicament. But I can't just abandon my task and let the rage take over, I may be able to solve whoever has been screwing with me. I also may be able to wind back time and save my loving companion.

I take in a deep breath and compose my breathing. I hear Gulaxa open the door and have a brief conversation to the determined me. How crestfallen I felt when I realised I'd called myself, such a devastating outcome, and it deflated my rebellious rage instantly. After a short while I hear the two mental Gulaxa's squabbling over tablets and crunching them down like drug crazed psychopaths. Not long after their manic munching they realise the cat has gone. Ha! Screw you two! That's what you get for stealing my bloody hat you twat, whichever one of you it was. This feels me with a sense of achievement and I smile broadly at my awesomeness.

"Right you two doppelganging wankers, where in holy fuckery is my pussy!" the other/previous/earlier/later me blurts out.

I sure do know how to make an entrance, what a God damn legend I/he is/am. Once again, my brain hurts. I hear the floorboards creak once more as I enter the room, I have visions of me pulling back the shower curtain and confronting myself. I brace for impact at the incoming demolition of the entire known universe. But no, I remember clearly how I bent down and felt the soft indent of my deceased friend. If only he/I knew that I/he had him in my/his arms not two feet away while his blood still ran warm. I close my eyes and try to make sense of this totally messed up scenario, all this shit had better be worth it in the long run.

Hearing the other me in the next room flinging open the wardrobe, I manage a little smirk at recalling my cool nail checking skills in the mirror while wearing that awesome hat. Such a cool Adonis I am, no wonder the ladies swoon at my every movement. I close my eyes and wait a few minutes so as I know the coast is clear. I'm not sure if me or Gulaxa or some other invisible entity might be lurking about anywhere. I clamber out of the bath and head into the spare room for a towel to dry myself off. After excessive rubbing has ceased, I replace the towel from whence it came to avoid any unnecessary calamitous paradoxical outcomes. I am still a little damp though so decide a little change of clothing would not go amiss. I stuff my hoody and the rest of my attire into the corner of the cupboard and grab the nearest items I can find, please be men's clothing I pray inwardly. Get in! Black tracksuit trousers, black top, that'll do me, the cool man in black.

Right, now where the hell can I take a deceased cat with a snapped neck to get fixed...

BATMEN AND SOBBING

Gone is the quiet moody graveyard to be replaced by a busy restaurant that attacks my anxiety like a fervent wasp, and as I was in mid walk I almost bump into the idiot in front of me. Taking a step backwards I see he is talking to a very beautiful woman, I'm guessing it is his mother a few years on from our previous excursions. Time has certainly been kind to her, she has a natural beauty which even the ravages of the ages cannot catch up with. I can see the warmth and kindness in her eyes, it's very mesmerising and I am momentarily caught in her loving trance. I'm kind of hoping that I'm invisible as I would look like some deranged addict staring at her like this. As she turns around to speak to a waitress, the spell that she had me caught within is broken and I blink away the beauty that had befallen me.

So, looks like I'm bound together to my new time travelling companion, shitting hell! I've heard about this happening to others, but I never thought this type of degrading shit would affect me. I always thought I was too powerful, guess this guy is a lot stronger than me right now, better not piss him off. I watch on as he gazes up at a TV screen mounted on the wall, good thinking Batman, he is definitely learning to use his surroundings to work out what time he has arrived in. I don't bother checking myself, it will provide no use to me whatsoever, I am no longer in charge. I'll just blindly follow whatever this guy does in the hope that eventually I will regain my powers and can fend for myself once more. I know one thing for sure, once that day comes I will get as far away from him as I possibly can. I go to run my hand through my hair and forget about the stupid bracelet, causing it's incessant jangle to alert him to my presence. Time to get my acting guise back on.

"Nice restaurant," I murmur, this seems to be my opening quip now.

"Yeah, it's pretty good, I think it's called Chino's," he replies to the invisible man, causing his mother to turn around with a bemused look on her face and ask if he is OK.

I can't help but smirk at this, he must look like a right nutter. I could actually enjoy myself here, but I must tread carefully. Have to keep my cover under wraps.

"Stop talking to me," he whispers out the corner of his mouth as someone walks past, this is just too funny and I struggle to hold in my inner child.

"I was simply pointing out the lovely décor of our new location, no need to be so rude," I say in my usual award-winning monotone.

He glares at me with a comical angry look while attempting to placate a woman staring at him from a nearby table, this shit is hilarious and I struggle to maintain my poker face. He looks like a right lunatic. Turning away from the woman who is pointing in his direction, while likely explaining to her male companion that he is nuts, he tries to ignore the quite obvious jibing in his direction. Then right on cue his mother interlocks arms with him and they saunter off after the waitress. I stand stock still for a moment as I notice a guy dressed as Batman walking past. Very odd that I thought of Batman earlier and then there he is, coincidence? Probably not, just another random occurrence in this ever-changing world we live in. He does look super cool though, until he stumbles and nearly loses his balance, eradicating instantly the look of suaveness while having derogatory remarks made after him. Nice recovery though.

Something about Batman's demeanour grabs my attention though, it can't be, can it? No way, he wouldn't turn up here, there would be no reason for him to. As I attempt to dismiss the probing thought I see his mother, his younger mother, trailing behind him at quite a good distance. Hmm, the plot thickens once more. I'm guessing this restaurant has some sort of relevance in the grand scheme of things, maybe more will be revealed later.

"Honey, are you OK? You've gone all white," his mother asks from across the room. I'd better catch them up instead of wasting time stood here.

As I amble up closer I hear him say he has to go to the loo, I dutifully shadow him along the corridor towards the toilet area. But not before, out the corner of my eye, another version of him appears out of nowhere plonked at a table in the corner, wearing a woman's hat with a huge feather sticking out of the top. What the hell!? And then just as we are about to disappear out of view, another one of him appears sat at another table! What the hell is going on? Is this some sort of super-hub for different versions of him to be playing a game of hide and seek with each other? I'm glad we're leaving, this is too crazy for my overworked brain.

I stumble against him, causing him to bash into the wall due to my overstretched neck gazing at the chaos behind me. A man returning from the loo gives him a rather disturbed look, I bet that looked really strange. If only that guy knew how insane things were back there he'd probably shoot himself in the head. If I had a gun right now maybe that's what I could do. Wouldn't death be a better prospect than what is happening right now? I give my head a shake and focus on whatever it is that I am supposed to be doing at the present moment. As he enters the toilet I dutifully follow him like a little lost puppy into the nearest cubicle.

"Nice toilet," I say, gazing around in my usual deadpan manner.

He then begins to chastise me about my polite chit-chat and asks me questions about why he is here and what is happening, as if I have a clue what is going on. He's the one with a multitude of different versions of him in the same place. The conversation begins to grind on my already frayed senses and I wish I could just vanish away from this waking nightmare.

"Am I supposed to tell her I'm a time traveller, and hope she keeps quiet about it, I ain't buying it," he quips.

"And I'm not selling anything," I awesomely reply while trying to adopt a serious face, although I feel the sides of mouth raise into a little smirk, I think I got away with it though.

"You've been here, so why can't you remember?" he asks incredulously.

"Because time travel has a nasty side effect on the old noggin," I retort, which right now is very bloody true, my head is totally messed up at the moment.

My reply seems to have hit a raw nerve though as he stares at me in a weird sort of way, is he going to kiss me? He'd better not. I don't care how powerful he is, if he plants a smacker on me I'll kick him right in the nuts!

"Right," he says, with all the earnestness of a dead rodent. "Time to go spend some time with Mum."

Good luck pal. Hopefully I can just stay here and relax for a bit, that would be so wonderful right now, and then, as if he read my mind:

"Gulaxa, would you mind waiting here? I feel as though if you were nearby I would keep staring at you, which might cause unwanted attention, and break my concentration. I would really appreciate it, buddy."

I nod back, hopefully looking sad, but inside feeling immense relief.

"Wish me luck," he says, and exits the cubicle which swings shut behind him, allowing me some peace and quiet.

Before I have a chance to accept the beautiful serenity of solitude, Batman appears before me and clasps his hand over my mouth while moving his mouth very close to my ear and whispering.

"Don't make a fucking sound. We are on a perilous journey. We need each other. I can get you out of this. Just do as I ask. I'm going to throw a note over the cubicles. Before you leave, tell Batman about the note and say he looks cool. I love you," and with this he plants a kiss right on my lips, throws a ball of paper over the top of the cubicle, then vanishes.

Can my life get any weirder? I hear a loud thud from outside and exit the cubicle to see a well built man laid out on the floor, after what looks like a severe beating, with the idiot stood over him panting excessively. What has happened here?

Shit, is that Derek?

"What?" he asks. "He looked like he was going to kill me, so I got in there first. Here, help me drag him into a cubicle, we'll dispose of him later."

As he says this his face falls, I think at this point he realises who it is and that this was always going to happen. Serves you right you murdering bastard! Although this is on me as well, and the guilt once again attacks my fragile sate of mind. Running to the nearest sink he begins retching violently, I guess killing someone for the first time can have that effect on you, I've been there, I know exactly how he is feeling. He begins sobbing which nearly sets me off. I don't know why but I embrace him fully, feeling his pain mimic mine.

"I really need my mum," he says softly against my shoulder.

"I know, but we need to get rid of this body. You know where we need to go."

He sighs and pulls away, resigning himself to his fate.

"Can I come back here? Can I have this time again with my mum?" he enquires hopefully.

"I don't know," I reply honestly.

He kneels down, holds onto Derek's huge wrist, then vanishes. I turn around to see Batman looking at me, I have no idea who it is but do as instructed.

"Read my note. Wrong toilet. You look super cool!"

I give him a thumbs up, as this seems like the right thing to do, while he stares at me blankly. Please God, take me away from...

HELLO, OLD FRIEND

Now if you asked me why I came back here, I couldn't tell you. Just before I jumped I had a little brain wave that while this guy may be a little eccentric, he may be able to assist me. Although I had taken a disliking to the irritating git, maybe I could hold my emotions in check and ask for his help. Not really sure how you go about asking someone you hardly know to bring back to life a dead cat, but stranger things have happened, and to be honest, my bench is pretty small, I have no real back-up to call upon so thought I'd go with a good old fashioned punt on an outsider. You never know, he might just come up trumps.

As Mitch is just an awesome individual, and most likely the most intelligent being in the whole universe, I remembered about Hatson's hat that I borrowed and pictured myself wearing it when I arrived. Of course this worked an absolute treat as I appeared right outside his shop window with the stunning Stetson perched upon my noggin. One thing I had to ponder though: is this the same hat? Have I magically commandeered it from wherever it is? Possibly on that weird Gulaxa's head? Or have I conjured up a completely new hat?

Most important question of all, will Hatson be able to tell if it's the original one? Well, only one way to find out, here we go.

I check that my feline companion is still comfy, he seems to be. Well, he isn't moving so he must be OK. Well, he's not OK because he's deceased. He is still warm though, so it just feels as though he's having a little cat nap, which makes sense as it's only been mere minutes since he passed. I pat his head softly, expecting a little twitch and a purr, none arrives, and I feel a hard sting of guilt stab at my broken heart. Before I have a chance to let the darkness take over, I press on with whatever the hell I am doing.

Adopting my most charming and innocent smile, I push my way into his enticing store. Well, I attempt to, but the door is locked. Hmm, this wasn't in the script. I check the door and notice a closed sign hanging loosely in the middle swaying lightly like a forgotten leaf. Maybe he has just gone for a poo or something. But I really don't fancy hanging about here with a dead cat laid in my arms like some psychopath. Turning around to decide on where I should wait I am confronted by a little old lady.

"What a lovely little pussy cat, what's his name?" she chimes in, and before I have a chance to react she pets his head softly, will she notice he's not breathing?

"Erm, his name is Dead Cat, I mean he's not dead, he's sleeping. His name is Sleeping Cat!" I blurt out, come on Mitch, sort yourself out.

The old lady eyes me suspiciously while halting her petting. Long moments go by and I wonder if she is caught in some sort of time loop as she just stares at me. As I am about to ask if she is OK she speaks.

"Well, you're an odd one aren't you. What's your name then?"

"Branning, Mitch Branning," I reply suavely, while checking my nails, while holding a dead cat, who's dead arse brushes the old ladies face.

"Pfft," she moans. "Well I never, how dare you shove your animals rear into my face. Old Doris is very perturbed right now."

Doris? Shit, is this the Doris? She does look kind of familiar. Guess I have a penchant for causing misery to her life. This must be a time before she goes into the nursing home, doesn't really give me a good indication of when exactly, but that doesn't really seem to be a problem. I think it's nice to meet this lady while I'm fully dressed and not getting mauled by her toothless mouth. Maybe me and her could be the best of friends. I have nothing else to do while I wait for Hatson, so might as well chill out with her.

A light slap around my pork chops awakens me from my incessant inward rambling.

"Cat got your tongue, boy?" she enquires aptly before retrieving an antibacterial wipe from her bag and cleaning her Mitch stained hand.

Does she think I'm some sort of filthy rascal or something? Cheeky git! I'm most likely the cleanest (and cleverest) guy in the known universe, how dare she attempt to sully the good name of time travelling legend Mitch "Ace" Branning! I have a good mind to take her on a little trip to the beginning of time to meet her maker, who is in fact me. Because I, Mitch Branning, am a God, a master of all...another slap on the other side of my face once again breaks my inward monologue, just when it was getting interesting.

"Will you cease slapping my noggin you git?" I ask politely. I watch on once more as she feverishly wipes her hand.

"And what's with the wiping me old mucker? I'm as clean as a whistle, what, what?"

I've never done a double what before, it's cool as hell. Damn, Mitch is one hell of an awesome dude, I bet she's just about to swoon at my suaveness, better get ready to catch her before she falls. I hold out my hands in anticipation of a future event I have no idea will happen, forget I am holding a dead cat, allowing said dead cat to fall lifelessly to the floor like a decaying pet with a loud thump. Shit! Maybe she won't notice. The screams that enter my ear canal tell me she may have noticed. Or maybe she is screaming at my previous cool as hell double whatting? You know what, I'm going with the latter, step aside Negative Nancy, Positive Peter is back to conquer the world.

I hold my hands aloft in exultation at my humble followers. I accept the praise from my minions and stand aloft on the tide of love. I am here my darlings, my seductive suaveness knows no bounds, here me call...ow! A double slap on both sides of my beautiful pork chops!

"Bloody ow!" I exclaim. "What in holy moley is your problem m'lady?"

"You are a disgusting animal! Carrying around a dead cat like some perverted little man, you should be ashamed of yourself!" she exclaims.

I think clearly before answering in a very calm businesslike manner.

"Firstly, how do you know he is dead? Have you checked his pulse? Are you a bloody vet? Secondly, which is..." I count on my fingers "...actually fourthly now, I love my cat, so I didn't kill him, well I did, but it was self-defence. Fifthly, which might be fourthly because I don't think I asked a question last time. Wait, what was the question again?" I hold my hand under my chin in an extremely pensive pose.

Doris stares at me blankly like some sort of broken robot, I think she may have malfunctioned.

"Hello?" I enquire, wafting my hand in front of her face. "Is there anybody there?" I mimic a ghostly apparition in the hope of awakening her from her pensive slumber, it doesn't work.

"Mum!" somebody cries from across the street.

An attractive lady runs over and puts her arms around Doris. I'm guessing, using my deductive skills, that this is her daughter. I am so God damn clever.

"Branning, Mitch Branning," I state, a customary nail checking scenario follows.

"What have you done to mum?" she cries.

"Erm, nowt. I was just chilling here with some pussy, I mean my pussy, Shit, I mean me and my cat, that is the cat and I, were just hanging out. Then this Doris git came over and starting slapping me, she's proper nuts," the universal sign for 'she is mental' follows.

She glares down at Gulaxa, who's obvious dead eyes are staring blankly up at us as his tongue lolls loosely out the side of his deceased chops. The woman looks up at me.

"He's OK," I begin. "Just having a nap the little shit."

The lady seems unamused.

"I'm taking my mum home, then I'm calling the RSPCA you sick wanker!" and with this unreasonable outburst she ambles away with poor Doris.

Staring after them, I wonder if this is the beginning of Doris's journey into vampirism or zombification? All I know is that I tried to help her and it has nothing to do with me, Mitch is nothing but a good, decent soul. As I gaze around at my surroundings, and seeing I am alone once more, I ponder over my next move. Picking up my beloved pet I hold him closely to my chest while sticking his tongue back in.

"There, there my chubby little friend, let's come back earlier/later."

So that's what I do.

WHAT GOES AROUND

As I dutifully followed my new master I arrive to see him just standing there looming over Derek's body. He isn't moving, he's just staring off into space like some stoned zombie. I watch him for a few moments, hearing him mumble something about Mary Poppins and some other nonsense, before all of a sudden coming to alertness as though someone had just switched on his power supply. What a weird guy.

"Hey buddy," he says bluntly. "Enjoy your trip?"

"No," I also reply bluntly, not really in the mood for banter right now as I see Derek's eyes staring accusingly at me.

"Well aren't you a happy bunny, and before you say it I know you're not a rabbit, well I hope you're not."

What the hell does he expect me to reply to that? I just stare at him nonplussed, hoping he gets on with whatever nonsense he has planned for us next. I'm guessing first port of call is placing Derek into the bath, kind of the reverse of what we did earlier, I mean later. He heads over to his shoulders and begins to lift them up, I guess I'm not so lucky this time, I will have to stare into his judgemental eyes as we dump his battered body.

"Here we go, lifting time!" he say chirpily. He was all sad and depressed a moment ago after killing someone, now he's all happy and giddy. This guy is definitely losing the plot.

I go along with the charade and we lift and lower the deceased man into the bath. However, he drops his head before it has reached the edge, causing a thud and a little squirt of blood to exit the back. I almost vomit and let go of the legs, causing one to remain hanging over the side, is this how it was before? I don't care any more.

"I'm starving," he exclaims, before exiting the bathroom and strolling downstairs.

I have a brief moment to myself and retch repeatedly over the sink, nothing comes up and my stomach hurts after the exertions. Is this the withdrawals? Or is it the pain of what he has just done? Of what we have just done? After calming my heaving chest to a somewhat normal rhythm, I follow him downstairs to join him in the kitchen, only to watch him leave and head out to walk back up the stairs.

"Where are you going?" I enquire.

"To see if I need a bed time story," he replies with a stupid grin on his face.

"That is not a wise cause of action," I reply seriously, because it really isn't, does this idiot want to break the timeline?

Trotting past me he flattens himself against the wall like a fat toad and begins pulling gormless expressions at me, he's really starting to piss me off now, I wonder if it tells on my face. It seems to take an age to reach the top with his ridiculous shenanigans, and when he does overcome the final step he begins crawling on his stomach as if he is some sort of soldier. He looks more like a deformed crab than anything else, but I leave him to his silly games and follow aimlessly behind him. As he reaches the door we both look down and see the furry Gulaxa intermingling between our legs.

"Uh oh," he exclaims. "This could be bad."

Yeah, no shit!

"We need to go, now!" I whisper loudly.

He closes his eyes and I expect him to disappear, he doesn't. What the hell is he doing? Has he fallen asleep? He closes his eyes tighter, as if that is going to make any difference you moron!

"Err, help," he cries, as a thump from the next room tells me shit is about to go down.

Well, I would assist you, but you've stolen my powers you idiot, so I guess we're screwed. Blood starts to run from his nose, maybe this wouldn't be such a bad thing after all. If he has a brain aneurysm then maybe I can return back to my normal awesome self. As I'm pondering his imminent death he grabs my hand and drags me downstairs and into the hallway, closing the door behind us. If no-one heard us bounding down the stairs then they're bloody deaf, stupid, or both. I can hear the previous versions of us bickering outside the bedroom door, so we must have gotten away with it.

I really don't need all this shit right now. All I want is a nice relaxing time all by myself. Maybe I could check myself into a rehab or something. Would probably do me some good. At least I could get away from him for a bit. As for now though, I seem to be stuck with him. I wonder why he couldn't jump. Shit, it's obvious, he needs food in that fat belly of his. He stops gawping through the gap in the window like some perverted time traveller and his face goes all blank, probably trying to work out why he can't jump. We'll be here until the end of time before he works it out, better save his underutilised brain cells from overloading.

"Fuel," I say matter-of-factly.

"Come again?" he says stupidly.

"You need fuel to continue jumping," I say, just about hiding my irritation.

"OK, like...plutonium...or uranium?" he asks, seriously I might add. Pardon my French, but this guy is a complete fucking idiot, I don't know whether to burst out laughing or punch him in the face. I do neither, and use my award winning acting skills to compose myself.

"No, that stuff would kill you, and you're not a machine. You need food." There, simple.

His face adopts its usual blank expression as he begins another inner monologue. At one point he begins humming Yesterday by The Beatles, very random. Watching his lips move, and the odd twitch from his lips, I once again marvel at how he became bestowed with such a great power when in fact he is a complete imbecile. God certainly does work in mysterious ways.

Hearing footsteps ascend the stairs, I'm guessing the other him is coming down to listen to the phone call, never did find out who that was, not that I really give a shit. He pulls me close and attempts to flatten himself into the wall, once again resembling some podgy animal, how the hell does he think this is achieving anything? If anyone walks in does he think that he won't be noticed because he's squelching his saggy tits into a firm area? I struggle once more to hold back my emotions. We seem lost in each others eyes for a moment, I kind of feel some sort of empathy towards him as I see his lips moving along with his inner voice. Shit, does this bastard fancy me? I prepare my knee for an upward jaunt into his groin area.

As the other him ascends the stairs he releases his grip on me and his creepy gaze disappears, thank God for that. I hear a distant train rumbling by, which is weird because I'm pretty sure he doesn't live near railway tracks, then realise it's his sagging stomach aching for more microwave shit.

"Food time yet, boss?" he asks while raising an eyebrow.

Why is he asking me? He's the leader in this crazy relationship we have, I no authority here, I am quite simply a pawn. This sends a pang of resentment into my tortured soul, as not so long ago I was the king in this scenario, now I am the guy at the bottom taking orders from a moron. But, when at the bottom, I guess there is only one way to go. Before that though, better keep up appearances.

"Soon, and I'm not your superior."

He chuckles irritatingly. "When did I become so bloody serious? No wait, I don't want to know the answer to that."

Shit, I forgot that he actually still thinks I am him. Did I infer that to him earlier, or later? As if he stills believes it, maybe I can use this to my advantage somehow. Before I have time to think of something clever he leaves our hiding place and heads into the messy kitchen. I decide that I would rather not watch him stuffing his fat face and take a look around his living room.

The living room, like much of his home, is pretty shabby if I'm perfectly honest. A large TV adorns the far wall and is way to big for this room, along with obesity problems he will most certainly end up with eyesight issues further down the line. A battered old two-seater sofa and a lazy boy recliner perched in perfect viewing position (and probably smelling of a thousand farts) are pretty much the only other things of note. I head over to the far wall and check out some old photographs scattered around like fading memories. They mostly consist of him and his mum, and him with the fat, furry, feline. One picture catches my eye though, it's him and his grandad stood beside the sea when he was a little boy.

I see some sort of movement at the rear of the photograph, two figures seemingly dancing or fighting, it is very surreal. They advance closer to the front of the scenery, kind of bypassing the old man and boy as if they aren't really there. I wonder if the drugs are seriously affecting my mental psyche right now, am I imagining all of this? I shake my head to try to restart my brain, but this has no effect whatsoever. As the figures draw nearer, almost reaching out like a three dimensional movie, I see one is dressed as Batman, and the other is wearing a baseball cap. They are indeed having some sort of fisticuffs, I half expect some bam, whack and splats to come protruding from the screen like the old Batman TV shows.

The guy in the baseball cap suddenly disappears from view and only Batman remains, stood with his back to my view, hands posed on his hips in a superhero pose, although more reminiscent of Superman than the man of bat. As if sensing someone is staring at his arse he cranes his neck slightly, then turns around fully. I think I know who this is, it's Gulaxa, the other one, not Catlaxa, but Batlaxa. Shit, so that's where he ended up. Which doesn't make sense, how has he ended up in a moving photograph? I'm really confused right now. But Batlaxa maintains his stance and stares in my direction, what is he doing? He lifts up one of his hands and seemingly blows a kiss my way, how very gay of him. Somehow I feel the tender caress on my cheek and it feels kind of cold, freezing in fact, ow, it really hurts! I try to stand up and avert my gaze but nothing happens. I'm completely stuck solid. As I gaze on at the picture, Batlaxa belts out a silent guffaw before disappearing into nothingness. My eyes no longer blink. My brain no longer seems to function. Am I destined to stay like this for eternity? Lost in a void of maddening torture, forever poised like an ice sculpture of blind pain.

I hear the idiot return and start waffling words of which I cannot understand, of which I cannot comprehend. He tries to move me, to wake me. Please, help me! I need you! You are the only one who can save me from this mental torture! He leaves me. He abandons me. I am all alone. I'm sorry for all I have done. God, if you give me another chance, I will be more, I will do more. I will be a good person and help mankind as best as I can. Please. Please! He returns beside me, my guardian angel, my saviour. Help me! Take me away from this...

FROZEN IN TIME

I may have made a big boo boo. As I was jumping, my mind got a bit distracted, and for some strange reason I imagined myself eating an ice cream. So when I arrived back at Hatson's shop hopefully an hour later, I was no longer holding my furry friend but was clutching a rather delicious looking flake 99 cone. Shit! Why didn't I just hang about an hour instead of being so bloody impatient and jumping? And of all the times to picture eating an ice cream, why do it when I'm on a perilous mission to save the entire universe and revive my little baby. Double shitting shit!

Oh well, might as well enjoy my cone before it melts, Negative Nancy is not ruining my day today, she can piss right off! I slouch against the window like the cool dude I am and try to conjure up a way out of this untimely predicament. Unfortunately, the window isn't where I expected it to be, and I fall down onto my butt with a little jolt.

"Ow!" I exclaim.

Not really upset right now, just a little bonk of my backside, nothing to worry about or get angry over. That is until I notice the lovely white ice cream has vanished, along with it's brown crumbling companion.

"Hmm, where the bloody hell have you vamoosed off to?" I enquire to whoever may be listening.

After looking left and right I suddenly make a shocking revelation. I am not outside Hatson's hat shop. I'm actually sat by the beach catching some rays from a glorious sun that blazes overhead. OK, this was not what I expected. Where the hell am I now? More importantly, where the hell has my lovely dollop of ice cream buggered off to? Then the answer becomes very evident as I feel an icy coolness start to envelop my crotch area. Triple shitting shit!

But all is not lost. I reach my hands tenderly into my nether regions and retrieve the now slightly squashed and melting object and cram it unceremoniously into my waiting orifice (my mouth, not the other one!). Mmm, nice, I think.

"Mmm, nice," I mutter seductively.

As the juicy contents join forces in my mouth to make love to my taste buds, I am instantly attacked by the coldness. Standing up abruptly I proceed to dance around like a panicked newly-wed who has realised they have just made a fatal mistake. As the freeze begins to take a tenuous hold of my brain, every fibre of my being is telling me to spit the offending object from my eating area. I defy all of my instincts and keep the freezing fireball firmly within it's heated establishment. I will not give in to this glorious pain. I am stronger than the world. I increase the circumference of my insane dance routine in the hope my varied movements may get the never-ending mouth pain to politely bugger off, it doesn't work. Wafting my open mouth seems to have some sort of an impact though, so this is what I do rapidly while running around in circles like a dog chasing it's tail. After intense seconds, which feel like hours, the searing ice begins to cool down somewhat and I fall to the floor as dizzy as a roundabout.

As I chomp noisily on the now less than threatening lump of tastiness, I gaze around in the hope of finding the missing brown finger, this would go gloriously within my gob right now. Seeing it nowhere in sight I pat my pockets in hopeful exasperation, feeling something firm in the left one. It can't be, can it? Inserting my fingers gently I retrieve the dark coloured item, eu-bloody-reka! It's the flake, and I still have some ice cream left in my gob. Without hesitation I shove the whole thing in, having to snap it in half against the inside of my cheek, and crunch down on it beautifully. I savour the moment as I would savour sex with a beautiful woman, and my loving mouth has a little orgasm, nice.

Well, now that little escapade of excitement is over, where in holy hell am I? By the sea, obviously, as I previously stated that, but where by the sea? Also more relevantly, when by the sea? Hmm, best get my detective hat on, and speaking of hats, have I still got the good old Stetson on? I check, and the answer is I do have a hat on, but not the Stetson. Receiving said hatted attire from atop my noggin, I see it is indeed a green baseball cap with Lord of the Graft etched on the front, very odd. But I do smile somewhat as a cool looking pair of aviators are perched upon the rim. Watch out ladies, Mitch Maverick Branning is here to make you swoon. Slowly plucking the dark glasses from their perch, I place the hat with the mysterious slogan upon my head. Maybe that will explain itself somewhere down the line, or even in a different universe, who the hell cares?!

Holding the aviators aloft like a trophy I twirl triumphantly to face the sea. Slowly and smoothly I reel the cool shades towards my sexy blue eyes as a magically appearing camera rotates around me like a voluptuous butterfly, taking in every single moment, every single movement of my suaveness. I draw out the action, feeling the tension in the whole universe, feeling every woman on earth trembling in sexual anticipation. As the glasses settle on my perfectly formed nose, I click the fingers of my other hand and begin to do a little jig.

"You've lost that loving feeling..." I begin in perfect tune.

"Excuse me," a man's voice from my right interrupts my angelic melody. This had better be good.

As I turn coolly to face the offending gentleman, I am confronted by my grandad. As I am about to blurt out something probably stupid I spot a young boy stood beside him looking up at me. Oh shit, it's me! I close my eyes and prepare for a random jump to another time and location. Nothing happens. Very weird.

"Excuse me, are you OK?" my grandad asks.

Opening my eyes I see I am still in the same place, with two members of my family staring dumbly at me. Better speak or forever hold my peace, whatever that means!

"Yeah, cool as peace, man," I say, adopting a suave as hell slouch.

"OK," my grandad says slowly. "I was just wondering if you wouldn't mind taking a photograph of my grandson and I. But if you're busy..."

"Yeah, no problem grand...dude," well done Mitch you clever quick witted bastard.

I've just had a eureka moment. I've got my cool as hell shades on, so this must be preventing the young me and I from a paradoxical like scenario. Very interesting. Also very stupid if you ask me. So all I have to do to prevent random jumps with my other selves is to wear some sunglasses? Whoever made this shit up is either nuts or a God damn genius, let's go with the latter, shall we?

"Are you sure you're OK?" my grandad asks once more.

"I think he might be broken grandad," the other me says, cheeky git. But as he/I says these words a worrying sense of deja vu overcomes me, sending my brain into a bit of a head wobble, quite possibly the second time this has happened on my mind-bending journey. I actually remember meeting this guy (me) and felt some sort of connection with him. I remember laid in bed on the night time wondering if he was my dad, very weird.

"I'm not your dad!" I blurt out. Shit, what the hell am I doing. "Erm, I mean I ain't no-one's daddy-o!" I sing this last part and begin gyrating like a cool as hell rock star.

My grandad puts a protective arm around me (the younger me obviously, although considering my mental outbursts I could probably do with a little cuddle right now) and backs away slightly. I cease my awesome dance moves and resume a normal stance and demeanour, don't want to frighten myself too much.

"Hey, I'm just having a giraffe me old muckers," I say jovially. "Let's get that picture taken shall we? Where's your camera at?"

Before he has a chance to remonstrate, I spot the camera laid on a nearby rock and retrieve it quickly.

"Right let's get a lovely photograph of you awesome dudes shall we, what?"

"What?" my grandad asks.

"Never mind, I think if you stood over there with the sea glistening behind you, that would make an awesome shot. Go on, get over there little chubs, I mean buddy."

Thankfully the younger me seems not to have noticed my unnecessary insult, don't want to have any sort of negative affect on myself and turn me into some sort of raving lunatic. My grandad however must have heard my little snideful remark and gives me a nasty sideways glance. Better not piss him off, I may need his help later/earlier.

"That's it, perfect, like two little garden gnomes. Right, hold those stomachs in, bare those teeth, yeah, like a shark, growl like a rabid mongoose, snarl like..."

"Just take the damn photo, idiot!" my grandad says, before quite possibly realising who I am as a look of recognition falls across his face. Guess the cap and shades can only hide so much.

I hide behind the camera again and focus on them fully, both literally and figuratively, and possibly metaphorically as well, which might be the same as figuratively, I'm not sure any more.

"Right hold it, hold it, bang! Give me a what what!" and I take the picture. "Well done my Adonis like models, you two are all kinds of awesome. Right I'm off for a poo, see you later."

As I prepare to turn around and get the hell put of dodge, I notice that all sound has ceased. And by all, I mean literally all. The sea has stopped erm, seeing, or seaing, I mean waving. Screw it, you know what I mean. Everything is still, a bit like when I was with my mum on the bench by the other beach, or the same beach. Time, and everything encapsulated by it, has stopped working, has quite literally come grinding to a halt. Even the younger me and my grandad are stood there like frozen statues, stuck in a moment in time. What in holy hell is going on? It is at this moment that I recognise this scene, it's one of the photographs in my living room, and also the one that Gulaxa got stuck staring at. I'm guessing something very weird is about to happen.

I place the camera on a nearby rock and begin to approach my younger family. Waving my hands across their faces I try and snap them out of it, but to no avail. I try to move them, but like Gulaxa in my living room all that time ago, they are stuck fast. Very odd indeed. As I walk around behind them I feel a presence appear from my right. As I turn around I am confronted by Batman who is stood staring at me like some cocky crusader.

"Can I help you?" I ask, adopting my ninja like stance, primed and ready for attack.

"Can I help you?" Batman retorts in a childish tone, before laughing like a psychopath.

"Are you me?" I enquire, but I'm guessing by the tone of voice that this is not the case. "Gulaxa?"

"Not quite, you can call me...Batlaxa!" he says while flourishing his cape like a dick.

So, the immortal battle between good and evil finally comes to it's conclusion. This is going to be epic, fables will be written about this cataclysmic encounter for generations to come. Children will tremble in their beds at the chilling name Batlaxa. Children will be in awe of the mighty hero Mitch Branning – saviour of all time. Stories will be...ow! He's just whipped me with his cape the bloody sod. Right, that's it, fisticuffs time.

We dance around each other like stalking predators, sizing each other up, taking it in turns to strike out. Sometimes we hit, sometimes we miss, most of the time we just jostle like school children, kind of afraid of lurching in too much in case we hurt each other. As the time consuming, and time wasting, battle edges on, I fear we are not getting anywhere at all and decide to up the ante a bit. Feinting a weak left hook I then dodge expertly to the right and crack him one right in the nuts. Have some of that you pretend super hero bastard! He seems to have some sort of nether regions protector in place though which hurts my hand somewhat. What a sneaky bastard. I decide enough is enough and use my time travelling expertise to jump and arrive behind him.

"Have some of this you dirty git!" I exclaim to thin air.

I'm guessing I have timed my jump a little wrong. I am back in the same place as I see my grandad and younger self still stood stock still. But no sign of Batlaxa. I am however blown away by the thousand foot tall Gulaxa staring at me from the heavens like some Godlike statue. I try waving at him but he seems stock still, as if mimicking the other two frozen sculptures before me. I then see myself appear, looming just as large and also just as beautiful as I always thought I was, damn I am one sexy man. If he did a nail checking gesture right now I would most probably die of sheer delight. I wave my hands back and forth, letting him/me know how downright awesome they/I are/am.

But if I remember correctly, he/I will hold up a magnifying glass and attempt to search for me/him. Which in a cool sort of way I/he will look as big as he/I is now, but to me/him, in the past, or the future. God I love time travel. But wait, is this time travel if I am stuck in a photo? I think it might sort of be, I also may have pondered over this previously, so screw it, just accept things as they are and move on. As the magnifying glass looms high on the horizon, a massive beautiful blue eye which is as blue as the ocean that surrounds us stares unblinkingly at me. I for a second forget where I am and also what I am supposed to be doing. I feel as though I am falling up into the deep blue abyss, and as I point straight at the dark pupil like the centre of a black hole, I feel myself tumble out of sight, and out of time, down the darkest rabbit hole within the entire universe.

FEEDING THE CHIMP

S hattering through the glass of a frozen reality I land smack bang right where I had been previously, staring at the picture. Thankfully this time there are no moving bodies to send crushing kisses my way, freezing me to the damn spot. How in holy shit did that happen? I've been around a while now and have never experienced anything so dramatic as all the stuff occurring right now, it's totally insane. I kind of guessed that Batlaxa was me (or an alternate/future version of me) and the other guy was him, but how can people move in a still photograph? It seemingly breaks down the barriers of reality, I really don't get it at all.

After making sure that the picture is definitely a normal still one, I decide I had better find out where my hero has gone to. Although this guy was very likely the cause of my lack of powers, he is now becoming my savour. All the previous anger I felt towards him was beginning to drift away like a forgotten song on a breeze of love. This was not how this story was supposed to go. I hear the snap shut of a door, followed by a very recognisable sound that I can't quite place at first. Hearing a couple of beeps, followed by a soft droning sound, reminds my memory of my friend's favourite magic box. Better make myself known.

Creeping through the living room I have a funny idea to sneak up on him and try some startling tactics, that's what friends do, right? As I draw nearer to my target I prepare a scary growl. Then my attempts at hilarity are immediately extinguished as my hand catches the side of the bannister, causing my ever-present chiming companion to let off a little early warning jangle. Better prepare my opening quip.

"Nice kitchen," I say in my usual deadpan manner.

"Thanks," he replies. "So, what the hell happened back there?"

My first thought was actually to come clean about everything, and I mean everything. How I had been playing him, and about Catlaxa, and now Batlaxa (what stupid names, whoever came up with these ridiculous monikers is seriously nuts!). I'm glad I don't act on my first instinct though as this guy worries me with all his abilities, it may be wise not to piss him off. Best to keep playing dumb and see how all this plays out. So I look over my shoulder and then look back at him, hopefully with a puzzled look on my face.

"Before we jumped?" he enquires. "When you were stuck looking at that photo?"

"I don't know," that's it, keep playing the dumb card.

"I'm guessing that was me in the picture, which is why I passed out, yet another bloody paradox. But how was I moving in a still photograph? Being in it was crazy enough, but to actually be waving and pointing just doesn't make any sense."

I wish he would stop asking me questions, I'm just going to say I don't know all the time, so he's just wasting his time. As I go to speak my usual negative answer, the microwave pings, alerting him that his gourmet meal is ready to be devoured. I watch on as he grabs a less then clean plate from the cupboard and begins what must be a very well practised ritual. As he empties the contents of the microwave container onto the plate it seems very fortunate that it all lands where it should and does not go cascading onto the floor. The food resembles and smells like cat sick, instantly bringing back memories of Catlaxa once more – I wonder where he ended up?

"Would you like something to eat?" he asks, which kind of brings a warm feeling to my heart.

I decline, saying that I am not hungry, which is completely true. I feel kind of sickly to be honest. I don't know if this is because of withdrawal or the smell of his disgusting meal, probably both.

"You should still eat something, you'll waste away," he says, and as the words leave his lips a look of melancholy falls across his features. I bet he is regretting not spending time in the restaurant with his mum. He certainly does love her, it is very evident in his eyes. I feel a sense of envy overcome me, a feeling of regret that I never had the loving relationship that he has with his mother. I feel sad and crestfallen, I struggle to hold back my emotions. Is this the drugs again? I wonder if there are any hidden about upstairs?

"I'm still hungry," he exclaims, dragging me out of my drug fuelled compulsion.

He begins rummaging around in the freezer again and starts off another droning meal, and another, and another, as I watch on aimlessly, lost in my own thoughts. Watching him shovel the less than nutritious supplements into his body I cringe, thinking of the dreadful party happening inside his stomach. I cringe even more when I think of the sorry state of whatever toilet he has to use, it's a good job he lives alone, I don't think any woman could stand to share a home with this typical single guy. At one point he seems so self-obsessed and self-absorbed in his quick fire food shovelling that I try and edge away from the room, maybe have a little look upstairs for some blue babies. Just as I begin my sneaky escape he pretty much orders me to sit down and places a meal in front of me.

"Please, try and eat something," he says tenderly.

I sit down regretfully, full of despair and self-pity. I really like the fact he is trying to look after me though, and this brings a slight feeling of warmth to my battered soul. I pick aimlessly at the putrid looking meal, which to be honest actually tastes quite nice, but my stomach doesn't seem to agree with anything solid right now and I struggle to eat even half of it. As he gets up to look once more in the freezer I retch involuntarily, just about managing to keep the food down with sheer force of will, damn that was close. I reach up and pour myself a glass of water and glug it greedily, I hope this will stay down and settle my stomach somewhat.

After his extended staring into the freezer, I'm guessing he saw the meal he makes later and juggles with a paradox of some sort, he decides on a bowl of cereal. At last he goes for something a bit more healthy. Watching him munch it down like a ravenous beast I inwardly chuckle to myself at the vast array of food he has consumed. Glancing around the table it is as if a gang of chimpanzees have barged in and had a massive food party.

"Ah, that's better," he exclaims while patting his belly after burping loudly. His exclamation reminds me of Catlaxa and Batlaxa after crunching their delicious diazepam, and a deadly yearning attacks at my fragile mind.

"Now I need a kip! Shall I go and wake Goldilocks up and see if he wants to swap places?" he enquires, and I wonder briefly if he is being serious or not, never can tell with this guy, doesn't he remember what happened last time?

"I do not think that would be a wise idea," I reply in my usual monotone.

He stands up and leans nonchalantly against the wall, his full stomach protruding against his clothing. He definitely needs to address his weight issue, maybe all this time travelling will drop some pounds off him. I watch him carefully as he surveys the scene before him on the table, the after effects of his bustling banquet. His face slowly changes from one of relaxation after a good meal, to one of total anger, as he realises this has all happened before. Oh shit, he's going to jump. Before I have a chance to advise him to think, he disappears. Shit! I wonder how much time I have. Without thinking I bound up the stairs, feeling the contents of my tummy gurgling against the unwelcome running and head into the bathroom. Snatching open the bathroom cabinet I see the sweet relaxing packet of diazepam staring at me and breathe a sigh of relief, my pain will be eased soon. I briefly think, is this the original packet from before? If I take these will I mess up the timeline? Screw it, I need instant relief, come to me my little...

SECOND CHANCES

I bet you're guessing a random jump occurred and you would be downright right, or downright correct, which sounds a lot more sensible than the first statement. But this time is different, this time I have all the knowledge and experience of a time travelling superstar, and nothing in the known universe can affect my pure of heart awesomeness. Nothing and no-one can knock the confidence I possess right now. Mitch Branning is a bona-fide God of biblical proportions, people cower to him, they pray to him. Women all over the world want to make love to his glorious body like nefarious nymphomaniacs. Alien females from distant galaxies travel vast distances to use their many waiting orifices to pleasure the masterful Mitch in whatever way he pleases. The Gods who created the universe bow at his feet, revelling in...

"What's your problem pal?" a rude dude interrupts my awesome monologue.

I realise I have had my eyes closed, and as I open them I see I am standing in a telephone booth, very odd. Even odder (or maybe not) I see Chino's just over the road. This could get interesting. But then again, maybe not. What are the odds I have come back to the same time as when I was here previously? Probably quite high I would imagine. I decide to just close my eyes, turn away from the guy interrupted, and have a nice big sigh.

A disgruntled tap on the glass where I am resting my head startles me somewhat from my incoming nap, I'm starting to dislike this guy. I turn over the other way trying to ignore his incessant tapping. But this has no positive outcome as he proceeds to tap against the newest window I am leaning against. I open my eyes wearily and stare at the irritating twat. Oh bloody hell, it's the pony-tailed wanker from earlier, or maybe later, not entirely sure. I make sure my shades are in prime position (they are) before opening the door slightly and conversing.

"What's the problem me old mucker?" I enquire jovially.

"Are you pissing in there?" he asks seriously.

What is it with this guy? Does he just stand around random phone boxes accusing people of pissing? What a weird chap. If only he knew who I was then he wouldn't dream of asking such incriminating questions. I mean, I do actually need a wee right now, so would it be rude to whip my giant todger out and let one rip? Don't really want to embarrass him, maybe I could...

"You should be ashamed of yourself," he says. "Pissing in a public convenience, people might want to use it you know."

"Look, pal," I state firmly. "What gives you the impression that I have had a urination in this here establishment? Is there any evidence to back up such insane accusations?"

"Well, you looked very embarrassed when I turned up, as if I had disturbed you doing something you shouldn't. You then turned onto the other side and sighed very contentedly as if you were having a nice long wee. Plus, it stinks of piss in there,

I can smell it from out here, I have a right mind to call the cops on you. You're the second guy to do this today, bloody Batman was here earlier dribbling down his leg the dirty bastard."

I stare at him for long moments, probably longer than is necessary. I thank him inwardly for confirming my time and location, but curse him inwardly (and maybe outwardly with my cool as hell stare, which he can't quite see because of the sunglasses) for not allowing me to use my super deductive skills. I also take the time to think of my reply, this has to be something cool, something prophetic, something he will remember until the day he dies.

"Give me a what what?" I ask while suavely lowering my sunglasses slightly.

The stare I get back is one of either utmost devotion or total contempt, it is very hard to tell the difference.

"What?" he enquires quizzically.

That's only one what my two-legged friend, but I'll let you off you stupid bastard.

"Never mind, look. It's like this. My name is Mitch Branning, I am quite possibly the coolest mofo on this planet, probably all planets in all known universes to be honest. Women swoon at my suaveness, men envy my Adonis like frame. Animals yearn for me to pet them until their hair turns grey," (don't know where that one came from). "I have no need for insidious insults or petty remarks. Please, allow me to leave and venture forth to spread my seed to the world."

And with this I leave the communications chapel and stride past the pony-tailed one with my head held high floating on extreme pride

"It stinks of piss in here, you should be ashamed of yourself," my new found disciple cries.

"Hark, my angel, sing a song of sixpence and bury your shoe in the sky!" I cry as I recite a well known verse from probably Shakespeare or some other awesome dude. Damn my skills are just never-ending. As I leave the anointed arsehole sniffing up someone else's urine (although it could be mine if I have been here previously), I decide to have a little walk over to Chino's. I mean, what's the worst that can happen? I'm sure if I just stand at the periphery of everything then nothing bad can go wrong. Maybe the cat has magically appeared here, stranger things have happened in this crazy roller-coaster of a life I seem to be living in.

Making sure my shades are affixed perfectly to my beautiful face I stride purposefully over to the entrance, not before causing a little bit of mayhem in the road area. Cars beep and rev their engines unnecessarily as I coolly cross the road like an out of control drifter who knows no limits (which pretty much describes me down to a tee). I nod acceptingly at them, doffing my cap to acknowledge their adoration for the one true master of the universe.

"I know, I know," I say while raising my hand aloft and stopping in the middle of the road. "It is I. The God of the world. Please, worship me as you will. I am the Lord of the lambs, or sheep, or something else more prophetic."

"Move out the way you dumb shit!" a gentlemen shouts from his car, probably at someone behind me.

"Get your fat arse off the road you fucking tit!" a little old lady cries from behind her dinky Fiat 500, further cementing my internal argument that people are not shouting at me.

"Why don't you just fuck off you silly little wanker!" a young lad shouts from the pavement. He seems to be looking right at me, or maybe he is looking at someone right behind me, let's go with that.

Just as I am about to reply, I happen to glance into the window of Chino's and see a guy wearing a Batman costume trying to light some sort of cable. This seems a bit out of sorts. I know it wasn't me, or at least not a version of me before now. I'm guessing it's that Batlaxa psychopath. A sudden realisation dawns on me that an explosion occurred when I was here previously. I'm guessing this is why I am here. I'm here to stop a madman blowing up a building and killing lots of innocent people, I will finally be a hero.

I stride purposefully over to the window and tap on it lightly, startling Batlaxa into dropping his zippo lighter onto the floor which sparks immediately. Batlaxa looks at the lighter, looks at me, gives me the wanker sign, then disappears. What a cheeky little bastard. Just as I am about to run into the building and save the whole universe, the sparks from the lighter ignite the cable (which I assume to be a fuse) which sets off a cascade of fireworks trickling down the side of the restaurant like a running slide show of dancing hula ladies. Just before it reaches a whole barrel of what I presume to be explosives by the flammable label adorned on the side, I say a silent prayer and get the hell out of there.

PLANE TERROR

As my hand reaches out for my blue saviours they disappear, only to be replaced by the back of a seat, which I grab onto just in time as the momentum of my arrival pushes me back with supreme force. Where in holy hell has he jumped to now? This is in fact pretty evident as I stare out the huge window of an aeroplane as it bullets through the sky like a torpedo. Two pilots converse with each other animatedly as I try to come to terms with where we are and why he would bring us here. What purpose would he have of boarding an air bound plane?

I stare over at him to see he is lost in as complete amazement as I am at where we are. These powers he possesses are getting stronger by the day, it's not easy travelling through time as it is, but managing to jump to a different time onto a moving object is pretty complex. I am in awe of this guy. But now is not the time to be star struck, I'm making myself invisible so as I don't get shot or something. Not knowing what time this is, they may have guns in the cockpit, better to be safe than sorry. Checking invisibility has been achieved (by using the reflection in the glass) I prepare my opening quip. But not before noticing the bunch of flowers in one hand, and a gun in the other. This guy really is something else.

"Nice plane," I mutter.

"Thanks, it's not mine," he replies, a little too loudly than is necessary, this could get interesting.

He seems to realise his little mistake. He turns from me to the two pilots who stare dumbfounded at this random guy chatting to himself in a place where he really shouldn't be. I kind of expect him to clam up and shit himself, but the opposite happens. He deftly drops the flowers and raises the gun at the pilots.

"Do not speak a word, I'm not going to hurt you, I'm here to help," he says, with a slight waver of panic in his voice. I imagine in his warped imagination he thinks he sounds cool, good on you fella.

"How..." the pilot on the left says, I think he might be the proper pilot and the other guy is the co-pilot. He has a nicer hat on so I'm going with that, I wish I had a hat. Whoa! Where did that come from? I've never been a hat wearer in my life! Very odd.

"Quiet!" my hero barks. "This is not a time for discussion. You are about to be hijacked and made to crash into the World Trade Centre, I'm here to prevent that from happening."

You've got to be shitting me! The twin towers! This guy is nuts! Why oh why would you bring us to one of the planes that's about to crash into a building in a blazing ball of fire? I rather think he has a death wish or something. If only I could get the hell out here, but no, I'm stuck here about to be decimated into nothingness for no reason whatsoever. At least my death will be quick.

"I need you to..." he begins before a startled lady at the door breaks up whatever he was going to ask them by knocking frantically on the door.

"Captain, we have a situation out here that requires your urgent attention."

Both pilots look at each in utter confusion, probably wondering if their day can get any worse. Trust me guys, it will get worse, but enjoy every second because it's about to be your last day on this earth. The maniac beside me holds one finger to his lips, asking the two trained pilots to simply be quiet and hope the lady gives up and goes away. Yeah, like that's going to happen! Idiot! My dislike for him is starting to fester once more. Another bout of nervous door knocking ensues.

"Please, Captain, one of the passengers has fallen ill and requires medical attention, can you please open the door!?" the obviously under pressure woman almost screams, she sounds terrified.

"Give me a minute," the pilot says to the closed door with a supreme air of authority, this guy doesn't fluster easily. He turns to the crazy one beside me. "We must open the door, a life is at stake."

"If you open that door," he says quite confidently. "Thousands of innocent people will die, you have to trust me."

The co-pilot must be having a bad case of the heroics as he edges slightly off his seat, staring fixedly on the gun aimed at the pilot. Don't do it sonny, not worth it. Just in time the gun moves its aim towards him, breaking any resolve he once had, good boy.

"Don't be a hero son," my saviour beside me says, very coolly I might add. "Good choice fella," he says, seeing the utter look of despondence on his face. "Now..."

What now? What's your plan here? Just ignore the frantic knocking and ask these two professional pilots to divert the plane to somewhere else? Then what, disappear in front of their eyes? The other plane will still hit, so will all the other shit that happens. Then they'll be a bigger conspiracy regarding the disappearing cockpit invader. More desperate banging breaks me from my incessant rambling along with a woman's cries for help.

"What if I told you that terrorists were outside that door and are planning on flying this plane into one of the twin towers, killing everyone on board plus thousands more innocents?" he calmly asks. Well, at least he's honest. Get it all out there, might as well. I can't wait to see what happens next, although my pounding heart thinks otherwise. These are the situations that diazepam was created for, I'd do anything for one right now.

"I would say you were insane," the pilot replies calmly. "But the fact that you are in here at all tells me that something bordering on insanity is definitely going on. What do you suggest we do?" What, he's actually believing him? This guy is just as nuts as the dude with the gun!

For brief moments he seems stuck, probably lost in his own inward musings, in fact he is as I can see his lips moving. He turns to look at me for guidance, what the hell does he expect me to do? You got us into this mess, you can get us out of it. I adopt my usual dumb expression and shrug my shoulders almost imperceptibly. I notice the two pilots stare at each other, probably wondering who he is looking at, and rightfully assuming he is indeed mentally screwed up.

"Is there anyway anyone can get in here?" he asks sharply, returning his gaze to his onlookers. "Never been in a cockpit before, what's the procedure? Do you have some sort of heavy-duty door that can't be breached?"

"Not really," the pilot replies. "Any sort of high impact against the door will open it, failing that the flight attendant has a key as well."

With that devastating revelation the door is bashed open, sending crazy guy face first into the pilot's nether regions. I stifle a little laugh at this, always knew he had an eye for the men. My grin is instantly wiped away as an Arabic looking guy appears in the doorway looking like a deranged serial killer, which in actual fact he will be if he carries out the devastating act he is planning. This guy scares the shit out of me. I back away as far as I can, which isn't far as I knock against the rear of the nearest seat. His wide eyes seem to suck in the whole cockpit, he looks like he is high on some drug, his pupils are as huge as saucers. I fart a little at my fear and hope it doesn't smell, but then again everyone has more pressing matters at hand than a little stinky pump.

"Who are you?" he asks in broken English. I almost reply meekly and realise that he cannot see me, thank God. "You not pilot, how you in here?"

"I'm the man who's about to fuck up your day pal," comes the reply from the guy who has removed himself from the cock and balls of his new best friend. Although he tries valiantly to hide his fear, it is to no avail, it trembles like the tracks from an incoming train.

For long moments nothing seems to happen. The terrorist stares him in the eyes, seemingly without blinking. Another foreign tongue speaks up from behind him and I manage to peek past to see a few more guys with the same appearance holding sharp objects, some look like hatchets. I see the front row of passengers, all with their heads in between their legs as angry voices are bellowed at them. What I am assuming is the stewardess who was banging on the door is on her knees, a psychopathic monster stood over her, his blade resting on her neck. Shit, he's not going to do what I think he is, is he?

"If you do not do as I say, my men behind door will start cutting throats, you understand?" lead terrorist enquires without an ounce of fear. Everyone in the cockpit says nothing, frozen to his every word like a statue of fear.

"We'll do whatever you want," the co-pilot pipes up, shit he can speak, good on you son.

"The fuck we will," my hero interjects. "This bastard wants to fly into a building, killing us all." Well done, just let the guy know that we are aware of his plans, that's a great help, idiot! Although this does cause a moment of confusion to fall across his face, might be a card well played.

"How you know this?" he asks "You American spy?" Well, obviously not, because he's not American, although his accent did adopt a slight Yankee drawl on his previous statement. For some reason I wonder if he made the phone call to himself all those years ago, in the future. Probably not the time to be randomly obsessing about a future event which has already happened, or might not happen, because we're all about to die!

"No, I'm your worst nightmare," the hero replies with all the steel and determination of John McClane, get in there. I almost whoop for joy, before remembering I am not in a movie theatre and I am actually in a life and death situation. Get a grip Gulaxa.

"We will see," the terrorist replies coldly without a flicker of emotion.

He shouts incomprehensible orders over his shoulder at his army of fellow martyrs. Once more I peek around the side of the door, just in time to see his number two hack into the stewardess' neck with extreme violence. Her eyes momentarily fix upon mine as if she can see me. As the ragged blade rips through flesh and bone her eyes never leave mine, we seem to be locked into a timeless trance. I watch on forlornly as the light from her eyes dims and then flickers out of existence, to be replaced by a cold vacant stare that stares deep down into my soul. The accusing look blames me for not helping her, I feel anguish and sorrow at the loss of someone I could have helped. I am a worthless human being and I slump back against the back of the seat in abject dejection, hanging my head in shame.

"This," the terrorist booms, startling me from my depressive thoughts. "Is what will happen to all on plane, if you do not obey my commands. You understand?"

Apart from the occasional sobs from behind the terrorist, the world seems to fall silent. The cockpit crowd have lost all their heroic intentions. I look at my friend and see the look of utter terror in his eyes. If anyone needed a hug right now then it was him, I wish I could go to him, I need a hug as well. If we are going to die then please let it be in the arms of someone I know. I suddenly feel a surge of anger well up inside me. This murdering piece of shit! I reach for the only thing with any weight, a heavy bound folder and prepare to smash this sick psycho on the back of his stupid head.

As I'm about to unleash hell I hear a commotion from my right. The so-called hero is now face first in the crotch of the co-pilot now. Is this really the time for sucking someone off? I don't think so pal. It's then I see the pilot with the Berretta aimed our way, shaking profusely. Good lad, that's how you become a hero!

"Back off!" he bellows "Let everyone go and drop your weapons." Way to go sunshine! Have some of that you terrorist wanker!

He then begins to point the gun at his ex-crotch loving friend and the terrorist. Whoa there cowboy! One target at a time. Keep it trained on this twat over here, he's the real threat. Unless you count unwelcome penis invasion a threat, more like sexual assault really, but I suppose a threat none the less.

"Whoa!" my friend cries, holding his hands aloft in a surrendering pose. "I'm on your side pal."

"Shut up!" the pilot screams. "I want you all to back up, I'm calling this in."

As he takes his gaze off everyone to reach for his headset, I see out the corner of my eye lead terrorist give a little signal to his number two, some sort of hand gesture behind his back. Number two pulls back his blood soaked weapon, preparing a long throw. I go to open my mouth to shout a warning but there is no saliva there to deposit any noise. As I try to make some by running my dry tongue around my desert like mouth, lead terrorist bends down, allowing his accomplice a perfect target. And boy does he take his chance. The hatchet glides through the air like an angry arrow with practised precision to land square between the pilot's eyes. If these wasn't such a volatile situation right now, I would start clapping.

For a brief moment the pilot stands still, as if unsure what to do next, as we all do I suppose, before he falls onto his seat. As he lands, a deafening boom reverberates around the cockpit and I instinctively hold my hands over my ears. I hope he shot that bastard between the eyes. Looking up I see this is not the case as he is still stood there, there is however a jagged spiral beginning to make it's way across the glass separating us all from most likely certain death. Another shot fires, this one not as damaging to my ears as they are still recovering from the first one and I see the the bullet smack dead centre into the co-pilots eyes. Once again I feel the need to applaud, but just about hold my insane actions at bay.

As I wonder if this shit could get any worse I feel a massive jolt forward as we plummet into a deadly descent. I manage to hold onto the back of the seat as I see the terrorist go flying past me, hearing a sickening thud against the toughened glass. Gazing back through to door leading outside the cockpit I see a young girl crying her eyes out. I feel such sad remorse that this was allowed to happen. Only God can save us now little one. I make myself visible and give her a little wave. A moment of confusion falls across her pretty little face. I hold my hands in prayer and close my eyes. I wait a second and see she is doing the same. Good girl. Maybe the next life will be better for you. I feel us levelling up somewhat and wonder briefly if we have changed anything. Or is this it? Is this the end? Am I...

ALL'S FAIR IN LOVE AND MITCH

Right, that's it. No more random jumps. No more messing about. I have two jobs to do. Find Batlaxa. Find the cat. Easy, right? Wait, I might need to find Gulaxa as well, not the original one, the one who nicked my hat, could he be called Hatlaxa? Maybe, doesn't seem quite right to be honest. Also, you know what, screw also! I'm sicking of trying to find answers to unanswerable questions. Why can't I just have some chill out time, just me, myself and Mitch. Everyone needs a timeout now and again, even super hero time travelling legends require a little holiday to refresh their tormented souls. So that's what I'm doing. No more Chino's. No more Gulaxa, Batlaxa, and whoever else Laxa. This is my time. Time to put my feet up and soak up some serenity.

Arriving with all the grace of an unpickled onion I succumb to the sumptuous bed with a contented sigh. I don't bother to open my eyes, I trust my skills to the max. I know where I am and no amount of checking will solve anything. I turn onto my side into my usual foetal sleeping position, folding my hands under the soft pillow and sigh once more. You know what, let's have a nice big long loud sigh, I'm not going to disturb anyone,

I'm all alone. I roll onto my back and stretch as far as I can before letting out a huge exasperated noisy sigh.

"Ah, that's better!" I boom as loud as a trumpeting elephant, while flopping my hands to the sides, causing the left one to slap against what feels like a face, but it can't be, because I'm alone, right?

"Ow!" a voice exclaims from beside me.

This could get interesting, best pretend I'm asleep and hope I get away with it, so this is what I do. Deftly adopting the foetal position on the other side with all the grace of a disturbed bee I begin droning away, damn I'm good at this shit. Feeling the real or imaginary being beside me move, I hope against fruitful hope that I have got away with my unwanted slapping.

"Mitch, why did you slap me?" comes a woman's tired like question.

Shit, say something clever.

"I'm asleep!" I exclaim, yeah good job Mitch, very suave. I check my nails under the pillow to make sure they're OK, they are. I, however, may be in some sort of a predicament.

"Not fair!" comes the not quite happy reply, along with a very aggressive slap to the side of my pork chops.

Now this does not seem quite fair. My slap was a definite accident, but hers (whoever she may be!) was most certainly not. I probably shouldn't react, maybe pretend I'm still asleep. I mean, the side of my face is throbbing like a V6 engine and hurts like a bastard, but I'm sure Mitch can handle a little pain. So I sigh contentedly once more and begin my bee-like snoring. Good old Mitch, always gets out of tricky situations, maybe I should add contortionist to my repertoire of awesome skills. I think the shit that I can conjure (get it!) up is actually endless. I try and list the ways in which I am awesome: detective, counsellor, nurse, hero, God, maverick, contortionist and down right sexy Adonis. I wonder if there any others I could add to the list?

"How about irritating ballbag?" the slapper proposes from beside me.

Hmm, she can't hear me think, can she? That would be super weird. Best to stay silent and do nothing and hope she goes away. I am asleep after all. Ah, that's it. Eyes closed equals zero problems. It's so peaceful in the land of nod. Maybe I could sing a song in my head to help me zone out more. How about a nice jovial song. 'We wish you a merry...'

A slap around the side of my lamb chops, in the same bloody place, ceases my inward singing. That bloody hurt more than a bastard this time, which is a lot let me tell you. What in holy hell is this ladies problem!?

"It's June you pondering moron!" comes the disgruntled cry.

As my face heats up like the centre of the sun, I wonder if I could fry an egg on it? Then decide I had better not think anything. This psychopath beside me is some sort of she-devil. Better not piss her off. Maybe if I just don't think. Right, that's it, no more thinking. But if I don't think then nothing else happens, ever. And that would be shit. That would mean Mitch's escapades end here and that would be downright poo. Maybe if I just thought a little bit, like about how the sun is yellow but so is wee, so is the sun actually a big ball of piss? Or like if I were to eat a lump of poo, would I defecate the same lump of poo twenty four hours later, or would it be a completely different poo?

"Or how about if you like don't shut up with your nonsense then I might not kick you in the balls?" a question or a statement from my slapper friend? Hmm something else to ponder.

Bloody shitting ow! Another slap in the same God damn place! My face is literally on fire. I decide enough is enough, time to face the wrath of the slapping woman. I raise myself and prepare a proper cool as hell retort.

"Who in the holy realms of Jesus do you think you are slappering you crazy git?"

As I am now risen to halfway on the comfortable bed like a half folded ironing board, I gaze to my left. Hmm, no-one there. Very strange. Have I been imagining all this nonsense? Surely not, Mitch is all proper sane and that, he doesn't go off on wild imaginary tangents of women slapping him. I pat the bed beside me to make sure that there is in fact no-one there. All I feel is bed, but the bed is warm. My detective hat twinges with excitement, so someone was here. The plot thickens. But speaking of hats, am I still wearing mine and my cool as hell shades? The answer to both questions is no and yes. Shades on, hat not on. Maybe the vanishing slapper has stolen my headed attire. She will pay for this, whoever and wherever she may be.

Another vicious slap around my beef chops, same side, startles me once more from my inward deductive workings out.

"I am not a slapper!" comes a voice from the invisible female.

Hmm, I'm guessing it's not Gulaxa, unless he's talking in a high-pitched voice, or unless someone is squeezing his gonads. Maybe he's squeezing his own nuts, wait, what? Saying that, I wouldn't put it past the psychotic bastard, especially that weird one, the hat stealing git. Anyway, enough obsessing over nonsensical nonsense, where is this slapping git? Come on Mitch, use your skills.

Glancing around the room I see a huge window overlooking the sea, I seem to be drawn to coastal areas for some reason.

The sun is just above the horizon, making it about 815 in the morning, maybe, not really sure. Glancing to my right I see a pure white bedside table with a black alarm clock staring me in the face (personification raises it's weary head again, wait, is the personification personification now? Ow, my head hurts) with the time: 813, shit! So close. Guess I can add time worker outerer to my list of awesome skills, my talents just never cease. A painting clings to the wall on the right as if holding on for dear life, as if letting go will free it from the eternal nature of it's being. The clinginess of the frame doesn't bother me, but it is what is inside that startles my shaking heart.

Smack back in the centre, with the sea glistening behind us, is me and some other woman, a very beautiful woman I might add. Although this is not really a shock to me, I am Mitch Branning after all, ladies swoon at my feet at regular occurrences. It is the clothing we are wearing. Her in a long flowing sparkling white wedding dress, me in a dapper as hell James Bond style suit. Firstly, I look cool as hell, in fact in the photo I have one hand out and my eyes are drawn to my nails, awesome! Secondly, I guess I'm bloody married! Thirdly, who in the holy chasms of Moses is this woman? And fourthly...

Ow shtting ouch! Bloody shitting shit! Another slap, on the same side, this is just getting a little bit tedious now.

"That woman is your fucking wife you cheeky little wanker!" comes the not too happy reply.

Well I never, I think.

"Well I never!" I exclaim. "Look, let's all just calm our tits down shall we," I say calmly while patting my breasted area. I am somewhat unsure if this is the right expression to make to an angry female, so I prepare my beautiful chops for another bout of red hot heat. It doesn't arrive, maybe she has had enough of attacking poor Mitch. I'm not a bad lad, if only she would get to know me then maybe things would be tickety boo. As I ease my scrunched up face from its intended slapping I relax once more. Then, right on cue, another slap on my beautiful vegan chops, but this time I am sort of aware. As the none too friendly hand makes contact I make a sort of sound in my mouth area, which emanates deep from within my throated section, a sort of high-pitched/low pitched choking gurgling sound. I can't actually put this outlandish noise into speech marks for you people (whoever you may be!) to understand, you'll just have to use your imagination.

The invisible hand that is making sweet love to my beautiful roasted chops (or is it actually only chop because it's one side?) seems to have stayed in the same position. OK, this is nice, maybe time for some sweet tender loving, it's certainly been a while. So I gyrate like a sex starved llama against the hand, my hot flushing face now adopting a more soothing feeling, this is really nice. Better than being slapped by that God damn psycho lady. Shit! Don't think negative stuff, she might go and sooth some other dude, Mitch needs his loving as much as the next man.

After a few moments of gentle rubbing, all being done by my movements it seems, I am acutely aware that the hand is not moving. OK, this is just getting weirder and weirder. I stop my romantic swaying, reluctantly removing my nice feeling veal chop from the non-moving hand, and stare at basically nothing. Well, not actually nothing, it's the wedding photo on the wall. I reach out my hand to feel if there is actually anything there, nothing. Oh wait, I feel something. Feels like a pillow, or a lump of jelly, it feels nice, probably be OK I keep squeezing, shit! It's a tit, or a breast, to be politically correct.

Better let go, this might be seen as sexual abuse if the other person isn't moving. Once more reluctantly removing a part of my anatomy from a very nice place, I decide to adopt a more clever approach.

"Wake up! Wake up! Give me a what what!" I first snap my fingers twice in what I hope is the eye area, then cup my ear waiting for the incoming double what, none comes. Hmm, what to do the noo?

So, let's just have a little think here, get some logic going in the old grey matter. I have jumped to the future, or maybe an alternate future, where I am married to a beautiful woman. Who is invisible. And can read my mind. And who likes slapping me. So far, so normal. So what with all the freezing shit? And I don't mean cold, it's actually quite nice temperature wise in here. When I emitted my less than normal sound earlier, have I caused time to stop? Or have I just caused her to stop. I check the clock beside me: still 813. Hmm, so either the clock is screwed, or I have stopped time. If this is true, then I am just getting better and better at being awesome. Can't wait to try this shit out on someone, maybe that pony-tailed wanker outside Chinos, or maybe even that bastard Hatson. This is going to be awesome.

First things first though, what do I do now? Do I just bugger off and leave wifey here frozen in time, yearning throughout eternity for the tender loving embrace of the sexual God that is Mitch? I'm kind of guessing that when I leave she'll just become unstuck anyway. To be honest it would be quite funny as she would fall flat on her lovely breasts onto the bed, have some of that you slapping git. OK, screw it, I'm going to bugger off and have some fun. Goodbye darling, love you. Before I go though, maybe a little goodbye kiss. Which is what I do, but I think I kiss her ear instead of her lips, oh well, all's fair in love and Mitch.

SNAP DECISIONS

J esus fucking Christ! My inner core almost explodes out of my chest as I feel the heat of the plane hitting the building surround me like a fiery embrace. Then, in literally the blink of an eye, I'm somewhere else, hyperventilating with all the stress of the previous situation. Luckily my saviour is stuck in one of his pondering loops and he can't hear me gasping for breath behind him. Get a grip Gulaxa, maybe this will all be over soon. I close my eyes and take deep slow breaths, steadying my heart rate, maintaining a calm balance to my fragmented being. I would do anything now for a diazepam. I also know this would just cause more pain in the long run, got to hold out, I've got to be strong.

Gazing around I see we are in some sort of closet, I wonder if this is some sort of under the radar way of him coming out as homosexual? Maybe he doesn't know himself, and he did look at me in a weird sexual sort of way earlier. He also has most recently had a double helping of pilot crotch. I'd better prepare my nut kicking skills just in case. I've got enough going on without worrying about being molested by a time travelling pervert.

For some strange reason he has another bunch of flowers in his hand, it's actually quite poetic that he keeps arriving with these, as if the universe is trying to tell him something. Or maybe they are a way of masking the disgusting odour emanating from him, he truly does reek like a thousand unwanted smells, a shower should definitely be the next right course of action. Suddenly he snaps to attention from his inward monologue and rashly dumps the flowers into a nearby bucket. I guess he hasn't learnt the lesson someone is trying to teach him, maybe in due course. He sniffs himself and pulls a distasteful face, not very often your own body odour can repulse you, but his certainly does and I smirk outwardly at his discomfort. Good job I'm just out of view so he doesn't know I am here yet.

Walking over to the wall near the door he inspects a piece of paper attached to it, looks likes some sort of cleaning rota, but I can't quite make out the date. I try to lean forward slightly but catch my arm on the mop handle, causing my irritating jangle to alert him to my presence. God I hate that thing, better get my acting gig back on show.

"Nice closet," I say, just about hiding my insinuation of his possible gayness.

"Hey Gulaxa, how's tricks?" he enquires. What is it with him and stupid questions? No worries, I'm used to playing the dumb idiot.

"Are you insinuating I am a magician? If so, I am not. If you are not, then I am unsure as to the point of your query." Amazingly brilliant! I should be a damn comedian, how I keep a straight face is just down to the fact that I still deserve an Oscar for this performance, even after all the shit I'm going through right now. In fact, adopting a different persona is allowing me to come out of myself, a bit like mindfulness, it takes my thoughts away from my incessant craving.

"Bloody hell," he chunters. "It's a turn of phrase! How in the hell did I end up this messed up? That's rhetorical by the way. So, looks like we caused 9/11?"

Once again, he still believes that I am him in the future, not going to tell him otherwise, he'll figure it out some time, maybe. As for the idea that we had a hand in 9/11, did we? I mean, if we weren't on that plane, and we didn't cause all the chaos in the cockpit, and he didn't level us out, would we have hit where we did? Shit, that's disturbingly deep and I am not even going there, too much going on without prophesying how we may have had a hand in killing many innocent people.

"I don't think so," I reply unconvincingly.

He then goes on to say pretty much the same conclusion I have just come up with, before adding:

"Come to think of it, how would we be able to check whether we had altered anything or not? The history books would always tell us how things had happened even if we had managed to change anything. I guess the only way would be to change something we know everything about."

Very true statement, about sums up time travel down to a T, this guy is starting to get it, which could prove dangerous. Better keep him tamed

"It is unwise to tinker with time." Awesome, straight to the point and a lovely way to end the conversation, I change the subject to divert him from too many awkward questions.

"Did you bring more flowers?" I enquire while gazing into the bucket.

"Yeah, I seem to have a knack for this, maybe God is trying to tell me to give all this up and become a florist," he replies stupidly.

"Or maybe you're supposed to give them to someone you love," I say sincerely, don't know where the hell that came from. Am I becoming all sentimental with all the mayhem going on?

He picks up the flowers and bends down on one knee. Softly taking my hand in his he looks longingly into my eyes. No way! Don't you fucking dare! I will kick your stupid balls all over the known universe if you do this.

"G, I never got the chance to tell you this, but..." he begins. Just when I prepare my foot for the biggest boot of its life a loud rapping at the door startles us both. More importantly, it stops in its tracks whatever the hell he was going to say. But confirming to me that this guy fancies my arse, I'd better be careful. I'm keeping my back to the wall from now on.

"Get a move on in there," a harsh American accent bellows. "Your break finished ten minutes ago. Toilet blocked on floor sixty, explosive diarrhoea the likes of which I have never seen, get on it."

Where in holy hell are we? I mean, I could say America, but that might not strictly be true. Just because the voice outside is American, it doesn't mean that's where we are, we could be anywhere. And the 60th floor! Wait, oh shit, I think I know where we are.

"Yes boss," my newly crowned queen replies in a very shit accent, he certainly does not have my talents.

"We're all going for drinks after work at O'Hara's, see you there if you ever get that toilet fixed," the guy outside bellows once more. Don't know why he didn't just come in to be honest, but it's pretty bloody good that he didn't. Firstly, we don't belong here. Secondly, he would have been greeted to quite an indecent proposal.

"Certainly," he replies in a completely different accent entirely, which sounds more Irish than American, this guy is shit, we are definitely screwed now. But no, footsteps draw away, how did he get away with that?

"And the Oscar for best actor goes to...me!" he stands up to accept mock applause from his imaginary crowd. The only one getting an Oscar is me you dumb dickhead! My discontentment must show on my face.

"Tough crowd," he exclaims. "Right, time to go clean up some shit. We have no time to waste, for shit is what is giving us a bad taste."

Very strange turn of phrase to use, is he mocking my awesome cool as hell statement from earlier? Or was it later? I can't remember any more. He proceeds to grab the mop and bucket as if he is an actual cleaner or something, is he seriously going to clean up some crap? And wearing that clothing as well? He certainly is not thinking straight. Then right before my very eyes, as I am wondering about his sanity, he seem to literally come to his senses and pauses momentarily. He slightly opens the door to peek out. As he does so a multitude of people chattering along with the click clack of high heeled shoes and polished brogues attacks my wobbling brain. Thankfully he closes the door, but the footsteps still seem to echo inside my brain like ants throwing a house party. Prancing over to a nearby locker he opens the door, sending a foul stench of his body odour my way, thanks for that pal. But at least the stench distracts me from the insect infestation within my infected mind.

Grabbing a set of filthy grey coveralls from inside I see him look at them suggestively. He's not seriously thinking of putting them on, is he? It is very evident that they're two sizes too small for him. I'm guessing either his eyesight is screwed or he simply does not give a shit, because he clumsily climbs into the dirty disguise before standing in front of me looking absolutely ridiculous.

"How do I look?" he asks. With a slight risk and a drop in my usual monotone, I decide to be brutally honest.

"Like an idiot," I say with a smirk.

"I love you too," he pouts before twirling like an overweight ballerina. "Off to the ball we go!"

Well, this could be interesting. Better make myself invisible, this will surely cause him some unwanted attention and maybe add some light humour to my experience, every distraction is welcome. Exiting the closet with all the grace of a three-legged giraffe on steroids, while wheeling his new companions, he holds the door open for me, prompting a curious look from a guy in a suit who's walking by. He must think he's nuts, how this makes me smirk. 'Hank' nods and doffs a cap he isn't wearing and closes the door behind me.

I let him walk ahead of me as I observe how stupid he looks, this is very evident in the many passers-by who point and laugh in his general direction. Damn, this is hilarious. Adding a swagger to his walk increases my inward laughter and I struggle to hold my serious face. When he starts belting out Without Me by Sir Slim of Shady, getting pretty much all the words wrong, I just have to let go. I let him walk ahead and burst out laughing, thankfully the noise of the many business people masks my chuckling. Then he seems to stop dead in his tracks, right in the middle of the hallway, what is he doing? Then he continues on and goes seriously over the top on the chorus, grabbing his crotch and starts waving his hands aloft like he's in his own personal rave. The smile is immediately wiped from my face, there's something wrong with him, this is not normal behaviour. He seems to be warping from one emotion to the next, this could spell trouble. I've caught up to him by this point and as we reach the lift doors he looks over, seeing the worried expression on my face. He performs a less than adequate twirl and produces a high pitched Michael Jackson scream as the doors magically open, good timing my weird and wonderful friend.

A vast amount of businessmen and women spew from the lift like a flock of geese, causing me to dodge them all like I'm dodging bullets. Once everyone is inside the same scenario occurs but from outside to in, once again I'm bobbing and weaving with expert precision, although I do jab one lady in the ribs, causing her to look back accusingly at the invisible poker. This makes me smile somewhat, I forgot how much fun it was being invisible. Once the lift is pretty much full 'Hank' squeezes himself and his mop and bucket inside, leaving no room for little old me. I feel a pang of sadness stab at my sorrowful heart as he mouths the word sorry at me. I watch forlornly as the doors close on my only friend in this world.

I ponder briefly what is actually binding us together and also how far this strand would stretch to. It obviously pulls us together across different times, but how about distance. Could I theoretically jump on a plane now and bugger off to a different country and leave him here? Or would I snap back to him like an enthusiastic rubber band? I wonder if I could just wait here on this floor and then magically appear next to him on the 60th, that would make life a bit easier. But if it didn't work then I would be stuck here for however long and, to be honest (and this hurts me to say), I think I'd miss him.

I gaze over to what I assume is the staircase entrance and think briefly about walking up sixty floors. I dismiss this thought just as quickly as it arrived, screw that for a game of soldiers, I'll just wait for the next lift. Before I have a chance to take in any more of my surroundings I feel a very weird sensation in my entire being, as if I am being stretched, as if I am being pulled apart from inside out. It does not feel nice. I let out a little scream and drop to my knees, causing a security guard to stop his walking by and glance in my direction.

"Don't worry pal," I say through gritted teeth. "Your day is about to get much worse."

Just as I feel I am about to literally snap in half the pain instantly subsides. I am stood in another hallway watching a man with his trousers around his ankles wailing like a banshee while good ole 'Hank' watches on. Well, seems my previous questions have been answered, better not get more than sixty floors distance away from stinky man here, that was not a pleasant experience. He walks past me, doffing his invisible cap like an idiot.

"Nice to see you sir, off to the shitter me old mucker," he quips.

Following him like a faithful companion as he eases open the toilet door my nostrils are immediately attacked by a devastating aroma. Wow! Someone has either died in here, or has had a really bad poo, then died. Or many people have had many poos and all have died. I think you can gather that it smells pretty nasty in here. I feel like waiting outside, but decide against that just in case he needs me, what for I have no idea.

Opening up the first cubicle I lean over his shoulder and see thick brown liquid overflowing onto what was once a pristine clean marble floor. However, this is not really the major cause of discontentment here. Bobbing on the top with one eye winking at me is none other than Derek, seemingly following me throughout the channels of time, forever cursing me for ruining his life, for causing him untold misery. Even in death this man cannot have any peace, and my heart shatters a little more. How he has got here is beyond me. Who in their right mind would firstly chop off his head, then bring him here to parade him like a sick joke? Well, seeing as only two of us knew where Derek was, it can only be one of us, my bets are on him, the sick bastard! Although I wouldn't put it past either of the other Laxas.

"I think someone is screwing with us," he says in a suspicious tone.

"Maybe," I reply neutrally, not wanting to aggravate him.

"What about you MB, any clues?" I look at him puzzled, who the hell is MB?

"I think it was Gulaxa," he says in a weird voice, sloshing about the mop in the bucket. Is MB mop and bucket? "He's a dodgy little bastard who always buggers off when the shit hits the fan," he continues in his mocking voice.

Does he think I have something to do with this? I gaze at him, trying to gauge some sort of insight into his brain. For a few moments I study him. His eyes glaze over, as if he is not really here. I'm guessing he is in one of his pondering loops. I watch his lips moving ever so slowly, unable to make out any of the words. Suddenly his face seems to soften and fall, the humour that was once in his features is gone now. A look of complete dejection, as if the whole world is resting on his shoulders, falls across his face like a deathly shadow. What is happening to him? He blinks solemnly, waking himself from his inward trance.

"I'm sorry pal," he says softly. "I can't do this any more."

Leaving MB and myself in the cubicle he leaves the room. I'm seriously worried about him. I follow him outside, his shoulders are slumped, his whole demeanour is slouched. It is as if an invisible weight is bearing down upon him. Has he just been overcome with a snap depression? Is that even possible? I thought that stuff was a gradual thing? But saying that, he has been acting weird for a while, maybe this was always going to happen at some point. Ignoring the strange looks from passers-by he walks over to the window and gazes out. What should I do? Can I help him? Can I do anything? I decide all I can do is hug him, like we hugged each other before, that felt so real, so right.

Before I make my way over to him I hear him whisper something, something about an old friend, then he disappears from view. Before I have a chance to question anything I see who he was talking to. As the giant nose of an unwelcome death plane crashes into the window with an earth shattering scream, I close my eyes and hope that my death is a quick one.

BOXED IN

Right then, who to try out my new found skills on? Maybe I should try them out on myself, maybe go back to when I jumped with my little baby and freeze myself to take my lovely moggy back. Wait, maybe that's what I do anyway. Am I already planning a future paradox like scenario? But when would I take the cat? Surely I would notice if I stopped frozen in time, or maybe not. Or maybe, just maybe, I shouldn't jump into something too extreme straight away. Probably best to check it out on some random person first, or maybe a random animal, or maybe both, just to make sure it wasn't a stroke of luck.

I arrive with all the grace of a love sick penguin smack bang in the middle of a busy town centre, in a phone box, checking my nails. Superman thought he was cool with his billowing cape and phone box shenanigans, well move over underpants boy, the real man is here. I also attempt a clothes change while in mid-jump, never tried it before so thought I would give it a go. It sort of worked. I did envisage an all leather biker type appearance. However, I seem to be wearing a jet black tinted motorbike crash helmet, a ripped pair of red jeans, and a women's beige blouse which is untucked, and no shoes, but I am wearing socks, albeit Christmas socks with little elf's dancing gaily on them. Oh well, at least I'm wearing clothes, this is a win I reckon. Here to save the day, here to literally (hopefully) save the known universe, and all other universes which are not known. Mitch "cool as ice" Branning – time travelling extraordinaire, stopper of things that are goeth. When the going gets tough, the tough doesn't get going, Mitch just stops it all before it has a chance to start with his mighty power. He is a God, all will kneel...

"Excuse me," a voice from outside the enclosed space chirps.

Why do people insist on disturbing me in mid-flow? Do they not know of whom I am? I turn my gaze towards the unwelcome visitor, bouncing my helmet off the window, this is probably not appropriate attire for a tight space. Who am I faced with? You guessed it, the pony-tailed wanker. This could get interesting. But we aren't outside Chino's, yet this creepy weirdo is still hanging out around telephone boxes, maybe this guy has a fetish or something. Maybe this is my chance to save him from his perverse addictive behaviour. I am a counsellor after all, and a nurse, maybe I could add therapist into my repertoire of awesomeness, only one way...

An irritating tapping against the window once again breaks my train of thought.

"You'd better not be pissing in there!?" Not sure if this is a statement or a question, hence the exclamation and question mark, you lot can figure it out, again.

I decide to have a little fun rather than taking things all seriously. I just politely shake, but also nod, my head. That'll confuse the irritating git. I also do a little shimmy with one of my legs, hopefully imitating a release of urination down my inner thigh. I do this while staring straight at him, with my tinted visor drawn down, hiding my dark eyes. I then shake the other leg in what I hope is comical fashion, the pony-tailed one seems unamused. In fact, he looks downright outraged. This pleases me, does that make me a bad person? Mitch thinks not. I think I may have to try some interaction with this somewhat disturbed individual, maybe calm his tits down.

I fumble clumsily for the sliding door mechanism, pulling it closed rather than shut, further causing my newfound friend untold exasperation. I love how his face is all red and flustered, he looks like a constipated rooster. As he attempts to slide open the door from his side, I hold tightly from my end, grinning inside my darkened globe, master of my own internal world.

"It's stuck like a bastard!" I mumble through my visor.

"What?" he asks, cupping his ear in comical fashion, only one reply necessary methinks.

"Give me a what what?" I cup my own ear, mimicking his action but improving on it ten-fold.

A look of possible recognition falls across his reddened face, did I say this same phrase earlier? This leads me to believe that at least the time I am in is after the time before, which makes no sense whatsoever, but sort of does in a weird time travel sort of way. I decide to use a diversionary tactic. I pull open the door with the strength of a thousand dead rats, causing it to crash against the side of the frame. The once well held and perfectly sturdy glass shatters instantly like an overworked cymbal, drumming against myself and my compadre before clattering noisily to the floor. Oops, I think.

"Oops," I mumble.

The pony-tailed one looks at me with what I sense is complete awe at my supreme power, I also get the impression he may want to make love to me right now. But sorry pal, no time for sexual shenanigans, I need to...

"What is wrong with you?" he asks politely.

"I'm fine me old mucker," I mutter.

"I can't hear you, lift your visor up!" he shouts.

I lift it ever so slightly, don't want this bastard recognising me even more, or falling deeply in love with me like everyone else does. Right, say something clever.

"Nice hair," I blurt out, good job Mitch.

The look is one of either complete lust or utter contempt, let's go with the former shall we, always seems a shame to let Negative Nancy take centre stage the light hogging cowbag.

"Erm, thank you," the pony-tailed one replies, blushing somewhat and lowering his gaze. I guess my sarcastic comment has completely gone over his moronic head.

"So, what seems to be the problem pal?" I enquire while holding my chin for effect, well actually holding the chin area of my awesome helmet, suppose it still has the same cool as hell outcome.

His blushing disappears immediately and his usual angry face reappears, here we go, this should be interesting.

"Well, as per article 52, paragraph 5 of the sex offenders register, person or persons are not allowed to urinate inside a public area," he says this in a very monotonous tone, making me believe he is being deadly serious.

"OK," I reply, allowing him to continue unabated.

"Furthermore, person or persons may be liable to prosecution if such offences are committed. Therefore I, as a member of the British order, am compelled by law and order to command you to cease and desist. If you resist my attempts at citizens arrest, I will be obliged to use physical force."

"Hmm," I mutter through the small gap in my visionary area. "Well, hitherto me old mucker, I know not of what you speak. I am a simple man on a simple mission to save the world, I have no time for your haberdashery. Henceforth, and with great forthrightness, I hereby sentence you to soddens the off." I end my awesome monologue with a little curtsey for no reason whatsoever, while banging my helmet against both sides of my enclosed interior, and as I rise from my reverent like bow I check my nails like a God damn legend.

My newfound friend seems to stare at me for a little longer than is necessary, people seem to have a habit of doing this around me. I'm guessing I have a kind of loving affect on all who come into contact with my awesomeness. I watch him blink once, twice, three times a lady, and then he does something completely unexpected. Pulling open his duffel jacket slightly I see the butt of a handgun protruding from his waistband. I'd recognise a Berretta 9mm anywhere, I'm starting to like this long haired prick. I also feel a tad nervous, which is not at all like Mitch, he is usually as cool as ice in these type of situations.

"This is my friend," the pony-tailed one says quietly, and although I can hear him perfectly well, I decide to toy with him.

"Can't hear you pal!" I shout at the top of my lungs, which makes a passer-by glance over in our direction.

He looks at me blankly, unsure of whether I am extracting the urine, or if I can actually not hear him.

"This is my friend," he starts again, a little louder, but not loud enough for my liking, let's get this guy screaming.

"No comprende pal!" I boom while pointing to my hearing area and shaking my noggin, which bashes against the sides of the phone box like a clattering movie projector.

I sense a hint of anger in his features, I think he knows I am screwing with him. Just as I think he is about to shout I watch his hand reaching for his secluded weapon, this could get interesting. Might this be the time to try out my newfound time stopping skills? I think so, what do I do again? I try and remember back to my marriage room, the sweet sensation of roasted pork chops. I begin emitting a gurgling sound from my swallowing area, watching as the expression on the man outside the box changes to one of confusion, but not stopping his hand from advancing towards his cool deadly weapon. Maybe I should fluctuate the pitch of my gurgle slightly, which I do, almost choking on my own spit. Surely there's a better way to do this. But wait, it's working, his hand is slowing, slowing, and it's stopped. Boom! I am the master of space and time! I do a little jig in the phone box, bashing my head against the sides, causing splinters to caress across the remaining glass like ripples of frozen flame.

Ceasing my awesome dance routine I gaze at the stuck still statue before me, his face with that same unsure look upon it, his hand touching the butt of his weapon. This is so cool. What is even more awesome is the view I see behind him. All the bustling shoppers who were going about their busy days have stopped too, every single one of them. I see a boy sat on a nearby bench with a look of bewilderment on his face as the ice cream from his cone is halfway to the floor. Tears are imminent in his eyes as the devastation dawns harshly upon him, I feel your pain pal. I see a beautiful embrace between two lovers, a moment of absolute beauty that could be forever frozen in time, a love that will stand the test of the ages. Lastly I see a rather comical sight as a huge seagull in mid-pluck as it steals a battered sausage from a man's hands as his literal wingman distracts him from the other side.

I am quite literally the master of time right now. I feel more like a God than I ever have done. I feel more powerful than the sun. Speaking of the sun, have I stopped that from erm, sunning? Or producing fusion? Or whatever the hell it does? How far has this time stopping gone? Have I stopped the whole universe? My mind boggles at this profound possibility and I ponder what this might mean. As my racing thoughts interpose with each other I see movement from within the crowd. Has someone managed to break my time spell? Must be super powerful whoever it is, I am a God right now, so whoever this is must be some awesome dude.

As the figure draws nearer I recognise who it is, it's none other than Mr Round, the one with the awesome nose, and quite possibly the creator of me, I think. Wearing blue jeans, smart black trainers, and what seems to be a Death Stranding hoody, he strides purposefully in my direction. Shit, is he angry? I'll just freeze the bastard, no-one messes with Mitch. Before he reaches me he stops besides the boy who's life is about to end because he dropped his ice cream. Damn, this guy is going to save the day, how bloody awesome. But then again, maybe not. He stoops down and gulps the ice cream into his waiting gob and continues sauntering over in a cool as hell way.

Standing beside the pony-tailed one he chomps noisily away, fanning his mouth as I did earlier while dancing from one foot to the other, I like this guy.

"Nice to..." I begin, but am stopped mid-speech as he holds one finger up in the universal sign of 'one moment please'.

Once he gets himself under control he stops his leg hopping and stares at me intently. I wait for him to speak, he does not.

"Nice to meet you Mr Roundy man, sir!" I say, snapping off a sharp salute, which seems to be the appropriate greeting here.

"At ease, soldier," comes the awesome reply and salute. "So, pardon my French, but what the fuck are you doing?"

Hmm, straight to the point, I like the cut of this man's jib, whatever a jib may be.

"Well..." I begin.

"Never mind," he says, cutting me off like an irritating wanker. "And think of me as an irritating wanker again and I shall erase your entire existence. Look, it's like this, stop messing around and go and find the cat, again. Find the cat, save the universe, it's as simple as that. I can't be bothered coming in here every time. The last time was bloody fluke, how you ended up in my home as I was writing was complete nuts, I didn't even write that, so God knows what happened there. And as for me being here? I have no idea what is going on any more."

I stare at him with what is probably a dumbstruck look on my face.

"OK," I reply.

"The thing is," he continues. "I have no idea what is going to happen next, so I tell you what, you figure it out. But the cat is the key to everything. Oh, and before I go, it's up to you, but you don't need to make a silly sound to stop time, just think it like you do while time travelling. Good luck Mitch, you're one hell of a guy."

With his last sentimental gesture he vanishes into nothingness, leaving me staring at the space he once occupied. Things are getting weirder and weirder here folks, and if the writer has no clue as to what is going on, what hope do we all have!? I know one thing though, it's going to be fun. I emit my time freezing gurgle (just because it feels awesome) and just before the pony-tailed one retrieves his killing weapon, I flip him the bird and continue on my merry way.

LIGHTING THE FUSE

Just as a shard of glass came hurtling towards my warding off hands with fire and fury I pinged back into the past, or the future, I don't really give a shit any more. My heart-rate is pounding like a jack-hammer, each thump of my life giving muscle sends a shock wave of adrenaline deep into my shattered core. This shit is becoming too much to take, I was barely hanging on as it is with the withdrawals. Now ending up scattered amongst the ages like some time travelling tourist, doomed for eternity to snap into varying degrees of mayhem and torture. I don't know how long I can keep this charade up for.

Gathering my senses I see we are back at Chino's, he seems to be drawn to this place once more, maybe this restaurant has some significance in the grand scheme of things. Or maybe he just came back to see his mother. I see a fresh bouquet of flowers beside her, I bet he brought them with him. At last the infamous travelling flowers have made their way to their rightful destination. I wonder if they were always the same bunch of flowers, like the mirror and something else I can't quite recall, forever caught in a time loop, destined to be a pawn in the ever-weaving web of time chess.

I watch on intently as they both say they love each other and my heart breaks a little. I can actually feel the deep devotion they have for one another coming off them in waves, once again I feel a pang of regret at not having this precious connection with my own mother. I'd never thought about this before, but maybe I could go back one day and try and reconcile with her. That is if I ever get my powers back. I guess that all depends on him, my ever pondering companion. Also my mentally unstable companion, that was seriously messed up what happened in the towers; one minute he was fine and dandy, laughing and joking, the next he was severely depressed and hell-bent on ending his life. They always warned us about this nasty side effect of time travel, but he never received the induction, did he? Guess that's all on me though. Maybe one day I can make amends.

I glance around the room, trying to locate the other versions of him. One is sat a few tables away, pretty much in a straight line from this very table, nattering away to a waiter. Why in the holy shitting hell did he come back here? Does he not know the rules around time travel and paradoxes? I'm guessing not, that's why he came here again the nutter. Where's the other one? I lean around a pillar and see him sat at a table near the toilet. Well, at least this one is out of view, he has some sense at least. Maybe not dress sense though, what is that God-awful hat he is wearing? Looks like a woman's wedding hat, this guy is definitely suffering from severe mental health issues.

As he sits down on the chair I stumble slightly against the pillar, causing my bracelet to alert him to my presence, opening quip time.

"Nice perfume," I say from behind him as I breathe in a welcome fragrance.

I see him flinch slightly which causes me a little pang of joy. I watch on intently from behind him as they both converse, once more inhaling the aroma of sweet perfume, which actually seems to be coming from him. I'm guessing this is her attempt at covering up his distinct smelly aroma. Although the stench of his body odour and various other smells are still very evident, as least the perfume adds a welcome distraction, well played.

"You OK darling?" she says. "You look like you've seen a ghost."

Wow, how very poetic, if only she knew.

"I'm fine mum, how did the interview go?" he asks her.

"I think it went well, all in the big guy's hands now," she replies while holding both hands together in silent prayer.

This is such an angelic pose that I feel compelled to walk across and stand behind her, inhaling her scent deeply and meaningfully. I close my eyes and enjoy the moment, feeling the peace and serenity of this brief break in time, holding back for just a moment the constant anxiety threatening to claw away at my collapsing being. She seems to shiver before me, as if sensing my presence.

"Oh," she says. "Somebody just walked over my grave, I felt all cold all of a sudden."

I glance back across the table, seeing my master attempting to convey a message to me. His mother has the menu in front of her vision as he tries all sorts of weird and wonderful gestures to get me to politely go away. I struggle to hold onto my mask and smirk slightly at him, damn this is fun. He then proceeds to wobble his jaw and rock his neck from side to side, he looks like he's overdosing on some illegal cocktail of God knows what, what is he doing? As the waiter appears beside me, I guess he was trying not to look like an escaped mental patient, and failing miserably.

"Are we ready to order?" the waiter asks politely, giving his obviously disturbed patron a puzzling look.

As they order their food I feel my presence here is no longer needed and proceed to venture off to find some peace and quiet, I'm sure I'll come back when I'm needed. You never know, I might find some little blue bastards somewhere, but do I really want one? That is the age old question I suppose. I know those things are the cause of all the pain and anxiety I feel right now, but I also know they will alleviate all of the internal suffering I feel within me. I guess this is my own mind-bending paradox that I have to circumnavigate.

As I leave the doting mother and son to converse I head away down a nearby corridor. Arriving at the intersection I see Batman rolling a red barrel down beside the window that overlooks the street outside, a very odd sight to see. Didn't I see Batman earlier with his mum in tow? Surely this must be the same person, I can't imagine anyone else wearing the same attire, that would just be down right insane. But everything about my life right now is pretty much messed up beyond belief. I decide to introduce myself, what could possibly go wrong?

"Hey, need a hand there buddy?" I enquire jovially.

Batman briefly stops his momentum and stares in my direction.

"Ah, yes, it's you. Did you find the cat?" he asks, leading me to believe this is another version of me from earlier, or later. I'm guessing it's not Catlaxa by his seemingly decent grasp of the English language. So, I reckon we call him Batlaxa, what an awesome name.

"Erm, not yet," I reply. "Been kind of busy with other shit. Hey, are you me from the future? If so, when do I get my powers back? That bastard has screwed me up good and proper, I'm attached to him like a guide dog."

He chuckles heartily, not sure whether to get offended by this.

"Awesome simile by the way. Well, yes and no."

Hmm, not really great with explaining things is he, what an arsehole.

"I'm not an arsehole!" he retorts, standing facing me with his hands on his hips.

"I didn't..." I begin.

"Shut it! Quick, throw me that lighter on the table, I need to blow this fucking place up, it's a super hub for loads of versions of that damn fool!" he says this while standing up the red barrel and unravelling a spool of wire.

"How rude!" I say, folding my hands across my breasted area.

"Look! Throw me the lighter or I'll take you to your birth and slit your moaning throat!" he orders in a very menacing tone.

Better do as he says, I have no powers at all and he seems kind of serious, and aggressive, I hope I don't turn out like that in the future. I really hope this is a multiverse type scenario, would probably make a lot more sense, not that I understand any of this shit any more.

Just before I throw him the lighter I hear some beeping of horns and some people shouting outside. Oddly I see a very peculiar sight of someone wearing a motorcycle helmet, red jeans, a blouse and no shoes. Are they Christmas socks? That can only be one person, it's the bloody idiot. How many versions of them are here now? Guess this is some sort of super hub, I throw Batlaxa the lighter and decide to get back to the original idiot, that is if he is even the original one.

Heading back into the eating area I see mother and son holding hands conversing across the table. He seems deep in talks with her and doesn't seem to notice my arrival, I guess I wasn't missed and this actually fills me with a tinge of sadness.

"...why do you ask?" I hear his mother say.

He glances in my direction with that look on his face he so often has before he does something stupid, where the hell are we going now? But it's probably a good thing as this place will be a fiery hellhole pretty soon.

"Mum, hold my hands," he says while gripping her hands softly. "Let's go see grandad."

I guess we're going back to the past, this could get interesting. Within a blink of an eye they disappear. I glance around the restaurant and no-one notices a bloody thing, how is that even possible?

"Ah, that's better!" I hear a familiar voice chime in from behind me. "Oh right! I exclaim loudly and everyone notices, but when two people disappear into thin air no-one bats an eyeball! Idiots!"

Guess someone is as perturbed as I am about the case of the disappearing people. I feel a huge whoosh of hot air head in my direction, shit, I hope I don't get burn to a cri...

BROKEN PEACE

F ind the cat, save the universe, find the cat, save the universe, find the cat, save the whole God damn universe! It's as simple as that, he says. But how can it be that simple? I wonder if he knows I lost the cat? Well, he should do, he wrote it, didn't he? How in the hell can he not know what is going to happen in his own story? Surely all decent writers have some sort of plan as to what is going on, maybe he isn't a decent writer, maybe he's just an amateur writing on the side while he has a day job, that would be funny as shit. But wait, does that mean I am just a little side project for him to work on when he gets some spare time in his ever so important day? Makes me sound quite worthless if truth be told. But if we're being totally honest with ourselves here, the fact that I am just a figment of someone's imagination makes me feel somewhat less than awesome. Does that mean everything I have done up to now are just pointless lines in a stupid novel? With no real meaning to any of it? I really cannot accept this, isn't life what we make of it? Isn't our life our own to do with what we will? Come to think of it, at least I am the controller of my own destiny, I am master of my own fate, and that makes me feel God damn amazing! So Negative Nancy, you can piss right off!

So, back to the cat, back to saving the universe. No point me going back to my old home and swiping the cat from myself, that would be pretty damn stupid, and would highly likely cause some chaos with the whole space time continuum. Also, the idea of freezing myself when I held the cat before I lost him seems kind of dumb as well, what if I am immune to freezing myself? I mean, not like immune to getting cold, I could just jump to the top of Mount Everest and freeze my nuts off, if I wanted to, which I don't, so I'm not going to. No, I have to come up with a dastardly plan to solve this mind-bending puzzle. Let's try and think of this logically: I had hold of the cat when I jumped, I imagined an ice cream in my hand when I arrived, and that replaced the cat. So, by all reckoning the cat is where the ice cream is, was, somewhere. Shit! Not really much help. I can't exactly travel to everywhere on the planet that sells ice cream. But the cat can't have just disappeared into nothingness, that would make no sense, it must have rematerialised somewhere. Come on Mitch, think!

"Excuse me?" a lady enquires from my left. "Would you mind moving?"

I turn around and take in my surroundings. I am perched birdlike upon a bench overlooking a row of gravestones as a light drizzle falls noiselessly in the air. A crow stares at me forlornly from a nearby gravestone, as if sensing that I'm not supposed to be here. Wait, these words, and this place, seem familiar. Shit, grandad's graveyard, again! That means, oh double shit, this could get interesting. Good job I have a helmet on, I hope. I whack my head to make sure, yeah, helmet still on and visor down. Things always work...

"Please, young man, my boy and I just need to rest our legs, would you scoot over a little please?" my mother's cleansing voice ever so politely asks.

"Of course mum, I mean son. I mean, yeah, whatever, I'm cool as ice, so no worries," I blurt out. Cool as ice Mitch? More like silly as a sausage. Good job my visor is down and she can probably not make out any of the shit I am waffling.

I do as asked and move from atop my perch on the back of the bench to sit with one leg over the other in a feminine like pose (quite apt with with the blouse I am wearing I suppose), holding my chin for effect while gazing out at the vast array of perfectly lined gravestones. My mother and the younger me sit down on the bench, both seemingly unaware of my odd attire. Although the boy (me) does give me (him) a sideways glance, causing me to have a massive jolt of deja vu, like a surge of electricity coursing through my veins. Wow, this is a very surreal feeling. But what is more disturbing is the continuation of the experience within my fracturing mind. The helmeted one (me) turns and runs away after some sort of animal, a very black animal, a feline looking beast.

I snap out of my external reverie to notice a black shape skulking around behind one of the gravestones, is that my furry buddy? Guess I'd better get my ninja stealth mode activated and start following the little bastard. Not before bidding a fond farewell to my family though.

"Nice to meet you fine people, I'm off for a little jaunt for some pussy, pussy cat I mean. Bye mum, I mean me, I mean you two. See you earlier, or later." With these nonsensical words I vanish off into the night (even though it's day time) to chase down the black beast of Blighty with all the grace of a raving lunatic.

Now, where has that little git got to? Good job I don't have any shoes on. My Xmas socks are a perfect addition to my super secret stealth moves, cushioning my footsteps like smothering a baby, probably not the nicest of similes in the world, but I'm sure you get the meaning. Inching around a rather large gravestone I hear the nearby caw of a crow, I wonder if it is the same one? Still shouting at me in its own warped way, cursing me for disturbing the flow of time with the constant ripple effect I keep creating. I wonder how many such dips into the stream of the universe's continuum I can keep attempting before I cause a tidal surge of chaos? No point worrying about such trivial matters, I'm sure I'll find out in due course. More important things to address right now, where's that bloody cat vamoosed off to?

A soft meow from what seems a few feet away jolts me from my pointless musing, that sweet mewing sounds very familiar, surely it must be him. As I creep around another huge monolithic gravestone I see my little baby perched (non-birdlike) upon a waist high railing surrounding the entrance to the church. Found you, you little bastard.

"Here Gulaxa, here boy," I chime, as if calling a canine and not a feline. This familiar quip reminds me of my old pal, the human one of course, causing a slight pang of regret inside my aching heart, damn I miss him.

I stop a couple of feet away, assessing my old furry friend as he elegantly licks his butt, what a supreme being he is. Cats are definitely from a different planet, I'm sure of it. So regal and heavenly in their demeanour, I bet there's a planet far away inhabited by talking cats who rule over their human slaves. Maybe that's why they act the way they do here, would make a lot of sense I reckon. I edge closer, within reach now, my super stealth movements making me almost invisible to this super hearing creature. Damn I'm good at this shit. A twig snaps underfoot, causing Gulaxa to tense up momentarily and glance in my direction, shit! Just before he attempts to bugger off I entrap him in my clutches like I've just clasped the holy grail.

"Got you!" I cry triumphantly, as I pull him close to my chest and rock him gently back and forth.

"Rock-a-bye fatty, on the tree tops," I begin to sing softly. "When the wind blows, your flab will rock. When the bough breaks, your fat will break free. And down will come fatty, and go for a wee." Ah, my old nursery rhyme for my little baby, guess I can now add poet to my awesome repertoire, damn I'm good.

Feeling and hearing my sweet chubby feline's mesmerising purring I feel completely at peace with life. Rocking him slowly back and forth we both flow gently with the soft breeze that seems to cocoon us with its swaying arms. I feel as though things are starting to finally fall into place. I'm at last finding atonement after all the weird and wonderful escapades throughout my journey. I'm sure nothing else weird will happen now, I think it might be time to go for a nice little rest somewhere. Maybe a nice little cottage atop a picturesque mountain, where me and my buddy can live out our days in peace and serenity.

"Shitballs!" I hear a familiar voice exclaim from way off in the distance.

Nothing to worry about here folks, we're way out of range of all that nonsense. Just me and my little chubby checker gently swaying in the breeze like dancing angels. The drizzle still falling without a sound creates a mist which coats the both of us with a fine dew, kind of reminds me of a time before now, a time that I had long since forgotten. Wait, this has happened before, possibly in a dream, or a vision. Once more I receive a massive dose of deja vu, as if I am right now reliving a moment from my future.

Something happens. Something terrible. Someone takes him. No. I won't let them. I won't let anyone take him again. He's mine! He's my little baby! I feel a rage building inside. A surge of adrenaline. I can't control it. It is too strong. But the feeling, the devastating feeling that someone is coming to take him, fuels the fire. A flash of inspiration. A flash of anger. Before me. Batlaxa, grinning. Running. No. No! NO! I push towards him with all the will I have. I watch as he fades to nothingness. I watch as his face crumples into emptiness. I watch as I end his life. I am a killer. I am a murderer. I am wrong. I must leave this place. I am broken. Once more, I am lost.

Holding my friend tightly to my chest, I concentrate on him and him alone. Then we jump together to escape the darkness that is death.

SAVING GRACE

Arriving into a place of extreme heat I at first thought I was being burnt alive by the explosion that rocked the restaurant, damn it's hot in here. I pat myself down with my non-jangling hand to make sure I'm not on fire, all seems good, no flaming pieces of burning flesh, my suit is none the wiser and still in almost perfect condition. As I glance down at myself I seem to have lost a lot of weight recently, I look as gaunt as a starving sailor after a hellish outing at sea. I really need to look after myself more, I've let myself go not just mentally but physically. Maybe after all this is over I could check into some sort of clinic to restore my internal and external self. However, now is not the time, best prepare myself for more insane shit. Standing in another closet (maybe this guy really is a little bit on the gay side, would explain a lot of his previous behaviour) I see him and his mother about to exit the room while holding hands, this saddens me somewhat, but I manage my opening quip just about in time.

"Nice closet," I say gloomily.

"See you later alligator," comes his reply while smirking at me, wanker!

Now what? Do I follow him or just wait about here? From what he said before he jumped I'm guessing he has gone to see his grandad in the past, do I really I need to witness this? I think not. Once more I am overcome with sadness, a deep feeling that I am no longer wanted or needed. I feel as obsolete as a jilted lover, destined to live my life alone and unwanted, both by him and the world around me. I am nothing. I am a useless stain on this unforgiving world. I sit down on a solitary stool placed in the corner and face the wall. Holding my head in my hands I begin to cry uncontrollably. Huge racking sobs which make me vibrate like a jackhammer, I feel broken to my very core as my whole world comes crumbling down with all the grace of a dying sun.

I don't know how long I stay like this, it feels like an eternity. Gradually I manage to pull myself together somewhat and cease my pitying cries. Damn I'm such a weakling, when did I become so soft? Not so long back I was on top of the world, a king sitting high and mighty upon my throne, surveying all the minions below me with disgust and distaste. But maybe that was the whole problem, maybe this has been my defect all along, thinking I was better than everyone else. The longer I spend time with my new friend the more I succumb to my own internal fears, of which there are many. How has my life come down to this? Facing a wall, all alone, sobbing like a little child. I need to snap myself out of this morbid self-reflection and find my fighting spirit once more.

Raising myself up into a standing position I raise my hands high above my head, reaching out to the heavens, trying to touch the hand of God, that is if he has not forsaken me like everyone else. I wouldn't blame Him either, what have I achieved really? My life is, and has been, an unspectacular failure of biblical proportions, of which I have been the entire orchestrator of my own disastrous downfall. Not once have I bothered to take into account how my insane journey throughout space and time has affected all those I have come into contact with. My own selfish way of thinking has completely overridden whatever slither of human emotion I may have had. Coupled with occasional suicidal tendencies and varying addictive behaviour, my life has quite obviously been a car crash waiting to happen. Maybe this is my rock bottom. Maybe I needed to get to this place so I could rise up stronger and become a better person.

But somehow this deep, darkening depression manages to push me back down with invisible force, plonking me harshly into the lonely seat with a deathly thud. Woe is me as my world once again begins crumbling around my battered soul. My shoulders slump as my brief feeling of hope and gratitude is crushed with the might of darkness that swamps as viscous as quicksand, embalming me with feelings of darkness and decay. How in holy hell have I let it come to this? My life is nothing. I am nothing. I might as well end my life. No-one would miss me. The only person who ever cared for me is off gallivanting with his mother, someone who truly loves him, something I can never have.

Glancing to my left the solitary light from the room bounces off a glinting object laid beside a mop and bucket. I reach down to retrieve a Stanley blade, one of the old school ones where the sharpened steel is permanently stuck out, wouldn't get away with something like this nowadays. Feeling the hefty weight in my hand, I welcome the sturdiness of the object, I welcome the cold touch of the razor edge as I slide it effortlessly across my shirt sleeve, watching it split jaggedly like wrapping paper. Turning the blade over, the light from above dances along the sharpened edge, momentarily blinding me, but not thwarting me, from my demonic quest. I am lost in a trance of total destruction, I am caught on the crest of a wave as I see the future without me in it, a future of peace in that I will never be missed by anyone. I rotate the blade once more, now caressing my collar, itching the fabric, as I inch my way further into the sweet oblivion that is my perfect death.

The cold steel rests lovingly against my neck. It sends a shiver down my spine. I shake with ecstasy. I shake with anticipation. I shake with anger, with hate, with resentment. I close my eyes. Hello darkness. My old friend. My only friend. Take me. Take me away from this life. From this waking nightmare. Relieve me from the bondage of self. I've had enough. Maybe the next life will be different. Goodbye cruel world.

As I prepare to end my life, I feel a presence behind me, arms embrace me, love encapsulates me. Regretfully releasing my life-ending weapon, hearing it clatter noisily to the floor, I stand up on unsteady legs and turn around while my saviour releases their grip slightly. Holy bloody hell! It's him.

"Why hello Gulaxa me old pal, how's tricks?" he asks jovially.

I am unsure of my reply, which version is this? He's wearing different clothes from before, he's actually dressed in a James Bond style tuxedo, very smart. Do I act all dumb like before and continue my charade? Or do I revert back to myself?

"Don't worry," he says, lifting my chin softly. "You don't need to act any more. I came here to save you, just like you saved me."

"What…" I begin to say meekly.

"Shh," he shushes, holding his finger to my lips a little too uncomfortably. "It's all good in the hood my two-legged friend. Now, we don't have much time. You're going to be jumping soon, somewhere long ago, one more charade to keep up then we can bring all this shit to a mind-bending conclusion. Just one piece of advice."

I look into his eyes, his deep blue cheeky eyes, as they dart brightly across his vision. They cease dancing and his features soften, for a moment I see his tender loving mother looking back at me. I feel love of the purest form emanate from the very fibre of his being, I am transfixed by the serenity in his whole being.

"Never forget you are wanted, never forget you are needed, never forget you are loved. I love you my old pal, see you on the other side."

And then I snap back into the past with all the grace of a lovesick puppy.

WEDDING BLISS

D eath seems to follow me wherever I go, a constant companion that is always by my side, never letting go with its unrelenting grip. My mum, my grandad, both my loving Gulaxas, my guilt ridden father, now Batlaxa. Although the latter had no immediate emotional tie to me, in a way he did, he was once Gulaxa after all, in another time, in another universe. Maybe the bond that ties us together throughout the weaves of time are forever woven integrally within the eternal fabric of love. For isn't it love that will forever stand the test of time? That will last until the dying of the suns? That will remain eternally more, an immortal source of beauty that controls us without us even knowing? Even in death, love will conquer all.

I arrive back home safe and sound, hopefully avoiding all the chaos of a time long ago. The house seems so empty, feels so lonely without all the unrelenting noise of my most recent excursions here. I am thankful for this, I feel I need a moment's peace to prepare myself for whatever comes next. Sitting down gently on my bed I feel the welcome sigh of the springs as they succumb to my familiar weight. Cradling Gulaxa in my arms like a newborn child I rock him gently to and throe, cooing softly as I do so. Fast asleep and purring contently, he is the epitome of peace and I thrive off his serene aura like a flower soaking up God's miracle life giving sun. I stay in this moment for what seems like an age, that is until the fat little bugger's weight makes my arms ache.

"Sorry my little baby," I say softly as if talking to a toddler. "Dada needs to rest his arms cos you is a chunky little sausage." I ruffle his little belly affectionately as I lay him down leaning against my pillow.

He seems not to notice my unnecessary jibe as he curls into a cute little ball and resumes his cat nap. I feel reluctant to leave him alone seeing as though I went through hell to get him back, but I'm sure he'll be fine here, and I really need to use the urination station. Sliding clumsily off the bed so as not to disturb sleeping beauty, I back away on tip-toes while still keeping my eyes fixedly on him, afraid of losing what I obviously consider the closest companion in my life, the only thing left I actually love in this world. Expertly avoiding the bannister and entering the bathroom, still going backwards, I eventually lose sight of him and turn around, bashing my helmeted head against the door frame.

Literally giving my head a shake I attempt to stare at my reflection in the mirror, but alas the glass is all shattered, shards still litter the basin like a broken reminder of pain and remorse. I wonder how long ago that was, chronologically speaking? Don't suppose it really matters to be honest, as long as I'm not interfering with anything I don't really care. I do however appreciate the reminder of how close I was to committing suicide, and seemingly not for the first time. I guess I am a little like my feline companion and have many lives, I should be more grateful for the one I have, others are not so fortunate.

Removing my dark headed attire (which highly likely saved me from a lot of unnecessary stress) I give it a little kiss and place it softly into the bath, once more afraid of waking my sleeping baby. I give my head a shake to rid myself of the unnerving emotions floating around my cerebral cortex like limpets of self-pity, also because it feels damn fine to be free from the cocooned like state I was in. Ceasing my head shaking I prepare to empty my bladder, but not before sneaking a quick peek at my buddy, who is fast asleep, and quietly close the door. I do notice a pile of glass piled up against the side of the wall in the corner, very strange, not going to over boggle my mind over that though, I'm sure it happened for a reason. Now, time to go pee pee.

After a well deserved urination has been completed, along with cleansing of hands in the sink area, avoiding the pile of glass of course, I leave the room and head into the main bedroom. Seeing the furry feline is still fast asleep in the mirrored reflection I check myself out. Damn I look ridiculous! What in the hell possessed me to conjure up this awful clothing arrangement? Apart from the socks (which are God damn awesome!) everything else is pretty shit if I don't mind myself saying, and I don't, so I do, but not out loud, so I actually don't. I'm starting to talk, or think, nonsense again, I think this might be a sign I need to alter something. I'm guessing clothing might be the best course of action, and a hat, a great big bloody awesome hat, but without blood on it, obviously.

Carefully opening the wardrobe (who knows what deceased body may be lurking within!) I rummage through the garments with practised ease, waiting for something spectacular to catch my eye, and then, there it is, the outfit of all outfits: a wedding dress! Only kidding you nutters, I'm not that daft, well maybe I am, but not today. Today could quite possibly be the day I save the whole universe, so it's best I look the part and make an effort. Although nothing says making an effort like a wedding dress, so would it actually be that bad an idea? Screw it. Let's try it on and see what happens, I can easily take it off and change my mind later, I'm sure nothing will happen in the meantime.

Having not worn many ladies garments before (apart from the ladies blouse I currently have on, oh and a wonder woman outfit) I literally have no clue as to how to put this thing on. I guess first and foremost would be to take all my other clothing off, good old Mitch, always knows how to plan ahead, what would I do without him/me? Discarding my current attire and hastily chucking them onto the bed I giddily hoist up the wedding dress from upon it's hanger, holding it aloft like some prized chalice. Hmm, seems a bit on the small side, maybe the bride to be was a midget? I feel a slight pang of guilt as I recall the only viable person's dress this could be is my mother's. Am I really going to put on her prized possession? Is this what a normal person would actually do under the circumstances? Well, firstly, I am definitely not normal. Sane, yes. Normal, no way Hosé. And secondly, or b if you want to be politically correct, these are not normal times. I am a hero on a quest to save the universe. Drastic times make for awesome measures. Come on Mitch, show us your balls! But, like, not literally, keep those jewels hidden away.

So I unclasp the back thingy and sort of climb into the wide area near the rear, seems like the right course of action.

I stumble slightly to my left, but adopt a perfect one-legged yoga stance, while shimmying like a legend. This seems to have some sort of effect as I feel the garment silkily glide down my perfectly toned figure with ease. Popping my head out the top like a turtle I gaze at my reflection in the mirror. Wow, I look amazing! Well, when I say amazing, I actually mean awesome. Although the dress comes up to my mid-thighs and the sleeves up to mid-arms (elbows?), and it feels kind of tight in the crotch area, I think I look pretty cool. What really blows me away is the way my breasted area is fully exposed, very sexually sensual, women will be swooning all over the cosmos once I start doing the nail thing. I decide on leaving the Xmas socks on (because they're bloody fantastic!) and wearing a pair of brown Jesus sandals I see lurking about in the back of the wardrobe. They are a couple of sizes too small but who really gives a shit, they look the part so I'm having them.

Now, for the final piece of the jigsaw, an awesome hat. This has to be the best one ever, the icing on the cake, the cat that got the cream, the egg that beat the yolk, what am I saying!? Then, I see it. Yes! Thank you Lord, you always know how to please a man, and I don't mean sexually, but you know everything, so you probably know that as well. Anyway, a Fez hat stares at me from the back of the wardrobe, like a red beacon of hope guiding me nearer. Come to papa. Tommy Cooper you total bloody legend, I will wear this in your honour. Retrieving the hatted Excalibur with caution I close the door softly. Holding aloft my crowning glory I place it triumphantly upon my noggin as the angels sing a rapturous choir. See me my minions, see your God as he is before you, kneel before...

"What in holy shittery are you wearing?" a high-pitched voice exclaims from behind me.

I let out a rather similar tone while covering my bare breasted area like a shy Victorian maiden. Unable to see who, or whom, is behind me, I decide the best course of action would be to turn around. But something inside me says this is a bad idea, but I can't just stand here doing nothing. So screw listening to my idiot head, let's turn around and face the bloody bastard.

"How dare ye frighten this fair wench..." I begin, before being faced with me, shit!

HORSES FOR COURSES

Leaving my once serene and loving closet, where I had been saved by my knight in shining armour (possibly not for the first time!), I was immediately transported back into a world of overlapping chaos. Grimy water splashed and sloshed against me, pulling me deeper and deeper into a filthy abyss. Try as I may I could not fathom out which position was up, my equilibrium was completely shot to hell by the untimely jump. Had I jumped into the centre of a vast ocean, destined to drown helplessly on my own like a pitying pirate? This wasn't how my story was supposed to end, surely the Great Gulaxa should have an ending better befitting his powerful name. There was no other thing for it, I had to swallow my pride and ask for assistance, screw the opening quip, I need a hero.

"Help!" I cried, hoping that once again my saviour would come to my rescue.

Frantically caressing the waves of whatever angry sea I was dwelling within, I momentarily lose track of space and time. Each passing moment feels like it is being stretched out like a rubber band, an everlasting moment of pure dread, forever dancing a weave of terror that envelops my overworked imagination. Is this what dying feels like? Is this the beginning of the end of my entire existence? Am I right now passing from this world onto the next with all the grace of a blubbering seal? Great way to go, at least no-one will see my final embarrassing farewell, I suppose there's that to be grateful for. As I slowly succumb to my waiting demise, I feel a sense of calm overcome my once fragile state of being. Maybe death won't be that bad. It is what I have wanted in recent times. For a moment I yearn for the end.

"Hold on pal!" I hear a familiar voice shout from nearby, maybe this isn't my final bow after all. "I'll find something to chuck in!" he bellows once more.

Once again the moments stretch unnecessarily long, like a torturer baying his victims I await whatever outcome with breathless anticipation.

"Grab on to this you bloody idiot!" I hear my familiar friend shout. I ignore the unwelcome insult, although a part of me did feel this quite unnecessary considering my near death predicament.

I flail uselessly at a seemingly feeble piece of wood I could just about make out, flapping it away numerous times before finally grabbing a hold of the lifesaving instrument. At last, salvation will be mine. I pull myself up with a strength I never knew I had to a standing position in the middle of quite a shallow river. I'm guessing I was slightly mistaken that I was in an ocean, oh well, I will not let this affect my pride. That is until I see him burst out laughing, clutching his sides like a small child, and this really does break my broken soul, I feel like bawling my eyes out.

"Seriously!" he exclaims through bouts of hysterical laughter. "That has to be the funniest thing I have ever seen. You, my friend, are a God damn legend."

I stare at him with utter contempt, my well played out facade was breaking as he guffaws irritatingly in my direction. Struggling to hold onto the Oscar winning act I had been keeping up for so long, I attempted to hide my anger behind a veil of embarrassment. But inside I seethed and boiled, like a volcano ready to burst forth fire and rage. As he continued giggling I continued simmering under the surface of my cool exterior. I felt like bashing his brains into oblivion the fat fucking wanker!

"Come on silly boy," he childishly calls out while holding the rake at arm's length. "Grab a hold of the stick like the clever little sausage you are."

Clever little sausage? Who the hell does he think he is talking to!? Time to teach him a lesson. I grab hold of the flimsy piece of wood and pretend to reel myself in, when in fact I was baiting him into a false sense of security. As he grins once more at my embarrassing debacle I heave with all my strength, pulling him into the river to join me within the thrashing waves. Have some of that you fat bastard! This really takes away my anger and I feel a rather warm feeling envelop my once brooding chasm of fire. Once he regains his footing I smirk beside him. My veil has fallen, but who cares, this is too much fun.

"You utter bastard," he says, also with a little smirk on his face "I thought we were the best buddies in the whole wide world."

"Nice dive," I say, still smirking triumphantly.

We stand there for the briefest of moments, two friends smiling at one another. Life suddenly doesn't feel so bad after all, I...

"What the devil is going on here old chap?" a peculiar accent enquires, interrupting my inner monologue.

Turning our gazes from each other's eyes to the newcomer, we both stare at a smart looking soldier sat astride a huge, black horse. Sporting a striking upturned moustache the guy in question is most likely an officer of sorts. Wearing a full khaki military uniform it is very evident that there is not a mark of dirt anywhere on his person, or even his horse for that matter. If this had been a regular solider then a: they would probably be walking, and b: they would be full of dirt and grime. I wonder what year we are in? The moustache has echoes of very early 1900s, would I be wise to guess we had arrived somewhere in world war 1? Maybe that gravestone of mine we saw earlier has some relevance now.

"I asked you a question," soldier boy says, seemingly breaking both of us from our inward musings, while also holding a revolver and cocking back the hammer. We really need to be more observant of our surroundings.

"Just taking a dip," my friend says jovially, good man, adopt a non-threatening manner, although Mr Soldier does not change his more than threatening posture.

"I don't recognise your accent, where do you hail from?" he asks sharply.

"I'm from Landan, innit bruv," my soon to be ex-friend replies in that I believe to be a Cockney accent, while at the same time slouching back and hugging himself. What in the holy shit is he doing? He's going to get our bloody balls blown off!

Soldier boy adopts the same less than happy facial expression, I'm so glad he can't see me, think I might just side step out of the way to avoid a stray bullet. Then something very unexpected happens, he turns to face me and looks straight into my eyes. Guess I'm not invisible, shit!

"What about your boyfriend? Where is he from?" he asks, I'm pretty sure he's not asking me, even though he is staring right at me.

"What! You can see him?" my incredulous hero exclaims, which is going to make him look like a right nutter. I hope he has a back-up plan prepared. "Only kidding my old chum, he's from up Norf, proper Norvener like, know what I'm saying geezer?"

Adopting a very different accent from the first part of his sentence, quite possibly Mancunian or Geordie, not quite sure. Then switching to his less than perfect Cockney accent for the latter part of his ramble, this guy is very odd indeed, but fair play to him, he did adapt quickly to his initial outburst. I stare back at him in what I assume is an endearing way, only to receive a very confusing remark.

"No I don't," he says petulantly.

"What?" I ask, getting a little worried now, does he think he can read my mind or something? We seem lost for a moment in each other's eyes before being rudely interrupted.

"Sorry to break up your little soirée gentlemen," soldier boy says. "But you do know there's a war on, don't you? Huns all over the bloody place and you two sissies are fannying about in the swanny. You're liable to get your blooming balls blown off, what?"

I'm guessing my earlier estimation at what era we are in has most likely been answered: Huns equals Germans, which in turn equals world war 1, or 2. But I'm guessing as he's on a horse and not a vehicle makes the first world war more likely. Damn I'm clever. Although maybe not quite intellectual enough to work out why he said what at the end of his sentence. I had to check behind me to see if anyone else was here, and there isn't, so what in the holy shit is wrong with this guy?

"I didn't say anything," my friend replies, obviously as confused as I am as to this disturbed gentleman's last word.

"I have a good mind to shoot you both dead right now," confused soldier says, pointing the gun at my friend. Shit, this guy is definitely nuts, maybe a touch of the old shell shock has got to him.

"Whoa there cowboy," my hero cries holding his hands up in a defensive posture. "Me and my pal Gulaxa are just chilling out, no need to start pointing guns at us."

"Gulaxa?" confused soldier exclaims while lowering his pistol. "Your friend's name is Gulaxa?" he stares at me with utmost incredulity, as if I am the first human being alive.

"Yes," my friend replies "Why? Have you heard of him?"

I seem to not be involved in the conversation now, like being in the middle of two parents arguing over who should take the bad little boy home.

"Heard of him?" soldier boy exclaims again. "He's a blooming legend is what he is, saved a whole battalion once from certain death, I cannot believe it is he in the flesh."

This is all getting rather confusing now, and I don't really understand any of the relevance at all. Have I been here before? Or has a previous version of me had some sort of interaction here? I don't recall any of his apparent goings on, but then again I can't really remember much of my life until I met up with my nemesis/friend.

"Yes, quite the hero is my old mate here, aren't you?" my mate says from beside me, eyeing me up in a very suspicious way, as though accusing me of knowing more than I let on. Which is actually true, but I know nothing of all this nonsense soldier boy is spouting out of his stupid chops.

I gaze back at him, then to soldier boy, then back at the accuser before me, lost for words. Probably best if I play the dumb card, it always worked before. I watch his eyes cloud over briefly as his lips begin moving in quiet contemplation, I manage to make out the word comedian before our soldiering friend chimes in.

"Always was a man of few words, why talk when you can be a hero, what?"

We both look around us for the apparent imaginary person lurking in the shadows, does he think someone else is talking? Or did he think we said something? I am utterly confused right now, my head hurts a little.

"So what moniker do you go by then?" he asks, not sure who but I'm guessing it's not me as he already knows my name.

"Call me Mitch, Mitch Branning," my sidekick replies while for some unknown reason checking his nails in a, if I don't mind saying so myself, rather dashingly cool way. And Mitch Branning, that's not his name, I'm sure his name is...

"Mitch Branning!" the rude interrupting soldier shouts, quite possibly preventing a very pivotal moment in the whole saga. "What a ridiculous name, sounds as though you just made that up on the spot."

My friend's moment of coolness is instantly shattered, his shoulders sag heavily as though a bag of cement had just been placed upon him. He crosses his arms across his chest like a little child, and for the briefest of moments I half expect him to burst out crying. Soldier boy seemingly senses the darkness overcome him.

"Only kidding old chap, come on, you both hop aboard and I'll take you back to camp. The boys need some cheering up. Damn gloomy most days around these here parts."

We both stare at each other, then back at our weirdly proposing soldier friend. Does he really want us both to join him on the back of that horse? Seems a bit gay if you ask me. My friend senses my apparent incredulity.

"You want both of us to jump on the horse with you? Is there room for all of us?"

"Of course there is!" soldier boy cries. "Old Gulaxa there hardly weighs an ounce, and you look like a blooming morphine addict. Tally ho now, what?"

Again I glance behind me, there's no-one there, this guy is off his bloody rocker. I really do not want to join him on his giant beast but my friend hassles me forward, making sure I get stuck right behind him. We both jostle each other ungracefully onto the pure black stallion before gradually settling into position. This feels somewhat weird I must admit. I feel sandwiched between two very disturbed individuals like a prey caught in a Venus fly trap with no escape.

"Which one of you chaps is wearing ladies' cologne?" he asks when we'd struggled onto the massive beast. "Or is it both of you? Had a funny feeling both of you were a bit queer, what?"

You're the one who pretty much ordered us to straddle you, if anyone is on the homosexual side it's you pal, I muse inwardly as my friend behind me mumbles something about his mum.

"Only five miles to camp chaps, shall we sing a song to pass the time?" soldier boy says jovially. "Oh I do like to be beside the sea side..."

Not quite the way I was expecting this ride to play out when I hopped aboard, but this guy is a little on the mental side so I suppose it fits. I look around at my rear passenger in hopeful expectation that he would know what to do.

"Screw it," he whispers into my ear, causing a slight ticklish sensation. "Might as well enjoy ourselves."

So we join in with our comrade, all singing along in beautiful unison. I feel the previous echoes of my past endeavours wilt away into nothingness. A cool breeze ruffles the shiny mane of the shimmering black creature as it glides majestically across the lush grass, as if dancing across the stars to heaven and beyond. Maybe we are actually on a magical journey, one which will take us away from this desolate life to a new pasture filled with hope and serenity. As I succumb to the beautiful peace of the moment I take in a deep breath and become completely present. I sigh heavily and thank God for my life right now, before a sharp crack breaks me from my inward concentration and soldier's boy head explodes like a cracked egg, soaking me with dark blood. Holy shit! As the horse bucks wildly we are all thrown to the ground with all the grace of a smashing bottle, to fall in a heap on the ground. My head whacks against something hard upon the solid turf, the last thing I see is my friend disappearing and then...darkness.

SUITS YOU SIR

W ith my eyes closed I await a while before opening them. I dread to think where in the hell I have randomly jumped off to now. Probably gone to have a little chin wag with the dinosaurs, or maybe supper with Abraham Lincoln the night before he gets his head shot in. Or, more likely, I'll end up back at Chinos trying to avoid previous versions of myself like a game of dodgems. So I reckon just keep my eyes closed for a while and enjoy the serenity of darkness within my lidded eye cocoon. Maybe I could use my top notch investigation skills without using my eyeballs, see no evil but hear all of everything. I could become the blind assassin, but that sounds like a I might rape visually challenged men's bums, and I'm not really into any of that black hole of Calcutta shenanigans. So I'm just going to stand here and pretend I'm sleeping like a fish.

I hear a cough from ahead of me, hmm. Using my investigation skills I would hazard a guess that this person is a male in his sixties. Highly likely a smoker for many years, quite possibly blind, might have been sexually assaulted in the past hence his need to make himself known to me. Hmm, what else. Ah, yes, I think he may have been a pirate in days gone by. Wow, I think I might actually be the greatest human being every created, or the best God ever, or both. Wasn't Jesus a sort of super human type dude? Like a semi-God? Maybe that's what I am.

"Ahem," the voice ahead of me coughs.

"Do not fear, Mr Blind pirate," I say softly while holding my hands aloft. "Your dark passage is safe from me, I am no threat to you. Please be on your way and mind your step, peace out man." A two fingered peace sign follows.

"For God's sake," the voice mutters. Wait, is that who I think it is?

I decide to open one eye slightly in a nervous blink, see I am still in the bedroom I was previously, and then snap both eyes open in exultant fashion. And there I am, laid on the bed in a seductively sideways pose wearing a very smart black tuxedo, what a cool bastard I am, and quite sexy as well. Is it wrong that I am attracted to myself? I think not, I am also down right sure there is not any sort of gay attraction here. After all, masturbation isn't gay. so neither is quite literally loving yourself, so you lot can piss right off! It takes me a moment to realise that my furry companion is curled up against him. Hmm, not really sure if this pleases me or not.

"So, like, what the hell?" I ask politely.

"I could ask you the same thing," I/he replies, this could get confusing. From now on the other me will be referred to as Bitch.

"Wait a minute," Bitch says. "Why in the holy shitting hell are you internally calling me Bitch? Seems a bit harsh if you ask me pal," he says while adopting a very familiar arms across chest pose.

"Only kidding me old mucker," I reply jovially. "Now, may you please henceforth explain to me what in Jesus' underpants is going on?"

"Hmm," you know who replies. "Hey stop calling me Bitch or I ain't telling you shit!"

"I did not refer to you as that moniker me old Monica, it is up to the very talented reader of this nonsense to make up their own minds who they refer to you as. So, please continue," I twirl my hand in a hopeful continuing gesture.

"Double hmm," B says. "Right that's it, piss off! You sir are a wanker, I'm taking the cat back to the future somewhere nice and cosy."

"Hey, hey, hey," I coo. "I'm only kidding pal. Look, we're all friends here, let's just calm our breasts down and have a good old natter. How about a what what?"

The man opposite looks sulkily at me, but a slight smirk reaches the corners of his mouth.

"What what," he says quietly.

"I can't hear you," I say, cupping my ears. "Can you give me a hearty what what?"

"What what?" he says, grinning from ear to ear.

"Attaboy, ladies and gentlemen, we have a pure bona-fide what whatter in the house. A legend in the making. A superstar who comes from afar. It is none other than Mitch, Who Isn't A Bitch, Branning!" I drag out the surname like a boxing MC, hearing the crowd go wild. My opposite friend laps in the applause, what a guy.

"Right then, now that that's settled, what in the holy realms of chaos is going on? How come we haven't randomly jumped?"

"Well," my friend begins. "You see, we are not really the same person. Well, we are, but we are not. You see, and you do because your eyes work, I am from another universe, or rather you are, and I am. So we are not the same, you and I, or I and you to be politically correct, you get me? Or do I get you?"

Hmm, this guy is not making that much sense. I wonder if he has been taking any mind altering substances. I, on the other hand, always make sense. Each time that I speak, my words are like an intellectual discussion, everyone always knows of the words of wisdom that protrude from my speech mouth. But this guy, well he make not that much of sense. Maybe I just need to fish for information like a fisherman baiting erm, fish.

"So," I begin in earnest. "Let me get this straight. What?"

"Firstly," he begins. "Why are you wearing mum's wedding dress? Secondly, where did you find the cat? And lastly, but most certainly not leastly, will you help me, brother?"

I digest the words for a millisecond before answering promptly.

"A, because sometimes a man has to do what a man has to do. B, I found him at the graveyard, where grandad is buried. C, I will always help you, brother. D, are you my brother? E, or is that just a way to say we are more than just friends, like yo bro what's up?"

A serious shadow falls across his face, the features which once were jovial and light-hearted take on a more sinister tone. Is this what happens when my depression overcomes me? It's quite scary to witness.

"Time is upon us, my friend," he says sternly. "All the many journeys we have traversed, all the perils we have overcome, they are about to come to a head. You see, that Roundy chap isn't the guy you think he is. Although he is the author, he is also the end of all worlds. He resides in a place not of here, you have been there. Out of all us, which there are many, you are the only one who has managed to escape these pages. You are the chosen one. But you need help, you need this furry little monster, that much is true. But you also need the other Gulaxa, he is a changed man now, you need to rescue him. He is lost on a darkened path, a path as dark as ours, he needs your love. Will you be the saviour? Will you rise up and become greater than all of us? Time waits for no man, but it will wait for a God."

His statement echoes across my mind like a ghost train over the tracks of my misfiring synapse. Somehow, I know everything he is saying is true, I feel it in my entire being. I feel as though every version of us is speaking through him as though through some universal translator across the ravages of space and time. His last seven words strike a chord deep within my soul. They ignite a fire lain dormant as I feel a rush of adrenaline course through my entire system. I tremble all over with passion, with fury, with love. Gulaxa, my friend, my brother, I will save you. I stand straight and tall, like a solider ready for battle.

"Where must I go?" I command.

His features soften again.

"Well, if I were you, I'd change clothes first. You need to look the part while saving the universe, and our mother's wedding dress isn't quite the look I would go with."

He could be right. He is right. But is she mother to both of us? Maybe something to ponder over earlier, or later.

"How about you give me your tuxedo, brother?" I ask confidently.

He looks incredulous, then remembers that I am his master, that he serves me, and I have a bigger penis, and better in bed, and also...

"Cut it out!" he snaps. "You can have the suit, and our genitalia are the same size, probably."

He steps out of his suit as I step out of my dress, both clumsily tottering about like drunken teenagers, often holding onto each other for balancing support. After he reluctantly hands me his tuxedo, I dress with extreme excitement.

"How do I look?" I ask, striking a hands on hips pose.

"Your bow tie is crooked," he says, walking over with Gulaxa cradled in his arms. "Here, hold chubs while I adjust it for you."

I take a hold of my furry friend as my brother in arms stands before me with a perfect Adonis like frame. I see him smirk slightly at this awesome, and very true, compliment. He straightens my tie like a God damn legend before gazing into my beautiful blue eyes. The lust he feels for me is too overwhelming, he leans in for a...

"Fuck off!" he snaps, holding his hand across his lips.

"Only kidding pal," I say, patting him on the shoulder. "Thank you brother, for everything."

"You are welcome, good luck out there. Don't fall for any of Roundy's tricks, he's a sly fox. And don't attempt anything until you have Gulaxa, you need both of your soldiers beside you if you have any chance of winning this. Gulaxa is back at world war 1, recovering, go gentle on him. One last thing before you go..."

I gaze at him, no words are needed. We both check our nails in that cool as hell way, and then I jump back into the past to save my friend.

THE TRUTH

Figments of my fragmented imagination fall towards me like floating pictures. Avoiding them is impossible as I am frozen stiff inside a timeless bubble of pain and despair. My life seems to be a revolving door of mayhem, twisting and turning as if warped like a wobbling earth's axis. None of the seemingly random pop-ups make any sense, or rather they are all distorted in an unfamiliar way. I see many pictures of the cat, of soldiers, of devastating nuclear explosions, of Mitch checking his nails in a cool as hell way. But none of it has any sort of structure. None of it is falling together like a perfect narrative driven story. It seems chaotic, broken, unrecognisable in the grand scheme of my mind's eye. Maybe it is I who is the broken one. Maybe it is I who is falling in upon myself. Maybe I am dead.

"Wake up old chum!" I hear someone shout as a sharp jolt attacks my battered body

Once more my thoughts randomise, jerking spasmodically across my brain like lightening bolts of emotions. Jagged edges of thought protrude throughout my frayed senses as if burrowing from deep within, hell bent on arriving front and centre no matter what obstacles are in their path. Although not painful, it is very uncomfortable, like sat in a room full of people you don't know and having to make small talk. If only I could harness one of the thoughts I could…

"We're losing him!" I hear a voice shout. "Hit him again."

Another bash against my chest area startles the fireworks into some sort of order. Brief recollections of my previous excursions begin to form together. I was drowning, I was saved, saved by Mitch, my hero. I keep hearing give me a what what, but this makes no sense, this has nothing to do with my time, or my life, but somehow it makes me smile, it makes me laugh. I see a moustached face obliterated like a splattering water melon. I see Mitch vanish.

"Mitch!" I shout as I come to my senses and open my eyes.

Surrounded by white clothed figures I reach out furtively, grabbing the nearby sleeve of the closest arm I can reach.

"Mitch! Is he alive?" I half whisper, half rasp.

"I have no blooming idea who the devil Mitch is. Do you know your name, sir? Or how you came to be here?" the man says.

I fall back onto the unwelcoming surface below me, suddenly aware of the screams around the room, pitying cries of pain and anguish. Men in extreme physical torture echo around the tent like wailing banshees, each rapturous moan chasing after the other with unrelenting despair. I turn onto my side and see the leg of a man being aggressively sawn through as blood spatters his face like the pitter patter of rain drops the colour or poppies. I heave uncontrollably and empty whatever I had in my stomach onto the floor below me, a surface running rivers the colour of death.

"Take him away," a voice mutters. "It's just shell shock, get a guard on him though, we need him to answer a few questions."

As I am wheeled away on a trolley which probably has squeaky wheels, but which I cannot hear over the cries of misery which follow me away from the sickly room, chasing after me like living nightmares, I close my eyes and wonder what fate awaits me. I ponder inwardly if my life will ever have meaning any more. Will I ever see my friend again? Will I ever smile again like I used to, before I lost my head and became the evil tyrant wielding the sword of Damocles over my minions?

Eventually the squeaking trolley stops, the dying remnants of broken men numbed by distance, and I am left alone. Tempted by sleep I resist the urge to close my eyes, I pull myself to a sitting position and swing my legs so as they hang over the side of my less then comfortable bed. A stabbing pain bashes at my temple and I reach my hand up instinctively to the source, hoping to quell the torturous throb. A huge bump swells outward, I almost feel the thing get bigger against my palm, before realising it is just my ragged heartbeat. I would kill for a glass of water right now.

"Here, take this," a familiar voice speaks softly.

I see a glass of water from beneath my shrouded vision, a welcome offering at just the right time.

"Thanks," I rasp, taking the glass gratefully and downing it greedily.

"Someone's a thirsty bugger, didn't you not get enough in the swanny me old mucker?" the voice chuckles.

Raising my head I see my old friend leaning against a tent pole wearing a shiny black tuxedo holding a pure black cat. I'm guessing that is his furry old friend, but if my memory serves me correctly he died a long time ago, or rather a long time in the future, after he is born first, of course. Brief memories of the mad Gulaxas squabbling about the cat surface to my mind, I'm guessing he got to him first. What a guy.

"Hi Mitch," I say quietly, each word sends a little stab into my healing head.

A look of surprise falls across his face, then I realise that I have forgotten to wear my mask. I have let slip the whole charade I have been carrying around for so long. But I am too weak, I am too broken, I cannot keep this up any longer. I cannot and will not lie any more.

"Mitch, I have something to tell you," I say, raising my head proudly to stare him square in the eyes. Tears form in my eyes as I prepare to make amends to the only friend I have in the whole universe. "I have been lying to you this whole time," I begin, and then I tell him, I tell him everything.

He stands there quietly, listening intently, stroking his cat like a practised counsellor, as I pour my heart out like I have never done so before. Tears flow down my cheeks as a flourishing river runs over rocks, nourishing my soul, cleansing me from loneliness and despair. After I am done I feel lighter, I feel as though the room has become brighter, I feel the weight weighing me down for so long has been lifted. I feel reborn.

"I'm sorry Mitch," I continue, wiping my eyes with a tissue he has provided me with. "You are the only person in the universe I care about, the only one who has shown me compassion, the only one who has shown me love. If there is anything I can do to repay you, please let me know." I climb down weakly from the bed, his hands go to catch me but I hold my hands up in protestation. I kneel before him. "Please forgive me, my friend."

Long moments seem to go by without a word being said, but I stay on my knees. My words have been spoken, I have said my piece. Whatever outcome he decides, I will abide by. I have cleared away my side of the street, my wreckage is in the past now. Only He can decide whatever fate I deserve. I close my eyes and await the decision. Seconds, minutes, hours, I don't know how long goes by without a word, without a sound, and yet I wait, as patient as a leopard stalking its prey. Then He speaks.

"Well, me old mucker, quite the tale. You certainly had me fooled. And it takes a sly old fox to outwit such an intellectual mastermind such as I." I smirk slightly, hoping I don't show that I am being sarcastic. "Gulaxa, me old pal, please, stand up."

I do as he asks, standing somewhat slumped and broken.

"Straighten up, soldier!" he barks, and I do, hearing everything creak inside me. "You are my best friend, you are my only true friend in this world, in this life. I forgive you, and I love you," and with these beautiful words we embrace like the times of old when we traversed throughout the ages on our many adventures.

"Thank you," I whisper through racks of tears.

We release from our hug to stare into each others eyes, his big blue orbs gleam with cheekiness. I've seen this look before, and I like it.

"We have a mission to undertake, my friend. But I need you fit and well, and to be honest you look like shit. I'm going to come back in six months, it will be in the blink of an eye for me, but you will have to put the work in. You will see another version of me first, in an army uniform, keep up the charade with him, then you and I will save the universe."

"OK," I mutter, unable to take my gaze away from his.

"You once said time waits for no man, but I am no man. See you soon my two-legged friend."

And with that final cool as hell statement he vanishes with all the grace of God.

THE PARLEY

After visiting my old friend in his hospital tent I immediately jump forward six months to a time I remember well. Shit-city attacks my waiting nostrils instantly with practised perfection, it's prying fingers work their way devilishly into my defenceless senses to claw greedily. Of course I instinctively retch, as does my feline companion, I'm guessing even moggies are not immune to this terrible town. I hear a little trump from nearby, shit, better make like a statue and still my sounds. Become the ninja you were born to be Mitch, nothing can detect your stealth like mastery. But then the offending pump enters my nasal area like a ghostly fiend, joining forces with the other invisible entities causing the biggest loudest retch possible. Maybe I got away with it.

"Who goes there?" a smelly bastard exclaims.

Do I play dumb or slink away like a legend? Or maybe I just introduce myself.

"At ease soldier, it's just Captain Branning doing an inspection, carry on."

A moment of quiet ensues, probably a good thing, maybe everything will be OK. I hear slight rustling then a sound as though trousers are being pulled up and a belt fastened. I still think everything will be fine.

"I do not recall a Captain Branning on camp, state your business. And why are you wearing a tuxedo and holding a cat?" his eyes must have become accustomed to the gloom surrounding us, or the bright white of the shirt dazzled him somewhat. Anyway, better get my get out of jail excuse at the ready.

"Now now, soldier. Are you questioning your superior officer? I am not of this camp, I have been sent here as surveyor of your city of shit. To make sure everything is up to code, and I must say all is exemplary. The smell is quite potent, I was going to give your vulgar village a five star rating, but as you seem to be questioning my credentials I may have to inform your superior officer of your insubordination and have you deported."

A long silence occurs. I stroke Gulaxa to ease the tension and adopt my best straight backed stance.

"Sorry sir," he says quietly. "Never had an inspector here before, please don't get me deported, I promise I'll make everyone proud here."

"Very well young fellow, off you pop now, let me here a what what?"

"What?" he asks confused

"Ah, a single what will suffice, tally ho now."

And with this mind-bending remark the soldier snaps me a sharp salute and saunters off into the mist of murky shit. I must admit I kind of like this being in charge stuff, really makes me feel proper important and stuff, which I am, obviously. Now, I had better go find my old chum and see how he is faring up, better watch out for the other me though,

I'm sure to be lurking around here somewhere. I head off into the overgrowth, hoping against hope I am avoiding the highly likely shit bombs scattered around here, to the sound of familiar voices chattering away. Coming into range I peer around the nearest tent and see myself in an old army uniform, and Gulaxa all smart and tidy, looking completely different from the shell of a man I saw most recently.

"Go," Gulaxa whispers. "Your journey is far from over, you have so much left to do, so much to accomplish."

As I watch them both embrace I recall how difficult this was, how my heart was breaking in two from leaving my only true friend here, damn this shit hurts.

"I can't do this alone," the other me pleads.

"You can," Gulaxa affirms, full of confidence and bravado "You're stronger than you think."

"Goodbye, old friend," I/he mutters, my chest heaving through racking sobs, my emotions now mimicking his.

"Goodbye, sir," Gulaxa says softly.

Then he is left alone like an old abandoned friend, soaking up the pain with the guts and determination of a battle hardened soldier. Although quite obviously a changed man, I can see from where I am stood the pain in his eyes. His tears glisten like dew on a vast plain of a morning field, threatening to break free to dance among the fallen leaves of love.

"I can see you, Mitch," he says softly, raising his head to stare in my direction. "Please, I really need a hug right now."

I oblige my friend and stride purposefully over to hug him with one arm, being ever so mindful of the still sleeping moggy between us. Seemingly unaware of everything, he continues to purr contentedly against my chest.

"You're looking well," I say to my friend after we part from our familiar embrace.

"Thank you Mitch, you're not looking too bad yourself. And I see you still have your furry friend with you." He gives Gulaxa a little belly rub, causing more low rumbling but no movement.

"Why thank you," I blush, doing a little ballerina twirl for good measure. "I got this suit off a very handsome gentleman. And as for this little bugger," I ruffle Chub's little head. "He's not leaving my sight again."

We stand there for a moment, gazing at each other. He looks so different from the broken soul I saw only a brief time ago. Fitting his uniform to perfection his frame stretches the fabric like plasticine, his muscles rising and falling with each gentle breath. Unlike before, his features are no longer drawn and skeletal, they are weathered and chiselled like the sculpture of David. His time spent here has served him well, and although the exterior of the man is different, his eyes still possess the kindness that endeared me to him. Even though his admittance of playing me like a fool made me feel somewhat betrayed, the love in his eyes now, and near the end of our first journey, are something you simply cannot fake.

"So, what now Mitch? What's the plan?"

Now that is a good bloody question, I know that Roundy is the bad guy in this whole saga, but how do we find him? And how do we confront him? Surely he is reading this right now, or rather is writing it at this very moment, isn't he always one step ahead of us? Surely he could just put down his pen or close his laptop and the whole thing would be done. So how do we fight that which is our creator? How do we combat the very thing that gives us existence?

"You can't," comes a familiar voice.

I turn around to see Roundy leaning against the tent not five feet away from us, grinning like a lunatic.

"You see," he continues. "I own you, I am at this very moment writing these words, if I choose for you to die right now, swallowed by a black hole that appears out of nothingness, then that would be your fate. You call yourself a God, well maybe in this world you are. But outside of here, these pages, this digital world, I am your God. I am your master. You are my slave, Mitch, get used to it. The end is coming for you. You have been warned. Do not disobey me, or your world will end slowly and painfully."

With this final utterance he flashes his grin at me, then something unexpected happens. His eyesight seems to cloud over, as if he is not really here any more, as if he is zoning out. Is he distracted by something in his world? Has something grabbed his attention? Or is he simply lost in the creative zone of writing? Has he fallen into this world, and everything, even time, has ceased to be? I think I know what we have to do, and we may only get this one chance.

"Gulaxa," I whisper to my friend, seeing him stuck still. "Grab a hold of my arm."

He grips my arm tightly, eyes still transfixed on the Round one.

"Let's go get this fucker!"

And we all jump back out of the known universe with all the grace of time travelling legends.

CROSSED WIRES

Sometimes, when you least expect it, you have a choice to make. This choice will decide the past, the present, and the future. It will open up magical doorways that transcend time and space. This decision will be the most important and most impossible that you ever have to make. But make it you must, because without this choice, without this fork in the road, then you are quite simply a robot, created for another's purpose, made to entertain others while blinding following someone else's dreams. A slave until your services are no longer required and you are dumped onto the scrap heap of life to fester away into nothingness. The choice is yours.

Arriving back in Roundy's living room I immediately feel Gulaxa's grip on my arm tighten. I glance over at him to see he is terrified, his eyes bulging out of their sockets as if a vacuum is attempting to suck them away into oblivion. I see nothing in the room to frighten him so much. Still the two televisions and the poo coloured sofa, the same view out the window, nothing out of the ordinary. Maybe the jump out of the story has flummoxed him for some reason. I pat his hand softly.

"It's OK," I say quietly. "Give me a hushed what what?"

He turns to look at me, his eyes soften somewhat.

"What?" he asks, halfway there, that'll do for me. "Where are we?"

"That would take a little explaining, let's save that for after we get rid of this bastard."

Glancing around I don't see that Roundy bastard anywhere. I do however see his laptop open and running, a word document is open on the screen. The weird thing is the keys are clacking away and words are being written, but no-one is there. It is as if a ghost is typing away like a spirited wordsmith, creating its own narrative in true haunting style. Well this is unexpected, and weird, weirdly unexpected, you could say. So where is that Roundy git? And who the hell is writing the story? As I lean over I can see the words that are being written are the ones I am thinking right now. This shit is nuts. I go to close the lid but then have second thoughts, that could end everything if I am not careful. Best to leave it the hell alone. I turn back to my companion to see him gazing around the room.

"Nice cottage," he quips, bringing back memories of his previous one liners.

"It's not a cottage," I chime. "It's a, well, I don't know what it is, probably a flat in the middle of hell or something, but it's definitely no cottage, I think. Anyway, enough about cottaging, and I don't mean homosexual acts before you ask, where is the horrible bugger? I mean bastard? Shit!"

I look over to see Gulaxa smirking at my unnecessary remarks, at least he has chilled out a bit now, maybe he could be of some use. Use for what though? I really have no idea what the shitting hell to do here. We came here to stop Roundy, but he seems to be elsewhere. I wonder if he is in the story still, lost in his own words of wisdom? The keys are still muttering away to themselves, someone must be writing them. I glance over at Gulaxa.

"Are you writing this shit?" I enquire suspiciously.

The look I receive is one of dumbfounded confusion.

"I have no idea what you are talking about," he replies. "I literally have no idea where in the hell we are."

"Well someone, or something, is writing this story, look at the laptop."

He leans over and sees the offending object orchestrating our entire life.

"Very strange, I have seen something like this before though. You remember the book you found, at the book depository store? Well after you jumped I read it, and it was doing this exact same thing, typing words all by itself like a possessed demon, scared the shit out of me."

"Hmm," I ponder out loud. "But that book was in the story, this one is outside, but there must be a connection somewhere. And someone must be writing it, but who?"

A couple of seconds go by before we both look at each other wide-eyed, then we both glance down at Gulaxa, my furry feline friend. Surely not, no, that is too God damn mental! That does not make any sense whatsoever, but then again, nothing really has made sense for a long time now. I ruffle his tummy a little, but the words keep on typing and he keeps on purring. So, what next?

"I'll tell you what next!" comes a shout from behind me. I turn to see Roundy stood at the top of the stairs with his arms folded, looking very pensive indeed. "I told you not to mess about Mitch, I warned you what would happen if..." he stops mid-speech and stares at the laptop, a rather bemused look falls across his face. "What the hell? This can't be possible, who..." he trails off.

"Cat got your tongue, boy?" I ask confidently, hoping he gets the awesome joke. "Seems as though you are not the author any more, we are in control." I stroke Gulaxa, the cat, for added emphasis.

"Doesn't change a thing," Roundy says, retrieving a wooden Arsenal bat from behind him. "I smash the lap top, your world ends, no backups around here, boy."

As he strides forward with purpose I attempt my time stopping thing. I gurgle, I belch, I chunter, all of which just causes me to retch awkwardly, mimicking a choking chicken and watching on helplessly as he gets nearer to his intended target. Shit, think fast. Before I have a chance to, Gulaxa, the literal human soldier, charges past me and bounds into the Round one. Go on son, mess him up! But just as he makes contact an ear piercing howl emanates from him and he ceases to be, swallowed up into infinity by an invisible black hole. The Round one stops momentarily and grins at me.

"I wanted you to bring him here so you could finally watch him die, screaming in agony and sent into the blackness of hell." He reaches the laptop as he says these words, bringing the bat above his head. "Goodbye Mitch, you're one hell of a guy."

This is it. The choice. The choice I have to make. Gulaxa, my furry best friend, I have to send you back so I can save us all. I will see you again. I heave my chubby friend at the evil Round bastard. Everything slows down. For a brief moment times does indeed stop, and this time I was not its master. Gulaxa's eyes open, briefly. Roundy's eyes open, terrified. The end has come, for the both of them. Just as they both connect, the keys stop their incessant clacking and the story ends abruptly.

EPILOGUE

I sit here now bashing away on an Acer silver laptop. This poo coloured sofa isn't the comfiest, but for now, it will do. Not really sure what to do here, this is all new to me. I feel tempted to just close this thing up and leave this place. Maybe explore this strange new world I am now a part of. Might go rummaging around this new home I have commandeered, would be a waste to not have a loot in every nook and cranny to see what goodies I can find. Maybe later though, once I've finished my typing. It's kind of fun, being the creator and not the puppet. Feels powerful. Feels Godlike. Maybe this is what I was destined to become all along. Another notch to add to the collection: nurse, counsellor, detective, time traveller, contortionist, linguistic, time worker outerer, maverick, God, singer, now add author to that list. Mitch Branning, you're one hell of a guy. Let's go write some books, might even have a starring role in one of them. As for Mr Round, well, I'm sure he'll turn up somewhere.

The sun sets on the horizon outside the window.
Scratch that. The whole room disappears.
I am hovering above the earth wearing a wedding dress. No, not a wedding dress, wearing a black super hero costume with a big white M on the front.

A billowing red cape, erm, billows behind me.
Damn this writing shit is hard!
Come on Mitch, get a grip.
I close my eyes.
I check my nails in that cool as hell way.
I blast off away into the heavens with all the grace of Mitch 'Cool as Ice' Branning.
There's work to be done.
This is just the beginning...

www.ingramcontent.com/pod-product-compliance
Lightning Source LLC
Chambersburg PA
CBHW070625260626
47161CB00007B/2594